#PLAYER

The Hashtag Series #3

by Cambria Hebert

Published by: Cambria Hebert Books, LLC

http://www.cambriahebert.com

Interior design and typesetting by Sharon Kay
Cover design by MAE I DESIGN
Edited by Cassie McCown

ISBN: 978-1-938857-68-3

#PLAYER

CHAPTER ONE

RIMMEL

"You could find out her entire family is full of murderers and I would still love her."

"Funny you should say that, because it appears her father is the one who killed her mother."

It wasn't true.

Even my sharp denial wouldn't stop what I overheard pounding inside my brain over and over again until I swear my heart beat to the rhythm of those words.

And just like a heartbeat, though no one could hear, I sure as hell felt it.

I couldn't think about that right now.

There was no room to feel the implications of Valerie's accusation.

My focus could be only on the man who sat closely beside me. His body wasn't relaxed like normal. And even though he tried to smile at me with his easygoing, no-worries smile, it didn't quite come through.

He was worried. Anxious and probably in pain. Though, I'd have better luck pulling out my teeth with my own fingers than ever hearing him actually admit any part of him was in pain.

He didn't have to say it and I didn't have to hear it.

I knew. And Romeo was all that mattered right now.

"You doing okay?" I whispered, tilting up my head to look at his face.

His ever-blue eyes found mine and he smiled. "Waiting sucks."

It seemed like we'd been in the room for hours. Maybe it had been. I really couldn't say. The concept of time had been reduced to moments.

One moment after the next.

It had been that way since I stepped into the indoor football field, thinking Romeo had asked me to be there.

One moment I was giddy with anticipation, and the next I was hanging vicariously from a field goal post, strung up by rope and looking into the eyes of someone who'd clearly come unhinged.

I shivered, and Romeo's arm tightened around me. His hand came up and flattened against the side of my head as he gently steered it against him. "You still cold?" he rumbled.

I felt the words echo in his chest more than I actually heard them.

"No," I replied. He was too close for me to be cold.

But not even the steadfast warmth of the man I loved was going to be enough to completely erase the memory of what Zach had done to me. To us.

"Relax," Romeo whispered, trying once more to push me farther against him.

I held myself stiffly and lifted my head despite his effort. "I don't want to lean on you anymore," I said. "You're arm…"

"Is broken," he said. "And it's over here." He pointed across his body where he held it closely against him. The skin was a mottled purple color and the flesh was swollen. My stomach flipped over every single time I looked at it.

His arm wouldn't be like that if he hadn't climbed up on that field goal to get me down.

"You're on this side." He went on like he didn't realize just how upsetting it was to see him like that. "And you aren't hurting me."

I gave in and lay against him. He wasn't wearing a shirt and his skin was smooth, his body so solid and strong that when I closed my eyes, I could pretend nothing on him could ever possibly be broken.

"Rim," he whispered a few minutes later.

"Hmm?"

"I need you to tell me what happened." His voice was harsh. "Before I got there."

My eyes sprang open. Why would he even want to know? Why would he want to relive anything that happened on that field even a second more than he had to?

"It's over, Romeo. There's no reason to bring it back up."

"Hey," he whispered and slid his body out from under mine.

I moved, immediately thinking maybe my weight was hurting him after all. But before I could go very far, he turned onto his side to face me and palmed my hip, gently motioning for me to do the same.

I glanced down in alarm because the hand he was holding me with was attached to his broken arm. He hadn't moved it that far or even that much, but I didn't want him to move it at all.

Even as my body obeyed, turning on my side so we were face to face, my eyes went right to the place just above his elbow where the skin was clearly traumatized.

I really hoped they came in here soon and I hoped they brought a giant Band-Aid. I knew it wouldn't fix what happened, but maybe not having to stare at it every second would make it easier to process.

"Hey," he said again, his voice gruff yet commanding.

I looked up.

He shook his head slowly, silently telling me to stop. His hand stayed still against the curve of my hip. He touched me nowhere else.

He didn't have to.

The azure shade of his eyes caressed me to my soul. I swear he looked at me like no one else ever could. It was like there was nothing else in existence except me. It was like he wasn't just looking at me, but *in* me, and I was the most precious thing he'd ever seen.

I got caught up in that gaze. I got caught up in him. My chest felt like it caved in, but not in a disaster sort of way. Like it was sealing in everything he was saying even though no words ever left his tongue.

"How do you do it?" I whispered. My tongue felt thick against the roof of my mouth.

"Do what?" he asked. That look never once left his eyes. If anything, it swept me in tighter.

"How do you look at me like… like I'm everything?"

He made a low sound in the deepest part of his throat. Sort of like a growl, sort of like an agreement. "Because you are."

"Romeo." I sighed.

"Rimmel," he replied. "Don't forget."

I started to pull back from the moment, but his fingers tightened on my hip. I looked back up.

"Don't forget this moment. Don't forget the absolute truth in the way you feel right now. I love you and I'm not going to stop."

Emotion welled up in my throat and tears rushed to the backs of my eyes. His words were beautiful, but it was the reason he said them that had me so choked up.

This wasn't the end.

Beyond this moment, this quiet, whole moment with him, were many more. Many more that weren't going to be like this one.

We were going to have to keep fighting to keep what was ours.

• • •

"I'm not going to stop either," I whispered.

A smile stretched over his face and lit up his eyes. I leaned closer and sealed my vow with my lips. The rush of heat I always felt when we kissed tingled my toes and they curled into the blankets. I opened my mouth so his tongue could venture inside, and I sighed, so wanting to feel him.

But the moment was cut short.

The door opened and a man with graying hair, a white coat, and a file in his hand stepped in.

"Mr. Anderson," he said, looking straight at Romeo. It was like he didn't even notice the intimate bubble Romeo and I occupied. "I have your X-ray results."

The bubble burst abruptly and reality rushed back in.

Romeo's dad came in the room, his face concerned as Valerie hovered just outside the doorway staring into the room like it was some forbidden fruit.

I scrambled up to sit on the mattress, ignoring the protests of my sore body. Romeo did the same, moving a little more gingerly.

In the space between us on the mattress, our fingers intertwined.

"How bad is it?" Romeo asked. For once I heard fear in his tone.

I glanced at him.

He glanced at me.

Our moment was over.

The fight started now.

CHAPTER TWO

#FYI
The local pizza joint is delivering.
Use discount code: #AlphaDown for
twenty percent off.
#FeedingTheHungryWhileTheyWait
... Alpha BuzzFeed

ROMEO

This was it.

Whatever that X-ray showed would define my future.

I'd never realized how much one piece of paper could change my life.

I clung to Rimmel's hand with a desperation I hoped no one else noticed. But she was my lifeline, and if ever I needed one, it was right then.

Dr. Craven stepped farther into the room and cleared his throat. He shuffled around a few papers in the folder he was holding as if he were consulting his notes.

My father stood nervously behind the doc, waiting just like me.

"The X-ray was very clear," he began, and my gut tightened.

"Wait." Rimmel cut in, and all eyes turned to her. "She should be here." Her hazel eyes looked toward the door.

In the small glass cutout, I could see my mother hovering, anxiously bouncing from foot to foot.

"Rimmel," I said, harsh, about to shoot her down.

Just looking at my mother right now made me fucking pissed.

"Romeo," she said. Her voice held a hint of steel. "She's your mother. You're seriously injured. She's worried and deserves to hear what the doctor's about to say."

Dad didn't wait for my reply. He went and opened the door and gestured for Mom. She rushed in the room like there was a fire in the hallway.

"Roman," she said, stepping closer, and I gave her a cold look that stopped her in her tracks.

"You can thank Rimmel for you being in here," I said and then dismissed her and looked back at the doc.

Upon my expectant look, the doctor cleared his throat. "Your arm is definitely broken," he confirmed. "The good news is it's a closed fracture, meaning the bone didn't break through the skin of your upper arm."

The doctor pulled out an X-ray film and held it up to the light. "It's difficult to see in here," he began and pointed toward the image of my arm. "The break is here, above the elbow. It probably occurred by the way you fell. The distinct cracking sound you said you heard." Beside me, Rimmel stiffened, and I squeezed her fingers. "That unpleasant sound was actually a good thing. It was a clean break."

Dr. Craven looked away from the film to smile at me. It was like he was delivering some great news.

Excuse me while I don't have a fucking party.

"Here's the point of the break. It's transverse, which means it goes straight across the bone," he said, pointing at the film again. I did see a dark line in the white area of my bone. "It's a non-displaced fracture. The bones are still aligned, which means no surgery will be needed."

My mother let out an audible sigh of relief as the doctor tucked the film back in his folder.

"What does all this mean for him?" my father asked.

I was glad he did. I was having trouble posing the question.

I wasn't sure I was ready for the answer.

"This type of injury can be life altering for someone in your profession," the doc said, glancing at me knowingly. "But I see no cause for major concern."

A small part of me relaxed. "So I can still play?"

"I'm not quite ready to make any promises," he said, and my guts tightened. "But because it's a clean break, you're young, clearly in perfect health, and seem to have no tissue damage or nerve damage—*at this time*—I would say it's a high probability that your career will not suffer."

Rimmel made a sound and bounced on the bed as she flung her arms around my neck. I bit back a groan as her sudden movements jerked my shoulders and pain radiated down my arm.

"I would definitely suggest limited movement," the doctor cautioned, looking directly at Rim.

She pulled back immediately and went still. I patted her hand.

"How long?" I asked. I had to know.

"How long until you can play again?" the doctor echoed. He shook his head. "It's too early to say."

I growled. "How long?"

"If you do exactly as instructed, if you don't push yourself, and bearing no complications, I would say you could be completely healed in eight weeks."

Okay, that would put me toward April.

"But," he said, speaking over my thoughts, "the arm is usually in a weakened state and stiff after being cast."

"He needs a cast?" my mother said.

"A cast is one option," he replied, glancing at her. "But because of your health and your profession, I would recommend a splint with a shoulder support and sling. The compression support of the splint would assist with the swelling and increase the elasticity of the muscles."

"What does that mean?" Rimmel asked nervously.

"It means there could potentially be less stiffness once healed," he answered. "The sling will be for comfort but also to help keep the area still. You'll need to see an orthopedic specialist to oversee your care, and also, they can likely work out some sort of physical therapy, as I know you're anxious for that."

"Yeah, thanks," I said, trying to take it all in. It didn't sound like this was going to be a career ender (before it even started), and the relief from that almost knocked me over.

"I'll be back in a few moments with a sheet of instructions, the splint, and sling. I'm also prescribing some pain medication—"

"No." I cut him off. "No pills." I wasn't about to drug myself up. I didn't need that shit in my system. I tried to stay clean.

He nodded. "Then I suggest taking an over-the-counter anti-inflammatory at least for the first few days.

It will help the swelling and discomfort. I'll be back in just a few moments," he said and then left the room.

"Roman," my mother gasped when he was gone. "Thank God it's not any worse."

An uncomfortable silence stretched across the room when I didn't answer.

"Roman," my father admonished, and I shook my head.

"This isn't the time or place," I said. "Later."

"I'm going to go out in the hall and put a call in to John's Hopkins. Hopefully one of their ortho doctors can get you in," Mom announced. "And I'll also run and get you some pain reliever, some ice packs, and a few pillows. You're going to need to keep that comfortable."

"Thanks," I said and sighed. Fuck, it was hard to be cold to my own mother.

"I'll go with her," my father said. Before leaving, he turned back. "Rimmel, is there anything we can get you while we're out?"

She looked up and gave my father a smile. How she could smile at all was beyond me. "No, thank you. Just take care of your son."

"If you need anything, you let me know," he replied, winking.

She smiled, but once he was gone, she sank back into the pillow. "Did I hurt you?" she worried. "When I hugged you?"

"No, baby, you didn't hurt me."

"I'm so glad your arm isn't worse," she said, her voice catching.

"Takes a lot more than a lawn mower to bring me down." I joked.

She didn't laugh.

It was probably too soon for jokes. But that was damn funny.

Before I could say anything else, another doctor in a white coat came into the room. This time a female.

"Miss Hudson, the nurses told me you'd moved in here." Her eyes moved toward me, and I gave her a lazy smile. She flushed and looked away. "Would you care to step over to your side of the room so we can talk?"

Rim shook her head. "He can hear this."

The doctor nodded. "It appears your injuries are superficial. I saw no signs of internal damage or hypothermia. Though I would caution you to stay indoors and warm for the next few days."

"That won't be a problem," Rimmel muttered.

"Your cheek doesn't appear to have a hairline fracture like I originally thought."

I jerked upright. "What?" I ground out.

The doctor seemed startled by my sudden outburst, but Rimmel barely moved. She just reached over and patted my chest like she was humoring me. "It's fine."

I knew Zach had hit her—the bruise on her face was proof—but just the mention of it breaking a bone in her face made me want to find him and pound him all over again.

"Calm down," Rimmel said out of the side of her mouth and then turned back to the doctor. "Go on."

"The swelling should go down quickly and the bruises will fade. The rope burns on your torso and stomach…" The doctor slid a glance at me before quickly looking away. I took a deep breath. "Will also go away, but I would recommend some simple medicated cream for the area where the skin was rubbed raw."

Tension was building in my body, so much so that it was hard to sit still. I wanted to get up and pace. Yell.

"I can do that," Rimmel said like she was just having some conversation about oranges and not the state her body.

"I saw no signs of a concussion, so there's no reason to keep you overnight. I would like to check your torso again before you leave, but beyond that, I'll get your discharge papers ready."

Rimmel stood from the bed, and the one thing anchoring me was no longer there. I got up and started pacing.

Rimmel gave me a look and sighed. She turned to the doctor. "You can check me over here." She went over toward her bed, and the doctor followed. I started across, but Rimmel shook her head. "I'm fine, and you're already mad enough."

Then she slid the curtain closed and blocked her side of the room from sight.

It was cute she thought a curtain was going to keep me from seeing what those ropes did to her.

I started forward, about to rip away the stupid fabric, when my doctor and a few nurses came in.

"If we could have you sit down over here, Mr. Anderson," the doctor said, "we'll get this arm immobilized.

I glanced back at the curtain before swearing under my breath and going to sit down. Rimmel might have managed to evade revealing exactly what Zach had done to her right now, but she wouldn't be able to put me off forever.

CHAPTER THREE

#ERSighting
Someone finally got past NurseZilla.
Romeo's right hand left us all in his dust.
Did you know?
The #Nerd has a big bro.
... Alpha BuzzFeed

RIMMEL

I was naked.

Well, okay. I wasn't naked.

I was wearing a grossly thin hospital gown.

So basically, I was naked.

(Can't a girl get away with a little dramatics after she was hung from a pole and blasted with an icy water hose?)

I had clothes, but they were soaking wet and ruined. Plus, every time I looked at them, I remembered everything that happened at the field.

If I had a garbage disposal, I would probably attempt shoving them down and grinding them up until they were nothing more than shreds. But I didn't have a garbage disposal and neither did Romeo, so I consoled myself by balling up the drenched garments and shoving them in the small trash bag beside the bed. It was probably a barf bag.

But my clothes were pretty much the same.

Unfortunately, that left me wearing this hospital gown. There was no way I could walk out of here in this, so I used Romeo's phone (mine was MIA, along with my glasses) and called Ivy.

She answered on the first ring.

"Romeo?" Ivy gasped. The loud noise in her background seemed to halt.

"It's me, Ivy," I said.

"Ohmigod, Rimmel! What happened? Are you okay?"

The light sound of voices floated behind her, and I couldn't help but wonder. "Where are you?"

"I'm in the waiting room, duh!"

"You're here? At the hospital?" I was surprised. How did she know I was here?

"Are you kidding? Of course I am. Me and half the college. There is seriously not one spot open in this waiting room. I heard some people were waiting outside."

I peaked around the edge of the curtain. Romeo was resting on the bed, his parents at his side. His mother caught me looking, and I jerked back around behind the safety of the cloth.

"How does everyone know we're here?"

"The BuzzBoss has been blowing up the AlphaBuzzfeed for hours about it. Romeo's car driving to the hospital is not to be missed. And the way the cops swarmed the field… My God, Rimmel, I thought somebody was dead!"

"No one's dead," I said dryly. Then I thought about Zach. I actually had no clue what condition he was in.

"Then why have you guys been back there so long? Seriously. People have started ordering pizzas."

I laughed. "Are you serious?"

"The nurses are pissed," Ivy said, but she was clearly amused.

"Hey, that my little sis?" someone yelled in the background.

Ivy made a disgusted sound. I smiled as I pictured Braeden pushing through the crowd of people eating pizza and toward Ivy. Braeden was probably Ivy's least favorite person.

"So what—" Ivy began to say, and then her muffled outraged yell came through the phone.

"Rimmel?" Braeden said into the line.

"Hey, Braeden."

"Girl, I was about to go Rambo on somebody's ass out here. No one will tell us anything."

"Why didn't you just come back?"

He hesitated. "I wasn't sure what kind of shape everyone was in."

I heard the worry in his voice, and I felt bad for making him wait so long. He deserved better than that. "We're okay. Well, I am. Romeo is injured."

Braeden sucked in a breath.

“Why don’t you just come back?” I said. It would be easier to let him look at Romeo when he learned about the break. At least then he could see Romeo was going to be fine.

And he would be fine.

He had to be.

“Will do, tutor girl.”

“Braeden?” I called before he could go. “Romeo’s clothes are wet. Do you have anything he can put on?”

“Yeah, I got a duffle in my truck. I’ll bring it in.”

“Thanks, Braeden.”

“You sure you’re okay?” he asked. There was way more perception in his tone than I realized he possessed.

“It’s been a long night,” I replied wearily.

“Here’s blondie,” he said, and then Ivy came back on the line.

“Jerk face!” she snapped. “Rimmel?”

“Yeah. Hey, Ivy, I was calling because I don’t have any clothes. All mine got ruined. Is there any way you can go get me something at the dorm?”

"I have some stuff in the car. I can grab that for you."

"Awesome. Just tell the nurse I called and asked you to bring me some clothes."

"See you in a few," she said and then hung up the phone.

I laid the cell on the bed and stayed behind the curtain. Romeo's parents were still with him, and I wanted to give them some time alone.

A sudden feeling of loneliness washed over me. I didn't have any family here. If it weren't for Ivy, I probably wouldn't have had anyone to call for clothes. I missed my mother. I knew she'd be here right now if she were alive.

Her father killed her mother.

The echoed words cut me like a knife. My father was all I had left besides my grandparents. I just couldn't stand the thought—the *implication*—that he would dare take my mother away from me.

I sat down on the bed, my feet dangling over the side, and I looked down at my hands. My wrists were rubbed raw from where they'd been tied. I'd struggled, desperately trying to get free from the rope that bound them. One wrist was rubbed worse, and it was now wrapped. After the doctor looked at it a few minutes ago, she decided it should be covered just to keep the germs out of it for a while.

My fingers ached and felt stiff from the cold and trying to untie the knots. In fact, my whole body felt sore. Like I'd done an intense three-hour workout. The doctor said that was normal because my body had been tense for so long as I hung and that my muscles would hurt for a few days.

Inside the white, itchy socks the hospital gave me, my toes were cold, and I thought longingly of my white faux-fur boots Romeo gave me. I glanced over at the fur-lined boots I'd been wearing earlier that night—the only article of clothing that survived being tossed in the barf bag earlier—but they were soaked and I wasn't putting my feet in them.

I hopped down off the bed and my socks slid against the white tile floor. I caught myself on the side of the bed, but my side brushed against the mattress, and I hissed a little because my ribs and upper abdominals were really tender. Even through my clothes, my skin was rubbed raw. I hadn't seen the marks fully, only what I could by looking down at myself. It almost looked like I had some raging rash, the way my skin was mottled and irritated.

Once I was steady, I walked over toward the small wardrobe against the wall and opened up the door. On the inside, there was a tall mirror, and I braved a peek at my reflection.

I knew it was going to be bad, but it was way worse than I thought.

I was almost fortunate that my vision was blurry from the lack of glasses on my face. Seeing the mess that was me with full clarity probably would have scared me.

I stepped up close until my toes almost bumped the door and studied myself. My cheek was black and blue. Funny, I never thought the color purple could be ugly until I saw this shade. I saw now why the doctor had originally thought my cheekbone was cracked.

No wonder I'd stayed out so long when Zach hit me.

The top of my cheekbone was swollen and the bruise extended all the way around my eye. There was a cut in the center of the purplest part, and I wondered if perhaps my glasses had broken when he hit me and that's what cut my skin.

It was cleaned and a small butterfly bandage taped over it. Funny, I didn't remember the nurse even putting it there. Of course, when I was first led back, all I could think about was Romeo and his arm. Well, that and the fact that I'd been tied up and hanging from a pole.

I could still feel the icy-cold water pelting me, rushing in my face and nose, as I hung there unable to do a thing.

They'd given me some kind of shot, but I don't remember what was in it. It might have been pain medicine, because by the looks of my face, it should hurt a lot worse.

My eyebrow was slightly puffy and the other side of my face was pale white, the only color coming from the tired ring beneath my eye.

And my hair.

I mean, really.

It needed its own zip code. It was matted, half wet, half dry, and hung in clumps over my shoulders. I never really made an effort, but this was bad even for me.

My eyes traveled down the front of my hospital gown, which embarrassingly enough, I could see my hardened nipples through because I was so cold. God, I hoped I hadn't looked like this the entire time the doctors were in the room.

My ribs were hurting and the skin on my stomach burned. I grabbed a handful of the gown and started to hoist it up to see the damage, but loud voices out in the hall caught my attention.

"They asked for me!" Braeden yelled.

It took me a minute to place his voice because I'd never heard it that angry before.

"What part of sister do you not understand!" he yelled a few seconds later.

On the other side of the curtain, Romeo cursed. "They won't let Braeden back."

I dropped my gown and rushed through the room, past Romeo's parents, and for the door.

"Rim, wait," Romeo called as I threw open the door and skidded into the hallway.

"You better go ahead and call 'em, then," Braeden growled as he towered over a nurse. "Because I'm not leaving."

Beyond him, I could see Ivy bouncing from foot to foot with a bag in her hand. She saw me and waved. "There she is!"

Braeden's head snapped around, and the anger in his gaze made his dark eyes bottomless. "Rim," he said, and some of the darkness receded. A look of horror replaced it. "Your face," he practically gasped.

I resisted the urge to cover my injury and motioned for him.

"Nursezilla here doesn't believe you're my sister," he growled.

The nurse turned to me with a huff. "Sister?" she asked sarcastically.

"Actually, yes," I said with bold confidence.

Her eyes rounded, and she glanced back at Braeden, who folded his arms over his chest.

The nurse looked between me and Braeden for long moments before relenting. "Fine. Whatever. Go in."

He started down the hall, and Ivy followed. The nurse blocked her. "No more people back there."

"She has my clothes," I protested.

Braeden backtracked and plucked the bag out of Ivy's hands. "Thanks, blondie."

Ivy practically snarled at him. He didn't seem to notice.

As Braeden approached, he looked me over like he was checking for injuries. The way his mouth flattened when he stared at my face made my stomach hurt.

"You look like dog meat," he said fondly and slung an arm across my shoulders. I sank into him a little because he was so warm.

"Gee, thanks."

He steered me toward the room but stopped abruptly when he saw who was in the doorway. His entire body stiffened and the arm across my shoulders tensed. "Rome."

Romeo filled the doorway. A fresh splint and sling covered half his arm and wrapped his chest. His blond hair was a wreck, and there were shadows beneath his blue eyes.

"Aww, fuck, Rome. How bad is it?"

"Broken," he said, gruff.

"Zach?" Braeden said, his voice deadly calm. That calmness was scarier than the fury I'd heard only moments before.

Romeo nodded once.

An unspoken message traveled between them and with it, a current of unrestrained wrath. It made me uncomfortable, and I shivered.

"C'mon, sis," Braeden said, loud. "You need some clothes." He guided me into the room.

Inside the room, Braeden tossed the bags on Romeo's bed and turned toward his parents. I went back around the curtain and sank onto my bed. I wasn't up for looking at his mother right now. She had every right to be here, but I had every right to be angry, and it was all just too much.

• • •

I needed some space. I needed to breathe and deal with one thing at a time, but the problem was I didn't seem to be processing anything right then. It was as if I were completely numb.

Romeo stepped around the curtain, the bag Ivy brought in his hand. He sat it beside me and stared down, not saying anything.

The broken part of his arm was now completely covered. It was a pretty modern-looking splint, and I was glad because it looked fairly comfortable. It appeared like they slid a white wrap over his arm so it covered his bicep, upper arm, elbow, and forearm. It looked thick and soft but also like it was sturdy, like it would compress the area a little. Over the wrap was a white, hard plastic brace. It wrapped around his bicep just above his elbow and ended just below his armpit. There were white straps that wrapped around the brace, holding it tightly in place. The top of the wrap (really, it looked like a sleeve) was attached to a long white strip that wrapped around his chest and anchored his arm to his side.

I stared at the brace, wondering how badly it had hurt when they put it on him. I hadn't heard him say a word.

"You're hiding back here," he said, his voice brusque.

"I was with the doctor," I argued.

"She left a while ago."

"I called Ivy for clothes."

"You're avoiding my parents."

"Just your mother," I muttered.

He grinned.

I found myself smiling back.

"I sent them outside," he said, cupping my jaw with his hand. "You don't have to see her. Hell, I don't want to see her either."

I wasn't going to put him in the middle of this. "I'm going to get dressed so we can leave."

He squatted down so he wasn't towering over me, but instead, I was slightly higher than him. He reached for my hand and wrapped his larger, much warmer one around it. "You okay?"

"Are you?" I countered.

"As long as you are."

But that was a lie. I slid a glance to his arm. He wasn't okay. He was broken.

"Remember what I told you," he whispered.

My eyes went to his. He was so steady. So calm. It seemed like everything around us was complete chaos, but he remained still.

"I remember."

He stood and leaned down to press a kiss to my forehead. "Get dressed. I'll see about the discharge papers."

When he was gone, I reached into the bag Ivy sent in and pulled out a pair of black yoga pants and a pink T-shirt with a designer label. I smiled. Only Ivy would wear designer clothes to the gym.

I pulled on the pants, which were too long and too big so I folded the waist an extra time to keep them up. Cold air rushed over my bare skin when I pulled off the hospital gown, and I hurried to get the shirt on. I tried to ignore the fact that it was pink. I hated pink.

There were no shoes in the bag, so I just left on the hospital socks and snatched up the brush to start the process of combing out my hair.

"You decent?" Braeden said and then pulled back the curtain.

I made a sound. "What if I'd been naked?" I gasped.

"You aren't." He shrugged.

I went back to fighting with the brush and my hair. After a couple seconds, my arm sagged. I was too tired for this.

Braeden took the brush out of my hand and started working it through the tangles. I was momentarily shocked at the gesture, but when I recovered, I said, "You're brushing my hair?"

"I had to. The way you were mistreating it, I'm surprised you aren't bald."

"Ha-ha," I quipped.

For such a big guy, he had a surprisingly light hand, and frankly, he was doing a better job than I had been. "You're pretty good at this," I observed. "Does this mean we can have sleepovers and paint each other's nails?"

"What do you think I am? A drag queen?" He gasped as he continued brushing.

I laughed. "Is that a no to the nail polish and face masks?"

He let out a curse, and I laughed again.

"That's a hells no." But then he grunted. "But you know I'm here for you, right?"

The genuineness behind his words pierced my chest. He'd gotten in. I hadn't meant for it to happen, but Braeden had wiggled his way right into my heart. "That's what big brothers are for, right?"

"You got it."

Overcome with emotion, I spun and hugged him around the waist. He hesitated for a second but then returned the embrace fully. I couldn't help but sniffle against his shirt.

Embarrassed, I pulled away. "I'm sorry. Tonight's just been a lot. I know you aren't really my brother." He was here because of Romeo. I needed to remember that. Getting attached to so many people wasn't a good idea.

"Fuck that," he argued. "We might not be blood, but you're my family. That's not going to change."

I turned away and suppressed a sniffle. I couldn't have this kind of conversation right now. I was too busy trying to hold it together. I clung to the numbness that cloaked me like a lifeline, because once it was gone, I was afraid I might fall apart.

"Hey," he said, gruff, and grabbed my arm to pull me around. "You hear me?"

I nodded. "I hear you."

"You're trying to be tough for Rome right now. I get that. But I'm not him. I'm not gonna go postal if you tell me how messed up you feel right now."

Tears flooded my eyes.

He understood.

He held open his arms. "Bring it in."

I half laughed, half groaned.

"You gonna leave me hanging?" he said, his arms still spread wide.

I stepped forward, and he folded me against him. A few tears slipped out from beneath closed lids and a sob racked my body.

"It's all right," he murmured and patted my back. "I'd cry too if my face looked like yours."

I started to laugh, but it turned into a weep as the floodgates opened. It hurt to cry, the way my body heaved and shook. I was already so sore and so tired, but once I started, I couldn't stop.

My God, I was making an ass out of myself, crying all over Braeden like this. But he didn't say anything. He just hugged me.

Well, occasionally, he assured me my face would go back to normal.

A few minutes passed, and I forced myself to get it together. The last thing I wanted was for Romeo to come back and see me crying all over his best friend. He didn't need to deal with the hot mess I was right then.

I pulled away from Braeden and wiped my eyes with the backs of my hand. "I'm so sorry," I murmured, my voice thick.

"Nothing to be sorry about," he said, no trace of sarcasm in his tone. "You know Rome is a lot stronger than you think."

I nodded. I knew that. Romeo was the strongest person I knew. But I didn't want to be a burden. I didn't want to be someone he had to look after.

"This place officially blows," Braeden announced once I was finished getting myself together. "Let's find Rome and get the hell out of here."

"Yes, please!" I didn't have to fake the enthusiasm in my voice, because getting out of the ER was definitely high on my priority list.

Braeden grabbed the bag off the bed and my wet boots by the wall. "This it?" he asked.

I picked up a white plastic bag the nurse had given me with extra bandages and ointment for my wrists and nodded.

He threw back the curtain and led the way to the door, stopping to pick up the now empty duffle he'd brought in for Romeo.

Before he opened the door, he turned and regarded me with serious eyes. "BBFL?"

I blinked. "What?"

He seemed appalled I had no idea what he was talking about. "Big brother for life," he said like it was obvious. "BBFL."

I grinned. "Yeah, BBFL."

He held up his fist, so I bumped mine against his. It was my first official fist-bump as a sister.

Seconds after we stepped out in the hallway, Romeo rounded the corner and smiled when he saw us. But his smile slipped when he drew closer and his eyes narrowed on my face. Then he slid a glance at Braeden, his stare dropping to the front of his shirt. I followed his gaze and noticed the wet spots on his chest from where I cried all over him.

Romeo's narrowed eyes snapped back to me.

He knew I'd been crying.

"Dude, you get the papers or what?" Braeden said, drawing Romeo's attention.

After a lingering look at me, he glanced away. "They're up front. The nurse said we could just sign them on the way out."

"Good. Let's go," I said, hurrying past the guys.

Romeo caught my hand with his. "Wrong way. Nurse's station is this way."

"Is anyone else hungry?" Braeden wondered out loud. "I'm starving."

Romeo grinned. "Dude, I could eat a horse's ass right about now."

He glanced at me and winked. I relaxed, and we walked hand in hand down the hall.

"Pizza?" Braeden said. "I'll go get us a few pies and bring 'em back to your place."

As we rounded the corner, Romeo and Braeden had a lively discussion about what toppings and who could out eat who per slice. I didn't really remember the last time I'd eaten, though the idea of food didn't really appeal to me just then, but I knew they'd bully me into eating it.

As the guys argued over pizza consumption, my eyes went all the way down the hall to where it opened up on the left at the nurse's station. The elevator a little farther down dinged open, and two uniformed police officers stepped out onto the floor.

My steps faltered a little, and Romeo's hand tightened around mine. Both guys stopped talking and stared at the officers as they spoke quietly to a nurse who pointed toward a room across the hall from the desk.

The officers went immediately to the room. One opened the door and waltzed in, while the other took up station outside the door.

A sick feeling dropped into the pit of my stomach. Sticky tentacles of foreboding wrapped around the back of my neck, and my skin crawled with goose bumps.

Our steps slowed as we approached. The nurse saw us and smiled, but my face had frozen and I was unable to smile back. I peeked into the room where the officer was and saw nothing but a drawn curtain. The breath I'd been holding leaked out between my lips like I was a flat tire with a hole.

The tension in my back eased, and we stepped up to the paperwork the nurse had ready.

"Sign here and here," she said to Romeo. As he did, she went on to say, "Your parents have taken care of the rest of the paperwork for you."

Then her gaze turned to me. I saw the flash of pity in the depth of her eyes before she replaced it with professionalism. "Would you mind stepping over here? I have a few more documents to go over with you before you're finished."

"Sure," I said and released Romeo to step farther down the long counter.

Romeo's dad appeared, and the three men started talking quietly.

"There's been a problem with the insurance card you provided," the nurse said, drawing my complete attention.

"What?" I took it out of her hand and glanced down at the insurance card I'd used practically all my life.

"This policy has been cancelled."

My brows snapped together in confusion. "That's impossible." I glanced up at her. "I've had this insurance my whole life."

"Through a parent?" she asked.

I nodded. "My father."

"Has he recently lost his job?"

"No," I denied. "He's a contractor."

The nurse seemed slightly uncomfortable. "Maybe he forgot to pay the policy."

He's in deep debt. He has a gambling problem.

Valerie's accusations assaulted me once more.

I shook my head. "No."

The nurse thought I'd been talking to her and took a step back. "I'm afraid, without insurance, we're going to have to bill you. Would you like to pay a portion up front, right now?"

My head was spinning, my face was beginning to throb, and the nurse was looking at me like she expected me to pull out a wad of fifty-dollar bills and toss them on the counter.

"I don't have my bag with me," I stuttered. "I don't know what happened to it."

It was lost with my phone and my glasses.

I glanced up. "I don't have any money."

Some of the kindness left the nurses eyes. "We're going to have to bill you."

"Okay." What the hell else was I supposed to say?

"All the information you put on this form is correct?" She turned it around as if I needed to verify my own address.

"I didn't lie," I said, a bite in my tone.

"Sign here." She pointed to a line.

I grabbed a pen off the counter and signed.

"Here." She pointed again.

I tried not to show how badly my hands were shaking as I signed again.

"The billing department will be in touch."

"Thank you," I said, a little hollow, and tried to smile.

But it was a lost effort.

A muffled yet familiar voice rang out through the hall, followed by a bit of maniacal laughter.

"Well, look who it is!" he yelled.

My body jerked and my head whipped around so fast that the room tilted on its axis.

There in open doorway of the room being guarded by police was Zach.

CHAPTER FOUR

Did anyone else notice a certain Xpresident being wheeled thru the ER escorted by the Po-Po? #TheCrazyIsIntheBuilding

... Alpha BuzzFeed

ROMEO

Her eyes were puffy.

Well, her one eye. The one that wasn't practically swollen shut thanks to fucking Zach.

Her skin was blotchy, and if that weren't enough to prove to me she'd been crying, the tear stains on Braeden's shirt were.

I decided calling her out on it right there in the hall wasn't the way to go, so I bit back my frustration and the slight jealousy I felt knowing it was Braeden she cried to.

Knowing Rimmel, she probably was trying to hold it all in because she thought I'd been through enough.

My girl was stubborn like that. And that stubbornness extended deep into a protective streak that I wondered if she even realized she possessed. It was like an automatic reaction with her—an instinct, like a momma bear with her cub.

She protected herself fiercely. It's why it took me so long to get in and why she still struggled to let in anyone else (like my mother who freaking went and ruined it).

But I got in.

And now that protective instinct extended to me.

And from the looks of Braeden's shirt, I'd say he'd somehow gotten in too.

Her family was growing, but her future was threatened on so many fronts.

She was probably scared as hell.

My mother finally got the hint that I wasn't going to soften no matter how many regretful looks she threw my way and left, but my father stayed behind so he could drive the Hellcat back to my place. I couldn't with my arm all jacked up, and Rim was in no condition to be driving.

As we walked down the hallway, I resisted the urge to pull her close. Instead, I kept our hands entwined and joked with B about pizza. That little piece of normalcy felt good, even if we were experiencing it in the middle of the ER.

When the cops stepped off the elevator, I felt the change come over Rimmel. The wariness in which she moved and watched the two men.

We'd already talked to a few officers hours ago when we'd been admitted, but they would have more questions. From the way they questioned me, I knew they barely got a thing out of Rim. I heard the nurses in the hall telling them she was in shock and they'd have to talk to her later.

I answered as much as I could, but the truth was I hadn't been there for all of it.

Only Rimmel had.

• • •

There were gaps that only she could fill in. Gaps I was terrified to know the answers to.

Out of the corner of my eye, I watched her exchange with the nurse at the end of the counter and I could have sworn I felt a change in the air the longer the two women spoke. It seemed like Rimmel recoiled from whatever the nurse was saying and the nurse was overcome with a sudden air of snootiness.

I didn't like snooty bitches.

Especially when their snootiness was aimed directly at my girl.

I was about to inject myself into the conversation when there was a bit of a scuffle from across the hall. The officer standing at the door jerked upright, his posture going rigid. I couldn't help but notice how his hand hovered over a Taser in his belt.

"Well, look who it is!" a slurred voice rang out.

What. The. Fuck.

My entire body went rigid and the rage I thought had faded out with all the adrenaline suddenly burst to life inside me.

I reacted without thought and bolted across the hall. The officer at the door jumped forward as if to block my path. "Why isn't he in a cage?" I growled.

Braeden wrapped an arm around my waist as if to restrain me, and my father moved to my side.

"Roman, this is not the place," he said calmly.

"That cast looks good on you," Zach said, trying to move closer to the doorway.

There were two officers in the room with him. One in uniform and one wearing a suit with a badge clipped at his waist. Both men moved on either side of him, ready to spring.

"No contact with the victims," the one in the suit told Zach.

"Victims!" Zach guffawed. Well, he tried.

His face was jacked the hell up. He couldn't even talk right.

As he stood there, he swayed on his feet like he was going to fall over. The left side of his jaw was about twice its normal size, a deep purple color, and looked a little crooked. Zach's lip was split and had just a bit of dried blood at the edges. Both his eyes were black and his nose was swollen. Judging from the white strip across the bridge of his nose, I guessed it was broken.

His "boy band" hair was completely ruined, matted with blood and a small section above his right temple shaved where a gash had already been stitched up.

The way he hunched over as he stood made me think he probably had injuries I couldn't see, and just that thought calmed me down.

I hoped he was suffering. He deserved every last one of those bruises, and I was proud I put them there.

Zach noticed my appraisal and his mouth turned up as far as his swollen face would allow. Then his gaze swung away from me, beyond where we stood.

I knew exactly who he was looking at.

My muscles bunched and Braeden's arm tightened. "Rome," he cautioned.

"Stop," said a low voice from just beside him. "You might jar his arm."

Braeden pulled back, and Rimmel stepped up in his place. Her small hand lay on my chest with ever so light pressure. "C'mon. I want to go."

I tore my eyes from Zach and looked down at her. She was exhausted and scared.

I wrapped my good arm around her and started leading her away.

"Can you still feel the water flooding your face and blurring your vision?" Zach's words floated out into the hall, and Rimmel's body tightened. "I still think about the way your body folded to the ground when my fist connected with your face." He wheezed out a breath. "Your cheekbone must really be throbbing."

I spun away from Rimmel. "You son of a bitch!" I lunged past the officer, but he caught me and shoved me back. Pain radiated down my arm and across my chest. The feeling only fueled my anger.

I kept going, and Zach laughed. The laugh turned into a cough and the cough turned into some kind of asthma attack.

All three officers jumped toward me, and I relented, holding up my hand in surrender. Before I walked away, I glanced back at Zach. He was still coughing like a fiend. Rimmel called my name, and everyone else stood by on alert, waiting to see what I would do.

I didn't do anything.

Because Zach fell over.

He literally crumpled to the floor in the midst of his coughing attack.

The officers all moved away from me and rushed into the room, one of them yelling for the nurse. She rushed past us into the room, and we all stood there watching as Zach gasped for breath on the floor.

Rimmel appeared beside me, and I pulled her against my chest.

"Get him on the bed," the nurse instructed. "I'll go get the doctor."

She rushed out of the room and down the hall as the officers picked up Zach and towed him toward the bed. His head fell back as they moved, and from an upside-down angle, his empty stare fastened on where we stood.

And then he smiled.

He had fresh blood on his teeth.

Rimmel shuddered, and I pulled her away. The four of us headed toward the elevator as someone stepped off.

Behind us, the doctor and nurse were rushing into Zach's room, and one of the officers appeared back in the doorway.

"What the hell is this!" the man who just stepped into the hall bellowed. His voice was very commanding and oddly familiar.

"Robert," my dad said, a tone of regret in his voice.

It was Zach's father.

"Why is the doctor rushing in my son's room? Why are you out here? What the hell have you done!" The last question was directed at me.

"You should be asking about what your son has done." My voice was level.

"Excuse me?" The man rose up to his full stature.

But I was taller.

I made a point to look down at him.

"This isn't the time nor place, Robert," my dad said. Then he turned to me. "Let's go, Roman."

"It seems like the perfect time," he intoned. "Especially since your son is walking out of here and my son is admitted."

"He isn't going to jail?" Rimmel asked immediately. The fear in her tone pissed me off all over again.

"Yes, but he's entitled to medical care first," my father explained to her. "That's why the police are here. He's still in their custody."

"And who is this?" Robert asked haughtily.

I dropped my arm and stepped away from Rimmel, angling so he could actually see all of her. "This is the girl your son strung up like some circus piñata and tried to drown with a garden hose."

Robert's eyes widened and he looked over Rimmel.

A look of regret passed behind his eyes, and then it was gone. "And your face?" he asked.

She cleared her throat. "That's where your son assaulted me."

Her voice was strong and clear.

It made me want to kiss her.

Robert seemed to take in her small size once more before clearing his throat and turning back to me. "I will be pressing assault charges against you."

My father stepped forward. "They won't stick and you know it."

"My son was battered tonight."

"My son didn't walk away unscathed." My father's tone turned hard and cold. The shark lawyer in him was beginning to surface.

"But he is walking away."

"It was self defense," Rimmel said.

"And what of the blows my son received after he was already incapacitated?"

"You mean when he hijacked a lawn mower and hit a pole?" I asked. Then I shrugged. "I don't recall hitting him after that."

Robert's eyes narrowed.

"I didn't see anything." Rimmel agreed.

"Well, his dislocated jaw, fractured nose, missing tooth, and head laceration say otherwise."

"This conversation is highly inappropriate and is borderline harassment," my father said with an air of authority. "If you want to go over the case, as documented by the authorities, call my office on Monday."

The elevator was waiting, so when Dad stepped around Robert to push the button, it opened immediately.

Braeden and my dad filed in first, and then I moved so Rimmel could go ahead and I blocked her from behind.

As soon as the elevator doors closed, Braeden looked at me. There was a bit of pride shining in his eyes. "Dude."

My lips twitched. "What?"

"You inflicted all that damage on Zach?"

My lips twitched again, and I glanced at my father. "I can't recall."

He held up his fist and we pounded it out.

Rimmel sagged against the wall of the elevator, and I moved in close beside her.

"Do not talk to anyone about this," my father cautioned. "This is now a legal matter. The less you say in public the better."

We all nodded as the elevator slid to a stop. As the doors began to open, Braeden glanced at me and Rim. "Warning, you got an audience. Get ready to address your people."

"His people?" Rimmel muttered.

I shrugged. "My people."

She rolled her eyes but straightened away from the wall.

"I'll meet you at the entrance with the Hellcat," my father said.

The doors opened, and an entire crowd stood watching to see who was going to step off. The minute the four of us came into view, a murmur went through the horde.

Dad moved fast and disappeared, swallowed pretty quickly by the crowd. Braeden moved to Rimmel's other side so she was between us. I reached for her hand, and she gave it eagerly.

The three of us stepped out of the box as one unit. Every single eye went to my arm. A few people started to cry.

Ivy broke out from the edge of the crowd and rushed toward Rimmel.

Everyone else just stood there.

Waiting.

Watching.

I couldn't say much, but I had to say something.

I'd always known I was popular here. But the amount of people who sat waiting for hours…

I was surprised.

And oddly, I was touched.

Clearly, dating Rimmel was making me soft.

But I'd never admit that out loud.

"Wolves stick together," I said loud. "And the loyalty I'm looking at right now says it all. We are one pack united!"

Everyone erupted into cheers and applause.

When they died down, people still looked at me expectantly. Many gazes were on the brace fastened around my arm. They truly wanted to know if I was going to be okay.

"What you see here is only temporary," I spoke out. "It takes a lot more than a broken bone to keep this man down!"

Everyone cheered and whistled. A few people in the back of the room chanted my number.

No one stopped us from leaving. They all parted so we had a clear path to the door. Outside, more people lingered, and I fist-bumped a few on our way to the Hellcat, which was already waiting.

"Pizza?" Braeden asked over Rimmel's head. I knew he needed more info than the small amount he'd gotten inside.

I really wanted alone time with Rimmel, but I would make sure we got it.

"For sure," I replied.

Braeden didn't hesitate. He looped an arm around Rimmel and pressed a kiss to the top of her head. "I'll bring ya some extra anchovies," he joked.

Rimmel stuck out her tongue, and Braeden jogged off.

Ivy had followed us out and was standing nearby. After Rimmel hugged her and promised to call, we were finally able to get in the car.

No one said a word the entire drive home, and my thoughts centered on Zach. I'd always thought his vendetta against me was somehow fueled by jealousy.

I'd been wrong.

I was beginning to see it wasn't personal at all.

The more I thought, the more I replayed everything that happened and the vision of the way he stared at us with those maniacal eyes back in his room…

I understood.

Zach was seriously imbalanced.

AKA: crazy as hell.

And that made him even more dangerous.

CHAPTER FIVE

RIMMEL

I was half afraid his mother would be at his place when we got there.

But the idea wasn't enough to make me linger outside in the blustery winter air. In just a few hours, the sun would start to rise, and I really hoped to be in bed when it did. Exhausted didn't even begin to cover the way I felt just then.

I left Romeo and his father standing in the driveway, talking about details from tonight, and pushed the door open and went inside. The warmth of the room seeped into me, and I sighed as I walked farther.

Murphy was curled up on the couch, and he blinked up at me when I stood in the doorway. The kitchen light was on, so I kept going, thinking maybe Valerie would be there.

But she wasn't.

It was clear she had been, though.

A new, very large bottle of over-the-counter pain reliever was sitting on the counter beside several cold packs that could be activated by breaking them up between my hands. There were also several sheets of instructions on how Romeo should care for his arm.

I picked them up and read through the information so I would know how to help him.

Beside those things was a brand new box of apple cider packets. The kind you just dumped into a mug and mixed with hot water.

They were for me.

Why would she do something so sweet when she'd made it perfectly clear how she felt about me?

I left the cider where it sat and padded into the bedroom to find my slippers.

The front door opened and closed, and Romeo called out my name.

"In here!" I answered as I grabbed the soft boots and sat on the edge of the bed to pull them on.

Leaning over for even just a few seconds made my face throb, and I sat up quickly.

Romeo stepped into the room, moving more stiffly than ever.

"We need to get your arm propped up on some pillows. The elevation will help with the swelling. And then I'll get you some meds."

He seemed amused by my instructions.

"Take off your shirt," he ordered.

"I don't really think now is the time for that."

He gave me a wolfish smile. "Baby, I could be half dead and it would be the time for that." I rolled my eyes, and he grinned some more. "But that isn't the reason I want you to get naked."

I started to ask why, but I stopped myself. "Seeing the marks on my body won't change anything."

Romeo prowled closer. The way his hips swiveled as he walked drew my attention, and I swallowed thickly. He stopped in front of me, and from my position on the bed, his crotch was directly in front of my face.

"I need to see the places I need to be careful of when I'm touching you." His voice was hoarse, and I tore my eyes from his nether regions and glanced up. Desire danced in his stare. "C'mon." He motioned with his chin and stepped back a little so I could stand.

I did because arguing with him was the last thing I felt like doing and also because I really hated this pink shirt. Carefully, I pulled it over my head and tossed it aside.

I wasn't wearing a bra. I'd thrown it in the trash. The air, even though warm, still felt cold to my flesh and my nipples tightened, but for once, he didn't seem to notice.

Romeo's eyes darkened and his mouth flattened in a hard line. "Damn, baby."

I wandered over to the mirror near the closet and stood before it, finally seeing the damage for myself.

It was pretty much what I expected.

I had purple rings encircling my ribs, just below my breasts. The skin was red and irritated; some places were puffy and raw. The rings extended all the way down to my belly button, and my lower back looked the same. What I hadn't expected were the rope burns wrapping vertically around my shoulders, cutting beneath my armpits. It's how he anchored the rope up around me and the pole.

Those marks were pretty angry-looking too.

Romeo stepped up behind me, his face filled with sadness, and he reached out to skim his finger over a bruise I had yet to notice on my upper arm. It was a handprint. I was glad these marks would fade. Looking at them was just a reminder. A reminder I didn't want or need.

It was bad enough the police took photos. They said they needed the pictures for evidence since this was now a legal case. It made sense to me, but I still hated the thought those photos would mean the bruises—the handprints Zach left behind—would never totally be gone. There would always be proof of this horrible night.

"I'm so sorry I wasn't fucking there." Romeo's voice cracked.

I met his eyes through the mirror. "I don't blame you for this."

"I know, and that makes me feel even worse."

I turned away from my reflection and faced him. He towered over me, and his right forearm rested across his middle so I couldn't press myself against him. Instead, I leaned forward and let my forehead rest against his chest.

Romeo skimmed his knuckles lightly down my back and dipped his fingers in the rolled waistband of the yoga pants. I wasn't wearing any underwear either.

They were still wet when we got to the hospital, and sitting around in them had been uncomfortable.

The fingers against the base of my spine jerked a little and delved deeper. It took him all of three seconds to realize there was nothing beneath the pants.

His entire body shifted slightly closer, and his hips titled toward me. One large, warm palm cupped my butt and kneaded the bare flesh. My eyes slipped closed as he massaged my backside. A long expelled breath floated above my head, and before I knew it, he was sliding his forearm beneath me and lifting me up his body.

I gasped and held myself still, trying to keep from bumping his arm. I resisted the urge to wrap my legs around him like I usually would, but he pulled me in closer.

"Do it," he growled.

I surrendered and wrapped my thighs around him, taking care to keep my legs low on his waist. Even though his arm was splinted and in a sling, his hand was free. His fingers caressed the bare skin of my waist, and his eyes searched mine.

He was doing it again.

Looking at me like I was all that existed.

My lips sought his and we fused together. I felt like I'd been wandering through a dry desert for days and I was suddenly bestowed the gift of drinking water. His lips felt like silk against mine, sliding over me with the greatest of ease. Boldly, I pulled his lower lip between my teeth and tugged. He smiled a little, and I sucked it farther into my mouth, milking every last drop I could.

He spun around without breaking our kiss and lowered onto the end of the bed so he was sitting and I was straddling his lap. The arm that had been supporting me came up so his fingers could tangle in my hair, and he tugged my head back so my neck was exposed.

His lips left a hot, moist trail down the sensitive skin below my jaw, and his teeth nipped and tugged so his tongue could come behind and soothe the bite.

I started rocking against him, a subconscious reaction to the hunger coursing through my system. As he sucked at the side of my neck, I shuddered because he felt so incredibly delicious.

"Romeo," I panted. "We can't. Your arm."

"I don't need my arm to make love to you, baby," he murmured between kisses across my collarbone.

I groaned and palmed the back of his head, reveling in how his messy blond strands curled around my fingers as I tugged him down to my breast.

His tongue wasn't as smooth as his lips, so when he brought it out to encircle my rock-hard nipple, I shuddered in his lap.

Somewhere in the house, the sound of a door opening and closing barely broke through the haze of need that eclipsed everything else.

Romeo's mouth stilled, and then he swore against my breast. "Braeden's here."

I sucked in a shaky breath and tried to calm my racing heart. "Okay."

Romeo chuckled, the sound causing me to rock against him one last time. "I'll tell him to leave."

I so wanted to agree, but the small part of me that wasn't totally overwhelmed my Romeo's touch knew it was better this way.

"No." My voice was hoarse. "You need to eat something and get your arm propped up. We need to get the swelling down as much as possible."

"What about the swelling in my pants?" he quipped.

I laughed.

"Yo! You guys decent?" B yelled from outside the room.

"Hells no," Romeo replied.

"More pizza for me, then," he called, and I heard him retreating to the kitchen.

Romeo raised an eyebrow and looked at me as if to say, "Where were we?"

I smiled and pressed a quick kiss to his fully intoxicating mouth. Before I pulled away, I whispered, "I love you."

"Does that mean you're going to help me out with what's happening downstairs?" he murmured.

Lightly, I caressed the rigid length between his legs. "Later."

He looked like he was about to argue, so I shook my head. "Food. Pain reliever. Elevate your arm." I climbed off his lap as I spoke and evaded his searching grasp.

"I think I'm going to take a shower," I said. "I still feel kind of chilly…" I glanced away. "And kind of dirty."

His jaw hardened and a stricken look filled his eyes. "What else did he do to you?" He pushed up off the bed and paced away, then right back.

"He didn't touch me, not like that." I assured him. "He never even alluded to any kind of sexual misconduct. I honestly think it never occurred to him."

Romeo muttered something under his breath.

"It was like he was beyond that," I said, lost in my own memory of what had happened. "I truly think something inside his brain just snapped. There was no remorse in his eyes, not even the shrewd look of vengeance." I shuddered and met Romeo's stare. "There was nothing but crazy."

He tugged me against him, pressing a kiss to the top of my head. "You want some company in the shower?"

"Nice try." I scoffed. "Go eat. Talk to Braeden. I'll come out when I'm finished showering."

He pressed one last kiss to my forehead and then left me standing in the center of the room.

Without him beside me, the room felt ten degrees colder.

I grabbed a fresh pair of panties off my little pile of clothes nearby and rummaged through Romeo's drawers for one of his shirts and took it into the bathroom with me.

I could hear Braeden's and Romeo's quiet voices as I shut myself in and went to the shower, reached in, and turned on the spray.

A sick feeling slithered down my spine, but I ignored it and went to the sink. As I pulled off the rest of my clothes and brushed my teeth, I avoided the foggy mirror because I already knew how terrible I looked.

When I finished, I reached for the shower curtain and pulled it back.

My body locked up.

Panic clawed at the back of my throat.

All I could do was stand there and stare.

CHAPTER SIX

ROMEO

Braeden was sitting at the counter when I walked into the kitchen.

My body was feeling the effects of the night, and the pain reliever they gave me hours ago at the hospital was starting to wear off.

The marks all over Rimmel did nothing to improve my disposition. The vision of her strung up on that field was never far from the back of my mind.

Braeden paused in devouring the slice of meat lover's pizza and looked up at me. I didn't say anything as I grabbed the bottle of pain reliever I was sure my mother put there and dumped some in my hand.

There were several bottles of chilled water by the pizza, and Braeden grabbed one, unscrewed the cap, and handed it over after I dumped the pills in my mouth. I grunted my thanks and downed the meds with a large gulp.

"What the hell happened, man?" Braeden finally asked.

I tucked a cold pack under my arm and motioned with my jaw toward the living room. "Out there."

Braeden picked up the three boxes of pizza and a couple waters and followed me out into the living room. Murphy was asleep on the couch, so I sat on the other end and slid one of the loose pillows beneath my arm. I hoped the meds kicked in soon because it hurt like a bitch.

I propped my feet up on the coffee table and set the open water bottle nearby. B offered me a slice of pizza right out of the box, and I took it.

He sat down in a chair opposite the couch and waited.

I talked as I inhaled the pie, telling him about everything. The rose. The note and the way I found Rimmel. I even told him about the lawn mower.

"A fucking lawn mower?" Braeden muttered.

"If it hadn't actually happened, I'd think it was ridiculous." I agreed.

Braeden frowned. "That guy is a lot more messed up than any of us realized."

I nodded. "Yeah, he's seriously screwed up in the head."

"They're gonna eat him alive in jail."

I shook my head and leaned forward for another slice. "My dad doesn't think he'll do slammer time."

The look on his face was incredulous. "Are you fucking joking with me right now, Rome?"

"Does it look like I'm joking?" I spat. "He thinks he'll get off on an insanity plea and go upstate to some swanky treatment center."

"Well, he is insane. Least he'll be locked up."

I lowered the pizza from my face. "It's not fucking good enough," I growled. "You should have seen her hanging there. Her mouth gagged and her body tense.

It was like watching a helpless fly struggle in a web while a tarantula stalked it."

The muscle in Braeden's jaw tightened. "So what are you gonna do?"

"I can't do anything right now. My father is going to see what he can do. We'll know more when Zach is arraigned. Until then, they're supposed to keep a guard at his door."

"How's she doing?" Braeden asked, motioning toward the bedroom.

I could hear the shower running, so I knew she was out of earshot. "You tell me."

Braeden's eyes met mine. His gaze was steady. "You accusing me of something?"

I stared at him for several long seconds. "If I was accusing you of something, you wouldn't be sitting in my house."

"She's my family now, Rome. I'm gonna be there for her."

"I think she's still in shock." I wasn't going to challenge B about his relationship with Rimmel because the truth was she needed more than me in her life. She needed someone she could trust, and I knew Braeden was trustworthy and loyal. Sometimes to a fault.

He nodded. "She just kind of melted down," he admitted. "I didn't know what the hell to do, man. Tears freak me out."

"She hasn't cried in front of me yet. Not since we got to the hospital."

"She's worried about you." He glanced down at my arm. "I gotta admit, Rome, I'm a little worried too."

I blew out a breath. The doctor's news had been positive. It was basically a green light to heal and get back on the field. The timing of this injury was the worst, but there wasn't anything I could about that now. I wasn't going to give up my dream. I wasn't going to let Zach steal that from me.

"I'm not down for the count. Give me a couple days to recoup, and then let's talk ball. I got some training ideas. If you're game, I can use someone to help me."

"I'm down," Braeden said.

I finished off the slice in my hand and listened again. The shower was still running. It seemed like she'd been in there forever. Rim wasn't usually a girl who lingered in the shower.

"What's up with Moms?" Braeden asked, drawing my attention.

I grunted. "She told Rimmel her father killed her mother."

"What the what?" he asked in a falsetto voice.

I smiled. "Yeah, as if being accused of plagiarism, her scholarship and education on the line, being tortured by Zach, and then being admitted into the ER wasn't enough, my mom had to throw one more devastating piece of info at her."

The amount of pissed I felt at a lot of people in my life right now was nothing short of record breaking.

"Why would she make up something like that?" Braeden wondered.

"Yeah," I echoed, my tone thoughtful. "Why would she?"

Our eyes connected and unspoken words passed between us.

"Well, fuck," Braeden muttered.

The shower was still running.

Maybe she was hurting worse than she let on.

"I'll be right back." I pushed off the couch and strode into the bedroom.

"Rim," I called out, but she didn't say anything.

When I reached the bathroom door, I didn't hesitate to walk right in. The humid air from the long-running water hit me immediately. The spray from the showerhead cascaded down, splattering everything around it before being pulled into the drain.

But Rimmel stood there, on the outside of the shower, the curtain crumpled in her grip, as her naked body visibly shook and the sound of her chattering teeth filled the room.

CHAPTER SEVEN

#ImportantMessage
Apparently my last notification could be construed as a death threat. I have been told to apologize or the #BuzzBoss will be deleted. I'm sorry for my illegal hashtag.
#DeathIsSeriousBusiness
... Alpha BuzzFeed

RIMMEL

Water cascaded from ceiling to floor.

It is astounding how such a simple, harmless thing could be anything but.

The sound of the drops raining against the shower wall, trickling down the drain, and splashing up along the sides of the tile would normally be beautiful. Relaxing even.

To me, it was the sound of hell.

My hand tightened around the shower curtain, hanging on to that bit of fabric like it was a lifeline to my sanity. Anxiety, clear and sharp, stabbed me like the sharpest blade I'd ever known.

As I stood there and stared, unable to wrench my gaze from the horrendous sight of the pelting water, everything in my vision tinged pink. That awful color of diluted blood.

I felt my chest heave as I grappled with what was real and what was only torment swirling through my mind.

But the lines between the two were blurred. The break between reality and nightmare had been breached far too many times, and something in me caved, unable to escape or assimilate the truth.

A rogue drop of water splattered against my chest, and I jerked like a bullet plowed into my skin. I gasped and used my free hand to wipe it away.

There was so much water.

So much water.

I felt the icy spray blast me in the face and then drag down my hair. I couldn't scream because my mouth was bound. Gagged with some type of thick fabric that soaked up the water faster than the driest sponge.

What would happen when the fabric could hold no more?

Would the water force its way down the back of my throat and slowly choke me? Would it fill up my lungs and drown me?

Images of my mother floating facedown in the pink-tinted water assaulted me, and I remembered how bloated she was when they finally pulled her out.

Is that what I would look like?

I tried to scream again, but it only resulted in an icy rivulet of water slipping down the back of my throat.

My nose burned from the water that forced its way inside as I heaved for precious air and fought against the drowning sensation stalking my body and mind.

I felt myself shaking against the fear and the cold, and everything in me began to go numb…

Then a solid, warm familiar feeling of safety enveloped me, and I smiled. My tired body sagged back against it, and it wrapped around me farther.

"Rim, baby," Romeo said beside my ear. I opened my eyes as he lifted his arm and shut off the shower. "What the hell happened?"

I blinked. Reality pushed its way back into my head, and I took in the water splashed outside on the wall and floor.

Romeo gently pried my hand off the curtain and folded it across my middle beneath his own arm.

"How long have I been standing here?" I wondered.

"A while."

I tilted my head back and looked up at him. "I don't think I feel like showering right now."

Shadows danced in his eyes, and he nodded. "You and water just aren't very good friends."

"I thought I was going to drown up there," I confided. "I know it wasn't a pool. I wasn't submerged, but the spray was so rough. I felt it going into my nose and down my throat."

Romeo hugged me close. "You're safe now," he whispered.

"I probably smell," I mumbled against his chest.

Laughter vibrated through him. "You expect me to notice how you smell when you're pressed up against me, completely naked?"

That earned him a giggle.

"You give me too much credit, Smalls."

The worst of the moment had passed, so I pulled away and reached for my clothes.

Romeo pulled the curtain closed and turned to watch me dress. "Don't do that on my account," he quipped.

"How's your arm?"

"Feeling good."

I gave him a look that called him on his lie.

After grabbing my brush to quickly brush out the tangles in my hair, I tied it up into a messy topknot on my head.

His shirt fell to my knees, so I didn't bother with a pair of pants. Instead, I pulled on the slipper boots, and we left the bathroom.

Before heading out in the living room, I filled my arms with pillows from the bed and carried them to the couch.

Braeden was looking down at his phone screen when I dropped them all on the cushions. "You two are the talk of all Alpha U social media," he informed us.

"My life is complete," I muttered.

"Pizza," Romeo said, motioning toward the open box.

I made a face. "Is there actually any pizza under all those piles of meat?"

"Does it matter?" Braeden asked and snagged another piece.

Romeo laughed and pulled out the box on the bottom and opened the lid to reveal an all-cheese pizza.

"Sit." I motioned to the couch. When he was sitting, I carefully piled some pillows beside him, creating a soft tower for him to rest his arm on.

But when I tried to direct his arm, I frowned, noticing the sling was keeping it against his side. "How are we supposed to elevate it for the swelling with that thing wrapped across your chest?"

Romeo reached up and pulled the Velcro apart to release the sling.

Gently, I tucked the loose ends of the straps beneath a pillow as he propped it up. The cold pack he had lying nearby was sitting ignored. I grabbed it up and crushed it around in my hand to break up whatever was inside. Cold burst against my palms, and I gently placed it near the splint.

"Can you even feel that?" I asked, frowning at the plastic wrapped around the break.

He nodded. "Thanks, baby."

I handed him another slice of pizza before getting one for myself (sans the bucket of meat) and curled up as close to the pillow tower as I dared.

Braeden turned on some movie about two guys who liked to drive fast cars. One of them sort of reminded me of Romeo.

Once my stomach was full, my body finally relaxed beneath a blanket and I rested my head on the edge of Romeo's pillow tower. His fingers played with the ends of my hair, and the background sounds of racing cars and Romeo's breathing caused my eyes to grow heavy.

I don't know how long I was able to sleep until a dream interrupted my peace.

My face felt hot and my head was heavy. I rolled onto my back, feeling the hard, cold concrete beneath me. Confusion broke through the pain, and I blinked, trying to see where I was. Everything around me was blurry and the lighting was low.

"She's waking up!" someone hissed, and I felt the rough tug of something being wound around my hands.

"You didn't hit her hard enough!" the chilling voice intoned.

My eyes sprang open as I desperately looked around.

Zach was towering over me, a look of crazed hollowness in his eyes.

"No, please," I whispered. Why was he doing this?

"Hurry up," he spat, and the rope around my wrists was pulled taunt. I cried out at the way it cut into my skin.

"This is wrong. She didn't do nothing," interjected the voice that was not Zach's.

He jerked forward and shot out his fist. The sharp slap of knuckles against flesh and the grunt of pain made me cringe.

"Stop it!" I yelled.

"Get me a gag!" Zach growled, and then he lifted his fist to me.

"No!" I screamed and jerked upright. I moved so suddenly I rolled off the couch and landed in the narrow space between the couch and table.

A string of curse words floated above me, and Romeo's hand slid under my arm and lifted. "It's all right, baby. We're at home."

A tremor ran through my limbs as I sank back onto the sofa. A dream. It had seemed so incredibly real.

"Come here," Romeo said softly and shoved all the pillows I'd arranged for his arm onto the floor.

I didn't argue because I was still trying to shake off the leftover panic I felt from reliving that moment with Zach.

It hadn't just been a dream. Just a few hours ago, that was my reality.

Awake, I'd been able to keep the thoughts—the memories—at bay, but in sleep, they came. They reminded.

I laid my head in Romeo's lap, my cheek pillowed on one of his strong thighs. The softness of his sweats made me want closer. Because of the swelling on my cheek, I had to lie so I was looking at his stomach. His free hand stroked through my hair, and I sighed.

"It was about him." he said, his voice flat.

I didn't answer. Everyone in this room knew who my nightmare had been about.

Braeden stood from his chair. "I think it's time for me to bounce. Give you two some alone time."

"You don't have to leave because of me," I said, sitting up and turning to face him.

"I know," he replied and leaned over the coffee table to hold out his fist to me. I smiled at it before bumping mine against his. "I'll see you later, tutor girl."

"Thanks for everything tonight," I said.

Romeo started to get up, but Braeden waved him back down. "Stay with your girl."

"Appreciate it, man."

Braeden shrugged and held out his arms. "I'm a saint."

Romeo grunted and yelled after him. "Keep telling yourself that!"

The front door shut, and Murphy, who'd been staring at me since I fell off the couch, stretched, then jumped down to strut out of the room.

I felt Romeo's stare and turned to study him. "I think it's time you tell me."

"Tell you what?"

"What happened at the field before I got there."

CHAPTER EIGHT

Muscles:
God's way of apologizing for men
#LadiesLikeMuscle
#IfTheySayTheyDon'tTheyRLying
...Alpha BuzzFeed

ROMEO

"It's over. There's no reason to go there," Rimmel said, weariness in her tone. She lay back down, her head in my lap and her knees pulled in toward her chest.

"I need to know. And you're going to keep having dreams like that until you get it out."

She didn't say anything for a long time, but her hand curled around the hem of my shirt and held tight.

"Damn this broken arm," I cursed.

She sat up immediately, her hazel eyes going wide. I was so used to seeing her with glasses that looking at her this much without them made her seem even smaller, more vulnerable somehow. She chewed her lower lip and scanned the right side of my body before asking, "Should I call your doctor? Does it feel worse?"

"My arm is fine," I growled.

She was so goddamned perfect. Everything about her, including the way she automatically thought of me before herself. It drove me mad, but it also charmed the shit out of me.

"I don't understand…" Her forehead crinkled as she tried to get the gist of my words.

"I can't hold you the way I want to," I explained. "I can't wrap myself around you like I should. How am I supposed to make you feel safe if I can't even hold you?"

My name fell from her lips. A broken whisper turned sigh. The sound rushed up my spine and tingled the back of my neck, and her eyes grew soft.

"It isn't just your arms that make me feel safe," she confided. The way she looked down at her lap when she spoke was more telling than her actual words. She didn't look at me because she was revealing some of her deepest, most personal thoughts. Rim held a lot inside; it was just her way.

It was my way to try and coax those things out of her.

When I succeeded, even a little, I felt like a superhero who cracked some secret code to save the world.

"It isn't your muscles or the way you tower over me when we stand so close." She continued. "It's the sound of your voice. The way your eyes always hold so much devotion, so much promise with every single glance. It's the way your body rotates just slightly toward mine when I enter the room. It's your awareness of me, Romeo. Your intuition. You could be all the way on the other side of the room, and I'd still feel more protected—more loved—than I ever have."

I swallowed past the thickness in my throat. The energy between us was so thick, so electric that it was almost uncomfortable. I felt so much and so deeply for her that it terrified me. I never in a million years thought someone could burrow so deeply inside me.

I knew in that moment I would do anything for Rimmel.

Anything.

I'd walk through fire.

I'd kill.

I'd give up my career.

But it wasn't any of those things she wanted.

All she wanted was my love.

And by God, I'd fucking love her with every cell in my body.

I had to bring the tension coiled up inside me, sucking all the air out of the room, down just a notch. Just enough so we could both breathe.

"Admit it, though," I said with a lopsided smile. "You like my muscles too."

She laughed. A real laugh that chased away some of the shadows in her eyes and made her shoulders shake. Then she winced and held a hand up to her face. "Don't make me laugh." She smiled. "It hurts."

I pulled her hand away from her battered cheek and leaned forward to press a feather-light kiss to the area.

She sighed.

I wrapped my free arm around her waist and lifted her across my lap, turning her so she could rest the unbruised side of her face against my chest and cuddle against me but still leave my arm without any contact.

Before she settled against me fully, she piled a large pillow on top of her stretched-out legs so I could rest my arm on top.

One of her hands climbed up to the side of neck, where she splayed her fingers out beneath my jaw. Her fingers flirted with the stubble sprouting out of my chin, and I groaned under the soft caress.

I couldn't help but notice the way the shirt she was wearing rode up on her thighs, exposing most of her creamy bare legs.

"This feels good," she murmured.

I tugged the shirt a little higher so her inner thigh was fully on display. She chuckled deep in her throat as her fingers found their way into the hair at the base of my neck.

The tension in the room dialed back up and crackled through the air. A rush of need so strong washed through my body, and my hand spasmed against her hip.

She glanced up at me, and I tumbled completely.

I lunged forward, capturing her lips with mine and reveling in the moist fullness. It was already like she was primed and ready. I sucked the supple flesh into my mouth, and her head fell back, giving me total access.

I worked her mouth over like I was applying for the last job on Earth. I licked and sucked and teased until her hand fisted in my shirt and she trembled in my lap, rotating her hips in search for more.

Rimmel tore her mouth from mine with a gasp and then dove into the side of my neck with skill of her own. As she did, her hand went to the center of my body and brushed across my bulging cock.

A shudder went through me, and I moaned.

"Bed," I demanded, more harsh than I intended.

Her cheeks were flushed and her eyes glassy when she climbed off my lap and went ahead of me into the bedroom.

Once there, she tugged off the shirt and stood before me in nothing but her panties and boots.

For once, I didn't see the marks covering her skin; I didn't pay attention to the other man's handprint on my baby's arm.

I didn't see her outer beauty in that moment at all.

All I could see was everything she was on the inside radiating out and filling up every inch of my chest.

"I love you so fucking much."

"I love you so fucking much."

I growled and stalked toward her. "Say it again."

"I love you."

"Say the word fuck again."

She smiled like the cat who ate the canary. "I love you so *fucking* much," she purred.

I said that word a lot, but it never sounded better than when it rolled off her innocent little tongue.

I yanked my T-shirt over my head to toss it aside, but it was still caught around my arm with the sling. Frustrated and impatient, I would have ripped it off my body, but Rimmel made a sound in the back of her throat and came forward.

Her gentle hands slid it off my broken arm without so much as a whisper of pain. When the shirt was gone, she took the loose straps at the top of the brace and wrapped them around my newly bare chest. Once they were fixed around me, my arm was anchored more solidly to my side.

I started to protest, angry at the limited movement it would afford, but her hand moved to the waistband of my sweats, and all thought fell away.

The pants slid down my body, and so did she. She kneeled before me and gently cupped my balls. Her fingers lightly played with the underside, and my eyes slid closed. As she gently massaged my sack, her other hand grabbed hold of the raging hard-on that proudly jutted from my body.

She held it out away from my stomach and slid her hot little mouth all the way down to the base. How the hell she managed to deep-throat all my inches I didn't know. And thinking about it right then was out of the question.

I jerked in her mouth, already feeling the urge to spill my seed.

I pulled out, one long, slow stroke, and her lips clung to the silky skin the entire way.

"Bed," I commanded, my voice barely audible.

But when we both got there, a little of her passion dimmed and her eyes slid to my arm. "I don't want to hurt you."

"The only way I'm gonna hurt is if you don't let me bury myself inside you."

Her teeth sank into her lower lip.

I lay on my back and crooked my finger at her. "You can do all the moving tonight."

She climbed up my body and straddled my waist. Her entire body was on display, and the heavy rings around her waist broke into my lust.

"Are you hurting, baby? Is this too much for you?"

Her response was to sink down on my cock in one fluid motion.

Words became impossible.

My eyes rolled back in my head as she moved and rocked. Rimmel kept her pace slow and deliberate. This wasn't like the times we went at each other with everything we had. Instead, she kept the movement to a minimum, bearing her hips down against mine and rocking her entire core against me.

The inside of her body was tight and hot. Her core was slick with desire, and the way she panted above me pulled me over the edge.

Just as I was about to pump myself inside her, I grabbed her hip and rocked upward, spearing her as deep as I'd ever gone.

Her mouth fell open, but no sound came out. She rocked in small little movements as her thighs trembled around me.

White exploded behind my eyes, and I saw nothing.

I heard nothing.

But I felt it all.

Once her body milked every last drop I had to give, she slipped off me and tucked herself between my side and arm.

"Maybe I kind of do like your muscles," she whispered.

I laughed.

She yawned.

We hadn't even bothered to pull the covers down on the bed. "Let me get you a blanket," I whispered.

"No."

"No?" I was surprised. Rimmel always wanted a blanket. She hated to be cold.

"You'll keep me warm."

I smiled up at the ceiling. "Always."

Everything around us might have been uncertain, but that was one promise I could make without a single doubt.

CHAPTER NINE

RIMMEL

Sleep was elusive.

After I drifted off in Romeo's arms, I managed to get a few hours of peaceful, dream-free slumber before waking up to a restless mind.

It didn't help that sunlight was peeking through the edges of the blinds in the bedroom and I had to pee. Romeo was still sleeping, his face soft and relaxed, and the last thing I wanted to do was wake him by lying beside him and worrying.

Slowly, carefully, I peeled myself away from his side and slipped beneath his arm. I stood at the edge of the bed, watching him for long moments, and I couldn't stop the feeling of gratitude that consumed me. It was a welcomed feeling.

Even after everything that happened, I still felt lucky.

I gathered up a couple ultra-soft throws and tucked them over him as he slept and then gently propped his arm up on a large pillow and placed a fresh cold pack on top. He barely stirred through it all.

As I pulled on his shirt, a pair of loose pajama pants, and my slippers, I prayed his arm would heal quickly and the NFL wouldn't drop him.

I didn't want to run the risk of waking him by making cider or coffee in the kitchen, so I fed Murphy a couple treats, refilled his food and water, and changed the litter box. Once that was done, I washed my hands and face and replaced the bandage around my wrist with a fresh one.

My body hurt today. I was stiff, and my eye area was still swollen. The bruising didn't look any better, and the rope burns on my torso still stung.

In the kitchen, I gulped down a couple pain relievers and wandered over to the window to look outside. It was snowing. Big, fat white flakes drifted from the overcast sky and danced across the yard outside before settling completely in their mission to cover the grass.

The pool cover was completely white already, and I could almost pretend there was no pool there at all. It was already noon, but based on the time we went to bed, I should still be sleeping.

But I couldn't stop thinking about my father.

And my mother.

And everything Valerie said.

Actually, she hadn't said much at all. Still, the accusation carried the weight of a thousand words. I thought she was warming up to me. I foolishly thought she was beginning to like me. And I was beginning to like her.

Had I read everything wrong? Had her offering to help me set up a fundraiser for the shelter been something to make everyone think she was learning to accept me as part of Romeo's life?

Or maybe it had been an excuse to keep an eye on me while she waited for that skeezy private investigator she hired to dig up dirt on me and my family.

When she couldn't find any, she made it up.

It was the worst lie someone could ever concoct.

My father was a good and decent man. He would never kill my mother. He loved her, just as he loved me.

I rushed into the living room and picked up Romeo's cell off the coffee table. I dialed my father's number without even looking at the screen. I knew it by heart.

The phone rang and rang, then eventually went to voicemail. Disappointment sank inside me like a stone in the middle of a pond. He was probably at work. It was the middle of the day. Maybe he was on a jobsite and left his cell in the car.

I left him a brief message, telling him I'd lost my phone, but I'd call as soon as I got another.

I carried Romeo's cell in the bedroom and plugged it into the charger beside the bed. He was still sleeping, looking as comfortable as ever.

I felt a pang of guilt as I watched him. He was caught in the middle of his mother and me. I meant it when I told Valerie I could never take her place in his life. I wouldn't even try. I thought I'd gotten through to her that day.

But I hadn't.

She kept poking around in my life with some stranger I didn't even know.

It made me feel dirty.

And angry all over again.

Maybe there was also a part of me that was curious.

Curious to know what exactly she thought she knew. I couldn't imagine her throwing around some insane accusation the way she had if she didn't actually believe it.

I wandered back to the window and gazed across the yard to the main house.

There was only one way to find out.

At the door, I didn't even hesitate. I walked out into the freezing air and falling snow. I wanted to know what exactly was going through Valerie Anderson's mind.

So I was going to ask her.

CHAPTER TEN

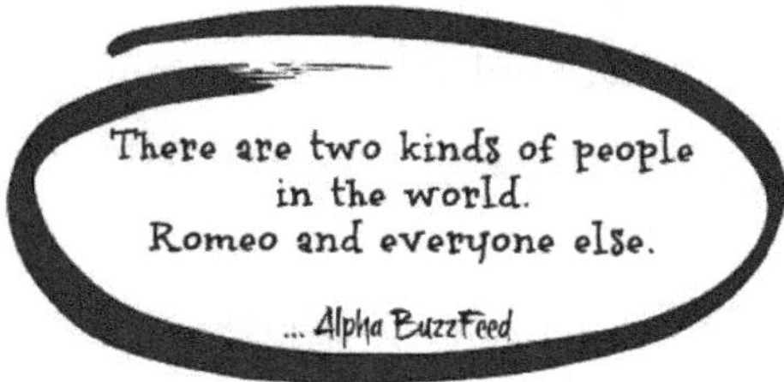

ROMEO

The sound of my ringing phone burst into my happy place.

My happy place = dreaming about sex with Rimmel.

I groaned and rolled to grab the offending noisemaker when the movement caused shooting pain up my arm.

The phone kept ringing, so I reached for it at a much slower pace and pulled it toward me. The charger came out of the wall when I tugged and the long cord dangled from the bottom when I answered.

"Yeah?" I answered gruffly.

"Good morning, son," my dad said into my ear. He sounded entirely too wide awake. I looked behind me for Rim to beg her to make coffee, but she wasn't in the bed. A couple rumpled blankets, a pillow that bore the indent of my arm, and an askew cold pack were in her place.

I blinked and looked toward the bathroom.

"Hey, Dad," I said with a lot less enthusiasm than he showed.

"I'd like to talk with you. There are some things we need to discuss."

"It's like the crack of dawn," I rebutted.

"It's after two in the afternoon."

"Oh." *Well, ain't that a bitch?*

"How's your arm today?" he asked, concern taking center stage in his tone.

"Same as yesterday," I muttered. I didn't hear any noise from the bathroom. Maybe she was in the kitchen.

"Well, as long as it's not any worse."

I grunted in agreement. Where the hell had the woman gone?

"So you'll come over to my office?"

"Sure, Dad," I muttered, wanting to get off the phone.

"Good, see you in a few."

I started to pull the phone away from my ear, when Dad called my name.

"Yeah?" I answered.

"Rimmel is here. She's in the kitchen with your mother."

Well, if that wasn't a bucket of cold water right to the balls.

"What the hell, Dad?"

"So far there hasn't been any yelling." He said it mildly, almost like he was more intrigued by the paperwork on his desk than the fact Rimmel and Mom were alone.

"I'll be right there," I snapped.

I could have sworn he was laughing when I cut the call.

CHAPTER ELEVEN

RIMMEL

I walked right in.

I figured knocking would have been too much of a sign of respect. She obviously didn't respect me, so I figured I should treat her the same.

Besides, Valerie wasn't a stupid woman. She had to know this visit was coming. I might be shy and I might even be easily intimidated, but I wasn't going to be pushed around.

It wasn't Romeo's job to shield me from his mother; it was my job to make sure he didn't have to.

The inside of the home was warm and quiet. I heard someone moving around in the kitchen, so I followed the sound and steered myself in that direction. When I walked around the corner into the spacious, modern kitchen my eyes went immediately to Valerie, who was standing at the counter with her back to me.

"I came to talk," I said from the doorway.

She didn't stiffen or whirl around in surprise. She merely turned and gestured toward a freshly brewing pot of coffee.

"Would you like some?"

So my instincts had been right. She was expecting me.

"I saw you coming across the lawn," she explained as she drew down two white mugs from the cabinet above. "I assume Romeo is still sleeping?"

"Yes." I moved farther into the room. "I didn't want to wake him."

"How is he doing?" she asked, concern clear in her tone.

"He was sleeping peacefully. His arm was elevated, and I put on ice on the area before I came over here."

"And what about you?" she asked, her shrewd gaze landing on me to stare intently.

"I think you know how I am."

She wasn't surprised by my tone or my short reply. Like I said, Valerie Anderson was anything but stupid. It made me all the more curious.

"Coffee?" She gestured toward the pot.

The heady aroma of the dark brew was delicious and my stomach was growling, so I moved forward and took a mug.

"Help yourself," she said and moved away toward the fridge where she pulled out some creamer.

I poured a healthy amount into the cup and took the caramel-flavored creamer she offered. Once it was added, I took a spoon from the counter and carried it over to a small nook lined with windows and sat down at the small café table.

The view out the window vied for my attention: the sweeping lawn, the falling snow, and the bare branches of the mature trees all lined in white. But this visit wasn't for pleasantries, and the view was most definitely pleasant.

I tore my eyes from the glass and studied Valerie.

She was dressed in a pair of thick black tights and an oversized cashmere sweater. It was the color of lilacs and had one of those uneven hems where one side fell longer than the other. Her feet were covered in thick lilac socks, and her blond hair was pulled up in a high ponytail on top of her head.

If she was wearing makeup, it was minimal, and there were slight shadows beneath her brown eyes.

She definitely didn't look old enough to have a son Romeo's age. It made me wonder how my mother would have aged over the years, if she would have been just as ageless as the woman who carried her own mug of coffee over to join me at the table.

"It seems I owe you yet another apology." She began.

I held up my hand. "I don't want an apology from you. I want an explanation."

"Fair enough," she said, tucking her legs under her and sipping at her coffee.

I mean, really. Did she have to look so put together all the time? I was sitting here bruised and battered with blurry vision, unwashed hair, and bandages around my wrist.

I picked up my coffee and took a fortifying sip.

"When Roman first started bringing you here, I hired a private investigator to do a background check. I wanted to know who my son was falling in love with."

"So when you found nothing that would keep him from wanting me, you decided to make something up."

"No," she denied. Her voice was clear and held a note of truth. "I know you won't believe this, but I liked you."

"You're right. I don't believe you."

"Maybe not in the beginning, but once I got to know you. The time we've spent on the fundraiser has really shown me what a special girl you really are."

"Just tell me about my father," I said. I wasn't having a heart to heart with her right now. I wasn't going to sit here and listen to her list all the reasons why she'd grown to like me when clearly all of those reasons had gone out the window the minute her snoop-for-hire called.

• • •

"After he did the background check, I paid him for the job. I didn't ask him to keep tabs on you or follow you. As far as I was concerned, the job was finished," she said.

I wrapped my hands around the mug and adjusted myself in the chair. My back hurt, but I forced my attention from the pain and sipped at the coffee.

"I guess some information he inquired about still hadn't come through when he gave me his report. It came through the other day, and he thought it was something I would want to know, so he called me."

I nodded.

"So I met him at his office so he could give it to me and explain the documents."

"What kind of documents?"

"Financial statements mostly. All dated from the year of your mother's death. Bounced checks. Notices from the mortgage lender who financed your house. There were also more current statements showing the same kind of pattern reemerging in recent months."

My hands tightened around the mug and a sick feeling twisted my stomach. "What pattern?"

"Your father is in debt, Rimmel," Valerie said without heat or accusation. "Very heavy debt. He's behind on the mortgage payment, the utility bills, and he was fired from his job."

"That's not true," I ground out.

"Was your insurance card accepted at the hospital?" she asked as if she already knew the answer.

"That's none of your concern," I said, brushing away the correct assumption. "My father went to work every day while I was visiting over Christmas break."

Sadness flashed in her eyes. "Are you sure it was work he went to?"

"Where else would he have gone?" I snapped.

"Apparently, he spends a lot of time at a nearby casino."

I laughed.

She ignored it. "There is also some evidence of him visiting a few off-the-books gambling houses, and some of the documentation leads to illegal gambling and betting."

"What the hell kind of evidence could you possibly have to support that?"

"My investigator has photos of your father going into the establishment long suspected by the local authorities there of illegal gambling."

I felt like someone sucker punched me in the gut. But even the sick feeling wasn't enough to convince my mind—my heart—that this was real.

"I want to see the documents."

She nodded, abandoned her coffee, and left the room. I took the moment alone to pull in a shuddering breath and run through the couple weeks I'd been home over break.

My father dressed in his construction clothes every morning before he left. He'd leave me at the table with the newspaper and kiss me on the head. He'd take the bagged lunch I made him and tool belt every time he walked out the door.

He was gone all day long.

A couple times, he missed dinner.

He would call and say it was going to be a late night at the job and he was sorry.

I believed him.

He wouldn't lie.

He had a couple days off while I'd been home. Those days he did seem a little distant, sort of preoccupied, but it wasn't because he was sitting there wishing he were gambling.

What kind of man would rather sit at a betting table than spend his time with his only child?

I thought back to when I told him about Romeo, about how I was surprised he wasn't more opposed to the idea of me dating. I still remember the look of doubt that crossed his face, the display of concern when I talked about my boyfriend. I'd thought for sure I was going to get a lecture, but then this look passed behind his eyes, and whatever he was going to say died on his tongue.

He said he only wanted me to be happy.

Was the reason he didn't tell me I couldn't date because he was doing something he knew I'd never approve of?

Valerie came back into the room carrying a plain-colored file folder. She slid it across the table in front of me without a word.

I set aside my coffee and opened the file.

Inside were full of bank statements, internet screenshots, security camera photos, and even information on the "underground" gambling ring going on in Florida.

It all looked so official, even if I wondered how the hell the PI got access to some of it.

At the bottom of the pile was a report. A copy of the official police report filed on my mother's death.

This was something I'd never seen before.

As I read it, I couldn't stop the rush of tears from falling down my cheeks. There was so much here that I didn't know.

How could I have not known about any of this?

I curled my hand into the too-long sleeve of Romeo's shirt and used it to mop up the tears dripping off my chin.

As I sat there and cried and read through the report, Valerie said nothing. She did nothing. She just sat there and watched.

I felt her gaze. I felt the shrewd way she stared. It was intrusive, and I hated she saw this vulnerability.

But I couldn't stop the way I reacted to all this information.

I sniffled a little and lowered the report to take a breath, still unable to tear my eyes away from what I was reading.

Somewhere in the house, a door slammed.

Romeo appeared in the kitchen, his footsteps halting when he saw the pair of us sitting together in the small nook. He noted the tears on my face, and I was sure he caught the bleak look in my eyes.

"What the hell did you say to her?" he growled and rushed around the table and grabbed the remaining empty chair. It made a scraping sound when he dragged it close to me and sat, angling his body toward mine and spreading his legs so me and my chair were partially between him.

His left hand fingered the top of the file I was holding. "May I?"

I refused to let go of the report. Instead, I turned it toward him so he could see what I was reading.

It took him a moment to understand. I heard him whisper, "*Tampa Police department, official investigation,*" beneath his breath, and then he gasped with understanding.

"You fucking have the police report from her mother's death?" he spat.

"It's a copy," she replied.

Romeo's hand fell into my lap and wrapped around my thigh. "You don't have to look at that, baby," he murmured.

"Yes," I said. "I do."

"Roman." Valerie began, and I flinched.

I wasn't about to listen to her offer excuses.

"You had no right to do this." My voice was cold and hard. "No right at all."

She didn't say anything. It was probably for the better.

"I don't know how you got half of this information, and really, it doesn't matter. I don't believe it."

"You can't ignore the facts. They're there in black and white," she rebuked.

I sucked in a breath and jumped up from my chair. "All you have is black and white," I said. "I have memories. In color. I have words and actions. I have hugs and kisses, holidays spent with two parents who loved me. Who loved each other. I don't know what I did to make you hate me so much, but this is vile. How dare you try and take away the memories I have left of my mother."

"I'm not trying to take away anything."

"No. You're just trying to make me think my father killed her," I spat. Romeo stood and laid a hand against my stomach, gently trying to pull me into him. I resisted and faced off against his mother.

"There is nothing to suggest that in here." I slammed the folder on the table.

"Finish reading the report," she said without heat.

I snorted. "The truth is you disliked me from the minute you laid eyes on me. You judged me in a split second based on the way I look. I may not be beautiful like you. I might not have money for fancy clothes or a stylist to make my hair look like I just stepped out of a salon. But my insides are beautiful. I have the kind of beautiful that can't be paid for. I have the kind of beauty my *mother* gave me."

She stood and opened her mouth. I made a slashing motion in the air with my hand.

"I'm sorry you don't approve of me. But I'm not going anywhere. I love Romeo and I'm not going to stop. I'm telling you from here on out to stay out of my life. I'll never keep you from Roman, but I want nothing to do with you. This"—I held up the folder—"is too much. I'll work with you on the fundraiser because I committed myself and because the animals need me, but once that is over, so is our relationship."

Valerie actually paled. She looked at Romeo with pleading eyes.

"You did this to yourself, Mom."

"I'm keeping this." I tucked the file beneath my arm and left the room.

My heart was beating so hard within my chest that the only sound I could hear was my blood traveling through my veins. My hands trembled and my knees felt wobbly, but I stood tall. Out in the hall, I sagged against the wall and pulled in a deep breath. A rogue tear spilled down my cheek and I wiped it away.

I heard the low exchange of Romeo's and his mother's voices, but I didn't even try to hear what they were saying. Seconds later, Romeo stepped into the hall and without hesitation, he pulled me into his chest. I sank into him and sighed.

Read the rest of the report. Her stupid words bounced around in my thoughts.

What good would it do?

My mother was dead and she wasn't ever coming back.

Did it really matter how she died?

Yeah.

Yeah, maybe it did.

CHAPTER TWELVE

ROMEO

Rimmel made it clear I didn't have to choose between my mother and her.

Yet it was my mother who had drawn a line in the sand.

She hadn't so much as said the words, but her actions… those were loud and clear.

I had no idea she had a copy of the police report from the Rimmel's mother's death. The stricken look on Rim's face when I walked in and saw her reading it told me she hadn't even seen it.

Why my mom thought it was a good time to bring this shit out in the open was lost on me. I understood she thought she was doing the right thing, but what I didn't understand was *why* she thought that.

I couldn't stand to see Rimmel hurt this way. It twisted my guts.

My mother was in for a rude awakening if she thought I wouldn't stand by my girl.

"Why'd you come over here, babe?" I asked Rim as I enclosed her tight against my chest.

"Because I needed answers."

"Did you get them?"

She tipped up her face. "I have more questions now."

I swiped the pad of my thumb across her cheek, removing the last trace of her tears. "Dad wanted to talk to us, but I'll tell him we'll come back later."

"No." She pulled back from me and straightened. "Let's talk to him now. I'm fine."

"You're sure?"

She took my hand and pulled me toward my father's office. He was sitting at his desk, staring down at some papers in front of him.

"We're here, Dad," I said in way of greeting.

He looked up and smiled. "How's the eye, Rimmel?"

"It's fine, thank you."

He glanced at my arm but didn't say anything. We sat in the two chairs adjacent to his desk and waited for whatever he wanted to tell us.

"I had a call from my computer guy yesterday. The one who went through your laptop, Rimmel, to see if he could find any trace of tampering with your programs."

She sat forward in her seat, her eyes intent on my father. "Did he find anything?"

"He did."

She sagged back in the chair like a ten-pound weight had lifted free of her shoulders.

"I knew it," I said.

Dad nodded. "It's really not a surprise to any of us. He's sending over a formal report of his findings today, and I'll forward it on to the dean."

"What did he find exactly?" I asked.

"Some kind of software that is undetectable to the average computer user was installed that allowed a third party to access the information store."

"So every time I saved my paper, with all the new information I added, he had access to it," Rimmel surmised.

"Yes," Dad replied.

"Will this be enough to get her scholarship reinstated and the probation lifted?"

"I have every reason to think so."

"What about Zach? Will he be expelled for this?" Rimmel asked.

"We would have to have concrete proof that Zach did this, which unfortunately, we do not."

"How the hell is that possible?" I demanded.

"Every time someone accessed her laptop and information, it was done through a different IP address. None of those addresses matched Zach's laptop. It was mostly done through public computers. Internet cafes, a library across town, etc."

"So he just gets off, scot free?" Frustration pumped through me and made it hard to breathe. How could someone who'd done so much not be punished?

"I wouldn't say that," Dad replied. "Zach is going to be put away for a very long time. There's no way he'll get out of what he did to you and Rimmel last night."

Had it only been last night? God. It felt like an eternity ago.

"Where is he now?" Rimmel asked.

"He's still in the hospital. Turns out his jaw wasn't dislocated. It was broken. They had to wire it shut."

Gee. I felt super bad.

Not.

"His nose is also broken, and because of the head injury from when he hit the pole, he was kept overnight for observation.

"But he's going to jail, right?" Rimmel asked.

Dad ran a hand over his face. He looked tired. I wondered how much sleep he'd gotten. It occurred to me that both my parents were under a lot of stress right now. This shit wasn't just affecting me and Rim, but everyone around us.

"There's a very high chance that Zach will be sent to some kind of treatment center."

"What do you mean?" she asked.

"He won't go to jail, babe. He's going to get locked in a padded cell."

She fell silent as she digested the information. "Well," she said after a few moments. "He definitely is crazy."

Dad laughed. "I'd have to agree."

"But he won't be able to get out?" she asked. The underlying worry in her tone made my fists tighten.

"Correct. He will be involuntarily admitted." Dad shuffled some papers around and continued. "But this isn't concrete. There's still a chance he'll end up in jail. There is going to be a closed hearing next week. You're both going to need to be there."

"What's it for?" Rimmel's tone was between curious and dread.

"His father pulled some strings. Used the fact that he's clearly unstable and injured to get a closed hearing in the judge's chambers instead of an actual trial. Basically, Robert will be representing his son, and I will be representing both of you. You'll go, tell the judge your side of the story, and then he'll bring down a sentence."

"Next week?" she asked.

He nodded. "This is fast. Usually, it takes longer. But because of Robert's position in the community and the fact that this has become a high-profile case, especially on campus, all parties involved want to get it settled."

"I'm glad. The sooner they ship him off to the loony bin, the better off we'll all be," I muttered.

"Yes. I agree," Dad said. "But don't use those exact words in court."

Rimmel giggled, and my father winked at her.

"When I know the exact time and date we'll need to be in court, I'll let you know. Let's get together in a day or so to go over everything so you're prepared."

"Thank you so much for doing this. You've really helped me, and I don't know how to repay you," Rimmel said.

"No repayment is necessary." He smiled. "Family takes care of family."

Her eyes turned misty, and I cleared my throat. "Thanks for all the info, Dad. If that's everything, we better go. Rimmel needs to take a shower. She stinks."

Rimmel gasped and stared at me with wide eyes. "I do not!" Then she fell silent. "Do I?"

Both my father and I laughed.

She picked up a pen off the desk and threw it at me. I batted it away with ease.

Rim shook her head and smiled.

Mission accomplished. I was tired of seeing that forlorn look on her face.

"Anthony," my mom said, opening the door and coming into the room. Her steps faltered when she saw Rim and I were sitting there.

Rimmel stiffened.

"Yes, Valerie?" Dad said.

"I didn't know you were busy," she said, glancing at me.

I stood. "We were just on our way out."

"Do you need anything for your arm? Is everything okay?"

I sighed. I was tired of conflict. It seemed to surround us. "No, Mom. I'm fine. But thank you."

Her eyes softened and she nodded.

"Come on, stinky," I said and held my hand out to Rimmel.

She snorted and took it. I shut the door behind me on the way out.

"Stinky?" she asked, lifting her eyebrow and glancing at me.

I grinned. "I know you have an aversion to taking a shower lately," I quipped, "but I feel the need to take one."

"And what does that have to do with me?"

"I'm gonna need some help. I can't wash myself with one hand."

I damn well could, and we both knew it.

"Hmm, well, that is a problem."

We stepped outside and started across the yard to my place. It was still snowing, and the fact that I wasn't wearing a shirt caused my muscles to tighten against the chill.

"If I protect you from the water, maybe you could wash all my two thousand parts?" I said.

The mention of the water took some of the humor and desire out of her face. I tugged her hand and pulled her around so she faced me.

"If it's too much, you just say the word," I told her.

She stared straight ahead at my bare chest. She lifted a finger and brushed against my pec. "The snowflakes are melting against your skin."

"It's because I'm hot," I replied, smug.

She smiled. "You definitely are." One of her fingers flicked over my hardened nipple.

I caught her hand and lifted it to my lips. Gently, I sucked the tip of her finger into my mouth and swirled my tongue around it.

Her eyes darkened.

"I'll try, okay?" she murmured, watching me suck her finger.

I had to think about what she was even talking about. In my mind, there was no conversation anymore. My body had taken over.

Oh. Right. The shower.

I released her finger slowly and nodded. "That's good enough for me."

I led her the rest of the way across the snowy ground.

I knew she'd be fine in the shower.

After all, I'd be in there with her.

No one could resist a naked Romeo. Not even fear.

CHAPTER THIRTEEN

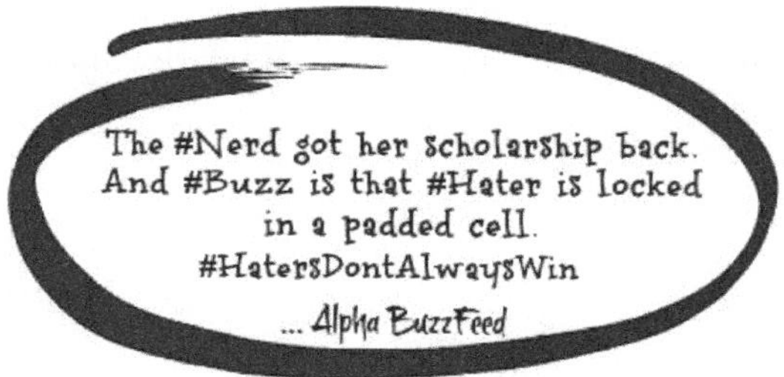

RIMMEL

Less than twenty-four hours after the report from the computer guy arrived, the dean reinstated my scholarship. My probation was lifted, and I was told to start attending classes again.

I missed about two weeks of classes, and the dean waived all the assignments I'd missed. He explained I shouldn't have to make up work I'd missed through no fault of my own. Of course, I was still going to have to play catch-up. The finals at the end of the semester, hell, even the midterms would cover things I missed.

On one hand, I was glad to be back to my regular routine. It helped things feel more normal.

On the other hand, I worried how well I was going to be able to maintain my high average during a time when everything was most certainly *not* normal.

Romeo and I talked to the police again about everything that happened on the field. We gave our official statements and were prepped by Tony on what would happen in the closed hearing involving Zach.

It should have been over by now, but the date was pushed back. Apparently, the person called in to evaluate Zach's mental health needed more time.

I didn't think it was a very good thing that a psychologist needed extra time to figure out what was wrong with him, but I kept that little opinion to myself.

Even though Romeo and I didn't talk about Zach or what happened that night, word still got around campus. No one directly asked me what happened, but the gigantic bruise on my face pretty much summed it up. It was beginning to turn an ugly yellow shade, but the swelling was gone.

It'd been almost a week since the incident with Zach, and I still hadn't spoken to my father. It was making me increasingly agitated. It wasn't so unusual for me to go this long without speaking with him. Sometimes when classes were really busy, I only called on the weekends. But I'd left messages. I'd gotten a new phone. He never called me back.

I'd be lying if I said it didn't make me suspicious.

And for that, I felt guilty.

But the seed of doubt had been planted, and my father's lack of communication only watered that seed, so it began to grow.

After a full day of classes, walking around campus in the freezing cold, and then spending my afternoon (and dinner) in the library catching up, I finally trudged up the steps to my dorm. I was tired and stressed. I felt like I could sleep for a week.

Ivy was sitting at her desk when I walked in, her back turned as she stared at her laptop. A pair of white earbuds were stuck in her ears and the cord was connected to the computer. I dropped my bag on the floor and kicked off my boots.

Ivy heard and glanced over her shoulder. "Hey," she said, her voice a little loud. She hit a button on the laptop and pulled out the earbuds and dropped them on the desk.

"You missed dinner," she said.

"I ate a granola bar in the library." I made a face to show how thrilled I was about it. Then I spun and let my body fall onto my bed, back first. My loud groan filled the room.

Ivy gasped. "Could it be?" she said, all dramatic like. "Are *you*—the most studious girl I know—getting tired of studying?"

I turned my head and tried to mirror her dramatic tone. "Are you—the most UN-studious girl I know—sitting there studying? On a Friday night?"

Before she could say anything, I pressed the back of my hand to my forehead.

"Have we entered the twilight zone?" I cried.

Ivy grinned at me and leaned so I could see her laptop screen. "Hell no, I'm not studying. I'm watching a makeup tutorial on YouTube."

I laughed.

"This girl has some good tips," she said seriously.

"All is right with the world, then."

Ivy turned her chair so she faced me. "They set a new hearing date for Zach?"

She knew everything that was going on, everything that happened, even the stuff Valerie said about my dad. It was nice to have someone to confide in. Someone I could talk to about it all. Romeo was always there for me, but sometimes a girl just needed another girl—*a friend*—to talk to.

"Not yet. Tony thinks they'll call Monday with a firm date."

"What do you think is wrong with him?" she asked.

"I don't know," I replied. "But I hope they figure it out, because Zach is seriously messed up."

She moaned. "I can't believe I slept with him." The blond bun on top of her head bounced when she shook her head vigorously. "I don't know what the hell they were serving at that party that night, but it must have been potent because I never would have touched him if I had even an ounce of sobriety in me."

I frowned. Ivy was a lot of things—a slacker when it came to school work, a clothes hog, a girl who liked to party—and she definitely wasn't innocent, but sleeping with Zach was absolutely not something I could picture her doing.

"How much did you drink that night?" I asked, concerned.

A look of concentration came over her face and then her eyes clouded over. "I really don't remember." She glanced up. "I really didn't think it was anything more than my usual. But, man, it seemed to hit me hard. 'Course, I had no idea what was in the punch we were drinking."

"Was everyone else as drunk as you?"

"Probably." She shrugged.

"Was Missy? Did she go home with anyone?"

Ivy snorted. "No. She's still hung up on Braeden."

I felt my eyes widen. "She is?"

"I think she is. She hasn't dated very much since coming back from break. She really did like him." Ivy made a face and muttered, "Although, I have no idea why."

"She hasn't been around much lately," I said. I felt bad I was just noticing.

"She's been around. You just haven't been."

"I've been a crappy friend."

Ivy shook her head quickly. "Are you kidding? Your life is like a soap opera. I couldn't even make up half the stuff that's happened you lately. You've had a lot on your plate."

Still. I should have been a better friend. I sat up as an idea came to me. "Call Missy. See if she wants to hang out tonight. We can watch movies or something."

"Girls' night? I like it." Then she lifted an eyebrow. "Don't you have plans with Romeo?"

"He can hang with Braeden. It's just one night."

"Hos over bros!" Ivy quipped and grabbed up her cell.

"That sounds like something B would say." I teased her.

"I think I just threw up in my mouth." She made a gagging sound.

I laughed. "Call Missy. I'm just going to try my dad again before we hang out."

• • •

She nodded and tapped the screen on her phone a couple times as she walked toward the door. "I'll be right back. I drank a giant Diet Coke earlier."

I waved her off and dialed my dad. The light mood brought on by the idea of having a girls' night began to fade the longer the phone call went unanswered. When his voicemail came on, I sort of lost it.

"Hey, you've reached Brock. Leave a message and I'll get back to you. Thanks."

BEEP.

"Dad. It's me. I've been calling you all week and you haven't called me back. I'm starting to worry… And I didn't want to do this over the phone, but I was attacked last week. I was in the hospital." The words just tumbled out before I could stop them.

The truth was I was angry. How could he just ignore his own daughter? So I gave him something he couldn't ignore. "Just call me back, okay?"

After a heartbeat, some of my anger faded. "Bye."

I tossed the phone on the end of the bed with a sigh. Maybe I should call my grandmother. Ask her to go over there and check on him.

Yeah. That's what I'd do.

I snatched up my phone just as it began ringing.

It was my dad.

So I guess my annoyed message got through.

"Hello?" I said into the line.

"Rimmel, honey? Are you okay? Oh God, sweetheart, I'm so sorry." The panic and regret in his voice fought against each other, making him sound slightly desperate and also a little crazed. "This is all my fault," he bemoaned.

His words struck something in me. That was an odd thing to say. "Why would it be your fault?"

"Tell me you're okay? What happened?" He was insistent.

"There's this guy on campus who hates Romeo," I said. "He, uh, he attacked me the other night because he wanted to get to him."

"This is your boyfriend's fault?"

Why did his voice sound so bewildered?

"Sir, would you like another?" a feminine voice asked in the background.

"Yes, please," Dad told her.

"On the rocks?" she asked.

Was he drinking? Where was he?

"Dad?" I said. "Where are you?"

"Sorry, honey. I'm just out grabbing a bite to eat. That was the waitress."

"Oh," I said.

"Your message said you were in the hospital?" he asked.

Ivy entered the room and gave me a thumbs-up and a smile. I assumed that meant Missy was on her way over.

"Yeah, but not overnight or anything. Mostly I was there because Romeo broke his arm."

"He was involved in this?"

"He came to help me and he was hurt."

There was a lot of background noise wherever Dad was. It sure was a loud restaurant.

"So you're okay, then?" Dad asked. "How bad were you hurt?"

"I'm fine now."

Ivy was digging through her clothes, and I hoped that didn't mean girls' night was something I had to dress up for.

"Thank God," he said. "Your message scared me half to death."

"Why didn't you call me back?" I asked abruptly.

"Honey, I didn't get your messages. There must be something wrong with this phone. I think it must be time for an upgrade."

"You didn't get any of my messages?" I asked, confused.

"Not until right now. I'm so sorry I wasn't there when you needed me." His voice sounded pained.

"It's okay, Dad. I was just getting worried."

"No need to worry about me. I'm doing just fine."

"How's work?" I asked abruptly.

"Busy as usual," he said. "We're gearing up for the spring rush."

I was about to ask him about my insurance card and why it had been denied when some noise erupted in the background. People were cheering and some kind of music was playing.

"Honey, my food just got here. I'm gonna let you go so I can eat before it goes cold. You know how I hate cold mashed potatoes. But I'll call you back when I finish, okay?"

"Yeah, okay," I echoed. If he heard the surprise in my voice, he didn't let on.

In fact, he disconnected the call without so much as a good-bye.

I held the phone out from my ear and looked at the screen in shock.

"Is everything okay?" Ivy asked.

"I'm not sure," I whispered.

There was a knock at the door and it opened. "Girls' night!" Missy sang, bouncing into the room.

"Girl, you look too good to not be seen." Ivy snapped her fingers, and Missy struck a pose.

She did look great in a pair of skintight black jeans with bright-blue high heels and a white blouse with silver-studded cap sleeves. In her hand she was carrying a bright-red coat.

"We should totally go out," Missy replied, running her fingers through her straight, sleek hair.

"Yes!" Ivy shrieked.

"We can go to that new club that just opened, the one near campus."

They wanted to go to a club? Like where people went to dance and drink?

Gulp

"I thought we were watching a movie?" I said.

"We're in college," Ivy said. "We're supposed to be going out, having fun." She glanced at Missy. "I hear Screamerz is supposed to be amazing."

It was called Screamerz?

Double gulp

"I'm excited!" Missy said, clapping.

"You two just go without me," I said.

"No," they both said at the same time.

"Missy, find her something to wear while I get dressed," Ivy instructed. Missy started going through my drawers, on a mission.

I bit my lower lip. "Clubs aren't really my thing."

"Football players weren't either, and look how well that turned out," Ivy said, a teasing light in her eyes.

"Ha. Ha."

"C'mon, Rimmel. It'll be fun. Weren't you just collapsing over there under all the pressure and drama your life has been lately? It's Friday. You already studied until your eyes bled. Your life is a disaster, and from the look on your face just now, I say you could probably use a drink."

"The way you just summarized my life makes me want a drink," I muttered.

Ivy took that as agreement and shrieked, "Girls' night!"

What the heck did I just get myself into?

CHAPTER FOURTEEN

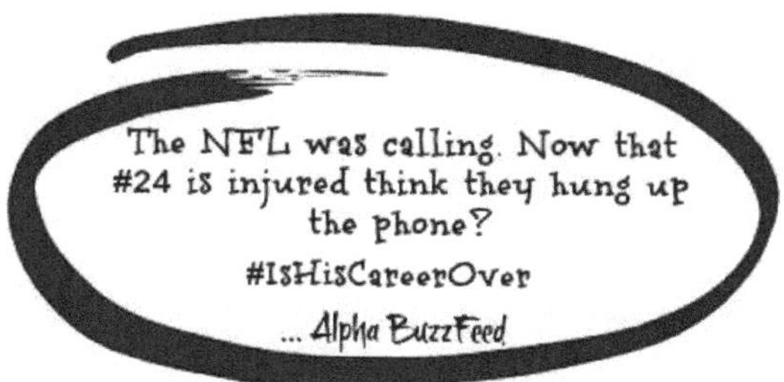

ROMEO

I'M HAVING A GIRLS' NIGHT TONIGHT

I smiled when I read Rim's text. I could almost hear her enthusiasm (or lack thereof) through the phone.

BUT I'M NOT A GIRL

WELL THAT'S GOOD NEWS. I WAS STARTING TO WONDER

WOMAN, ARE YOU QUESTIONING MY MANHOOD?

YES. MAYBE YOU SHOULD COME GET ME RIGHT NOW AND GIVE ME A LESSON.

I laughed out loud and wiped a bead of sweat off my forehead.

GIRLS' NIGHT THAT SCARY?

THEY'RE MAKING ME GO TO A PLACE CALLED SCREAMERZ.

My hand tightened around the phone. Screamerz was the new eighteen and over club near campus. I'd heard it could get pretty rowdy there. I hadn't been yet because I'd been too busy with football and now training. I wasn't sure how I felt about Rim going there. Without me.

THAT'S A NIGHT CLUB

HERE I THOUGHT IT WAS A BOOK CLUB

RIM…

I hoped those three little dots showed the warning in my tone.

YOU GONNA MAKE ME SLEEP ALONE TONIGHT?

THAT'S MY LINE

I groaned. Damn if that little hashtag heart didn't make me forget she was trying to sweet talk me.

From down the field, Braeden yelled, "Yo, Rome. We doing this?"

I'LL FIND YOU LATER. BEHAVE.

;)

Why did that little winky face make me remember why I had a bad feeling about this?

I gripped the football and threw in down the field toward Braeden. It was a shitty throw. 'Course all my throws this week were shitty.

But what else can you expect when a right-handed quarterback starts training to be a left-handed quarterback?

"You tired?" B yelled.

"Rimmel's having girls' night at Screamerz tonight," I told him.

"Guess we're going to Screamerz."

I grinned. "You read my mind."

"I'll call the team. They can meet us there. We'll have a *guys'* night."

I picked up another football out of the giant basket next to me. Braeden lifted his hands like he was ready to catch it. "Right here," he said, motioning.

I'd yet to throw him a solid pass, and we'd been working on this for days. It was frustrating as hell.

But I wasn't about to give up.

And I wasn't about to sit around on my ass and wait for my arm to heal while the NFL went and knocked on someone else's door.

If my right arm was out of commission, then my left one would pick up the slack. And when my right arm got better, I'd be an ambidextrous quarterback. It would only make me a better player. Learning how to throw from the opposite side of my body was sort of like learning how to ride a bike. The skill was there; I just needed to learn to master it.

I didn't mind the hard work, and doing this was better than sitting around while my muscles got soft and my endurance went downhill. I couldn't run, so I moved an elliptical into my gym (doctor okayed it). I couldn't lift or really focus on upper body, so I'd been hitting legs hard.

I did the exercises recommended by the team doctor, and I had an appointment with the orthopedic specialist on Monday and a physical therapist on Tuesday. I couldn't start therapy on my arm 'til it was healed, but I wanted to know everything I could be doing until then.

I refocused on Braeden, on the center of his body. My mind shut down all other thought: the stress about my career, the fight I was in to hone my body to perform… and yeah, the image of Rimmel at Screamerz. None of that mattered right then. It was me and the ball.

I concentrated on the way it felt beneath my hands and the breath filtering into my lungs. My arm pulled back and my balance shifted. I put as much force as I dared (still careful not to jar my other side) and launched the ball at B.

I watched with baited breath as it cut through the air. The ball slammed into Braeden's waiting hands, hitting exactly where I wanted it to go.

Braeden let out a big yell and threw the ball on the field and started doing some kind of mad victory dance.

Dude looked like he was in a bad remake of *Saturday Night Fever.*

"That was the money shot right there!" he yelled when he was done embarrassing himself.

I grinned. "Hells yeah."

"'Bout time you got in a good throw. I was getting worried, Rome." B shook his head. "I thought for sure you were gonna end up taking orders from some pimple-faced kid at a department store no one ever shopped in."

I gave him the finger.

"We good for the day? I'm gonna call the guys. Maybe you should sit down."

"You sound like a damn woman," I muttered. "My arm's broken. I'm not freaking dying."

In my pocket, my phone started ringing, and I grinned. It was probably Rimmel calling to beg me to get her out of going to the club.

I pulled it out, but it wasn't her.

"Dad," I said into the line. "What's up?"

"I'm afraid I have some bad news, son." That's the thing about my dad. He never beat around the bush. He just came out and said whatever it was. I respected that.

"What is it?"

"The two NFL teams that were interested in you have rescinded their offers."

I knew this was a possibility. Hell, I knew it was practically set in stone.

It didn't make it any easier to hear.

I plowed a hand through my hair and noted how damp the ends were from being on the field, throwing for so long. "Fuck," I swore under my breath.

"I think we knew it was coming," he said. "With your arm the way it is, no one's going to want to commit when there's a real possibility you won't be able to play this season. It would be a huge gamble on their part and could end up being a real loss financially."

"I know, Dad. You don't have to explain." I sighed. "They putting me back in the draft or am I just out 'til I can prove myself again?" Just the idea of that made me exhausted.

"I don't know. I'm waiting on a call back."

We both knew what that meant. The NFL was cutting their losses.

"Thanks for letting me know, Dad," I said.

"It's a setback. But it's not the end. You'll be even better next season, and you'll have more than two offers on the table."

It sucked to have been so close to something I wanted that badly only to have it yanked away at the last second.

"Let me know if you hear anything else," I said. *Like when they call and say I'm out.*

"Of course. And, Romeo? Take a break this weekend. You started training just days after your accident. Rest is just as important for your body as movement."

"Yeah." I agreed. "Okay." It didn't seem like a bad idea at the moment. "I'll talk to you later."

When I hung up, Braeden was standing nearby looking at me. "What'd he say?" he asked.

"I'm out. Teams withdrew the offers."

"That blows," Braeden said.

"Everybody on for Screamerz tonight?" I asked. Talking about the end of my NFL career before it even started wasn't high on my list of to-dos.

"Hells yeah."

"Good. Let's hit the showers." I picked up my stuff and we headed toward the locker room.

Suddenly, I was feeling like a strong drink.

CHAPTER FIFTEEN

All the cool kids are hanging at
Screamerz tonight.
Even the unofficial team mascot of
the Wolves
#NerdIsTheNewCool
... Alpha BuzzFeed

RIMMEL

I felt like a walking Barbie.

Ivy and Missy had entirely too much fun dressing me up.

Of course, it isn't like I protested much, so it really wasn't entirely their fault. Thing was right now, talking about clothes and hair and listening to them chatter on about everything they read in celebrity magazines was a great distraction.

It wouldn't hurt to not think about everything for a little while, would it?

...

Ivy curled my hair in those big messy curls like she's done before. I'd had it up so much lately it almost felt weird to have it cascading down my back and over my shoulders. Normally when she came at me with makeup, I would have told her no. I didn't like to wear makeup. It made me feel like I wasn't being myself.

But tonight I relented. Truth was, the makeup made me feel more like me.

She used a light hand and kept it natural, but her expert application managed to cover most of the bruising around my eye. When I slid on my glasses, the rims covered the small cut high on my cheek and I looked like I did before Zach used my face as a punching bag.

Aside from the foundation and light dusting of powder, she didn't do much other than add a little bit of stuff to brighten my eyes (she told me what it was called, but I really wasn't listening) and I added a tinted lip balm.

Missy picked out a pair of denim leggings I forgot I had. It was one of those purchases my grandmother insisted on when we went shopping over break. They were a faded blue and had rips all along the front from the thighs down past the knees. They were tighter than I liked to wear, but because they were leggings, they weren't uncomfortable.

I didn't really understand the concept of wearing jeans with a bunch of holes in them, but Grandma told me they were in all the fashion magazines.

She paired the jeans with a black knit sweater that was also more formfitting than I would have liked. At least it wasn't low cut or cropped so it showed my stomach.

"Do you have any heels?" Ivy asked hopefully.

I laughed. "You know I don't wear heels. I'd kill myself."

"Well, mine are all too big for you." She frowned.

"Mine too," Missy said.

They both looked so sad I wasn't going to be able to complete this ensemble with heels that I laughed. "I'll stick with my boots."

Ivy groaned. "You wear those all the time."

I shrugged. "They're warm."

Missy caught my eye and smiled. "Uggs as club wear, I like it."

They weren't really Uggs, but they did look just like them.

"Ugh," Ivy said. "Don't encourage her."

I gave Missy a grateful smile.

"Fine," Ivy muttered. "I'll just wear heels big enough for the both of us."

Missy and I laughed as Ivy slid her feet into a pair of high-heeled, knee-high black suede boots.

They definitely weren't Uggs.

With them she was wearing a pair of white jeans, a red tank top, and a black-and-white-striped jacket. Her blond hair was in a high ponytail that looked flirty and fun, her lips were painted red, and her makeup was flawless.

I eyed Missy's outfit again—the one that made Ivy think we had to go out rather than stay in. I had to admit she did look like she needed to be seen.

Her dark hair looked as sleek as ever, and every time I looked at it, I couldn't help but have a little bit of hair envy.

She caught me ogling her, and I smiled. "It's nice to hang out with you. I've missed seeing you around."

"Me too," she replied.

"Well, no more of that shit," Ivy said, drawing both our gazes. "No more brooding over guys who don't deserve it." She looked pointedly at Missy, who blushed. "And no more being stalked by some psycho who's finally locked up where he belongs."

I didn't mention that technically Zach hadn't been punished yet. I didn't think she would appreciate my commentary.

"Tonight we dance, we drink, and we have fun!" Ivy proclaimed and picked up her bag.

I didn't feel as excited as she sounded as I went to pull out the gold necklace that used to be my mother's. I added it to my outfit and slid on my boots. The gold bracelet Romeo gave me still adorned my wrist, and I paused to look at it before grabbing my coat.

When I stood up, a stack of mail on the corner of Ivy's desk caught my eye. The top piece was addressed to me.

"You coming?" Ivy asked from the door.

"Did this mail just come today?" I asked.

"Oh yeah, I totally forgot about it."

I nodded. "I'll be right there."

Missy and Ivy moved out into the hall, and I quickly tore open the letter.

It was a bill from the ER.

I swallowed thickly when I saw how much those few hours cost me. It was over a thousand dollars. I didn't have a thousand dollars.

At the bottom of the bill in bold letters it said: UNINSURED.

Way to rub it in.

"I'm not getting any younger out here!" Ivy yelled from out in the hall.

"Coming!" I yelled and slid the bill under my pillow. I'd deal with it later.

I had no idea how, but I would.

The inside of Screamerz sort of made me want to do just that.

I don't really think that's what they intended when they decorated the place, but it was the outcome all the same.

It reminded me of a warehouse, a huge wide-open space. The floors were polished concrete and the walls were covered with what looked like large sheets of aluminum. Beer signs and neon lights decorated the walls and track lighting covered the high ceilings.

The music was so loud it made the gravel in the parking lot vibrate beneath my boots as we passed a group of laughing people loitering at the entrance.

Inside, the music was even louder, the very air vibrated with it, and people were everywhere. A large crush of bodies was in the center of the wide-open space, all gyrating and dancing to the beat. Toward the back of the club was a giant DJ booth with a man at the controls. He had on a pair of oversized headphones, and the sight made me snort.

Apparently, the music was too loud for him too.

Around the perimeter of the room were a bunch of tables of varying shapes and sizes. The bar stretched the entire length of the place on the left side and had to be at least thirty feet long. Almost all the barstools were filled with people, most of them college age. Behind the bar, at least five bartenders were serving drinks, and I saw a couple waitresses walking around the floor with trays of drinks.

"This place is awesome!" Ivy said and grabbed my hand to pull me farther in.

I gripped her fingers as she tugged me through the crowd, afraid I was going to be swallowed up by all the people. I felt like Alice in Wonderland, like I'd fallen down a hole and ended up in some strange land.

And just like every strange land, everyone else looked entirely at home and it was me who was the odd one out.

I dared a glance at Missy just behind me. She flashed a broad smile and shimmied her shoulders to the beat of the music.

Clearly, I wasn't going to get any help from her.

Somehow Ivy found us an empty table. It was a small round one with four seats. The three of us plunked down, and I wondered if anyone would notice if I hid beneath it.

"Drinks then dancing!" Ivy yelled over the music.

I shook my head vehemently. "I don't dance!"

Missy laughed. "You do tonight!"

Oh my. This was a huge mistake. Screamerz was so not my scene.

Ivy laughed and put an arm around my shoulders. "You know what you need?"

I was afraid to ask.

"A drink. You need a drink to loosen you up."

I held up my wrist displaying the wristband they put on me at the door, a marker that I wasn't twenty-one. All three of us were wearing one.

Ivy grabbed the sleeve of my sweater and pulled it down over the band. Her and Missy did the same. Did they really think that was going to work?

There was no way we could just walk up to the bar and order a drink without them asking to see our wrists.

At that moment, some drunk guy stumbled into me from behind. My chair tipped forward and I smacked into the table edge, but Missy caught my shoulder and kept me from smashing my face.

"Hey!" she yelled.

The guy righted himself as beer sloshed over his glass and on his hand. "My bad," he said, taking in the three of us sitting there.

His smile turned into more than just a polite apology. He took in Ivy and Missy, his eyes appreciative. Then he looked at me.

His eyes narrowed. "Hey, don't I know you?"

"Me?" I squeaked. "No."

He took a swig of beer and squinted over the rim of his glass. "I totally know you," he said but offered no more explanation.

Ivy smiled. "You've probably seen her on campus, and maybe on TV? She's dating the quarterback of the Wolves."

His eyes widened. "That's it!" he bellowed, and a few other people looked. He grabbed his buddy by the neck and spun him around. "It's the nerd!"

I glanced at Ivy and Missy. "Did he just call me a nerd?"

The guy laughed and pushed himself between me and Ivy. His arm dropped over my shoulder, and he smelled like he took a bath in the crap in his cup.

Ew.

I tried not to wrinkle my nose when he leaned close to talk. "No offense, little nerd. You're like the new team mascot for Alpha U."

"Gee, thanks," I muttered.

"Where's number twenty-four?" he asked.

"Its girls' night," Missy said, giving him a flirty smile.

She could do so much better than beer breath.

"I dig it," he said, drinking more beer. I really wished he'd get his arm off me.

"You think any of those bartenders wouldn't notice the Alpha U mascot is wearing one of those bracelets?" Ivy asked, leaning close.

The guy looked blatantly at her chest. "No worries. Drinks are on us."

"Oh, you don't have—" I started, but he lifted his cup and shouted. "To the Wolves!"

Everyone around us started howling.

A waitress came by, and he finally let me go to put in an order for more drinks.

Ivy and Missy gave me amused looks.

"Don't look at me like that," I muttered.

"Team mascot?" Missy said, her grin getting wider.

"Free drinks," Ivy said.

The two of them laughed and high-fived.

Beer breath and his friends appeared through the crowd, dragging a table along with them and sitting it right beside ours.

And just like that, we were at a table filled with people who were all way drunker than I'd ever been.

Ivy and Missy were thrilled, and beer breath motioned at the seat next to him. Ivy gave me a nudge, so I moved down, with my friends taking up the space on my other side.

The waitress came back with a huge pitcher of beer, a few empty glasses, and a tray of shots.

One of the shots, and bright-blue one, was put in front of me.

"What's this?" I asked.

"Smurf balls!" Beer breath laughed.

I looked at the girls. They each had their own Smurf Balls. "He wants us to drink balls." I couldn't stop the giggle that bubbled out of me.

Ivy picked up her glass and saluted the air. "To balls!"

Everyone cheered and downed the shot.

I sipped at mine. It didn't taste bad for balls.

"Do it!" Missy yelled in my ear.

I shrugged and tossed it back. I felt the liquid heat of the alcohol all the way down to my stomach.

One of the guys across the table was sitting with his girlfriend. She was pretty with long red hair and a simple hoodie. I wished Ivy had let me wear a hoodie.

"I heard about what happened with Zach," she said, leaning across the table.

A few people who heard her looked at me.

What was I supposed to say to that? Clearly, they wanted me to say something.

"He's a real douche," I said.

"I'll drink to that," Ivy said and sipped at a beer that appeared in her hand.

"More balls!" the guy beside me yelled as another tray of blue shots appeared.

Missy took two and handed one to me.

I probably shouldn't have taken it. I probably should have given it to the guy beside me. But the reminder of Zach and the image of that hospital bill I just opened were too fresh in my mind.

I didn't sip the Smurf Balls this time.

I opened up my throat and tossed it down.

My eyes watered, but my limbs started to loosen up already. The thoughts of Zach, my father, and lost insurance faded away to be replaced with a warm, fuzzy kind of feeling.

Maybe Screamerz wasn't so bad after all.

CHAPTER SIXTEEN

#Message4MyBoys
Does your girl have a blue mouth?
It's the balls. Smurf Balls.
#LetTheUniversityStaffFigureThisOneOut
... Alpha BuzzFeed

ROMEO

We stopped at my place so I could put on something other than gym clothes before going to Screamerz. Braeden was ahead of me in his truck and pulled up into the driveway. Since I was going to drive us to the club, I didn't bother pulling all the way up the drive, but parked the Hellcat down near the road.

When I got out of the car and started up the drive, someone called my name. "Romeo Anderson?"

I spun around as a man in a windbreaker, jeans, and sneakers came jogging across the street. I glanced behind him at the car that was parked on the side of the road across the street from my parents'.

My eyes narrowed. "Who's asking?"

"My name is James Darling. I'm a writer with the *Maryland Tribune*—"

I cut him off. "You're a reporter."

I didn't have anything against reporters in general, but this guy was sitting outside my parents' on a Friday night, literally waiting for me. That made him an asshole in my book.

"I'm a writer. I was hoping you could give me a quote on both pro teams withdrawing their offer of contracts this season. Think there will be any new offers on the table?"

"How the fuck did you even know that?" I spat.

He stopped walking. "The teams updated the list. You were removed. It's public record."

"So you thought you'd sit outside my house to find out why?"

He glanced at my arm and sling. "Your injury is also public record. You've been quite the hot topic in sports lately."

This pissed me off.

I knew it shouldn't. Hell, I could probably spin this to my advantage somehow, but I was tired, and pissed off I was getting booted out of the NFL.

"Look, man, maybe we could set up another time to talk? Like during working hours?"

He seemed like he wanted to object, but then he relented. "Of course," he said. "I'm sorry if I bothered you. Sometimes being a reporter and getting an exclusive gets in the way of my manners."

I flashed him a grin. At least he was honest. "Next time, you should just lead with that."

He grinned back. "Yeah, maybe I will." He stuffed his hand into the pocket of his windbreaker and pulled out a white card.

"This is my card and my personal number. Call me on Monday and we can set something up."

I walked the few steps down the driveway to where he stood and took the card. "Will do."

The reporter glanced at the Hellcat and whistled. "That's a hell of a nice car."

I grinned. "Hells yeah."

"What's that retail for? Fifty grand?"

"Sixty-six," I answered. But really it was none of his damn business.

He whistled beneath his breath. "That's a pretty penny. But I guess when you're a star quarterback en route to the NFL, money isn't an object."

My back teeth came together. That sounded a lot like judgment from a total stranger. What a douche.

He turned and walked away. Halfway to his own car (a Toyota), he stopped and turned. "Oh, and you shouldn't be surprised if more media outlets reach out. Your performance on the field last season got a lot of attention, but the…" He paused as if searching for a word. "The drama surrounding you lately and that girlfriend of yours, that's the stuff that makes the news."

My muscles bunched. I didn't like that he brought up Rimmel. Not at all. I didn't say anything, but I stood there and watched him until he drove off. I walked up the driveway toward the house. Braeden was standing in the shadows, staring down to where I'd been.

"The media?" he asked.

"Fuck, man," I spat.

Braeden slapped me on my good shoulder. "Forget it. He was probably just trying to make himself sound important. Now you just go get pretty for our date tonight."

I chuckled. "Dude, you have some major screws loose."

"Nothing a few beers won't fix," he mused. "And maybe a hot woman."

I changed into a pair of jeans, a pair of shoes I didn't have to tie, and a short-sleeved T-shirt with the Wolves symbol on it. It was too cold for a short-sleeved shirt, but this damn splint and sling made putting on a long-sleeved a pain in my ass.

Once that was done, I threw on an Alpha U baseball hat so I didn't have to mess with my hair. Doing shit one armed took longer, and I was in a rush to get to the club.

Braeden was dressed in a pair of loose jeans, a black Henley, and a long-sleeved button up worn unbuttoned and untucked. He was wearing a silver dog whistle as a necklace on a long silver chain and had a watch with a thick leather band encircling his waist.

He took the time to do his dark hair so he didn't need a hat.

Ah, the benefits of having more than one hand.

Plus, he had women to impress. I didn't.

Some of the guys were in the parking lot when we pulled in. It was crammed full of cars and the music was already pumping through the night air. I parked the Hellcat in the first spot I saw, and we joined the guys who were waiting for us.

A line had formed at the door, but the bouncer recognized us as the Wolves and waived us in ahead of everyone else.

The lighting was dim and flashing inside. People were everywhere, at the bar, on the dance floor, and all the spaces in between. It was a huge place, but it was still crowded. This place probably made a killing on the weekends. With it being so close to campus, it was the perfect spot to hang.

I thought it was pretty cool. The music was loud and jamming, and the atmosphere was pretty chill despite the large crowd.

"Romeo!" Someone called my name and I turned, but it wasn't the girl I wanted to see. It was a group of cheerleaders for Alpha U.

"Ladies," I said, giving them my charming smile.

"Are you okay?" one purred, slipping up to my side and giving a look to my arm.

I angled my body just slightly away, not wanting to give her any ideas. "Feeling good," I replied.

She opened her mouth to say something else, but Braeden interjected. "Rome!" he said, coming up behind me. "Where our girl at?"

"Haven't spotted her yet," I answered, turning away from the cheerleaders.

A few guys I knew from campus walked by, and I slapped them high-fives.

Trent and a few of the Wolves who hadn't met us in the parking lot appeared. They already had beers in their hand.

"Beer's flowing tonight," Trent said with a grin. "This place knows how to treat the Wolves."

"Sa-weet," Braeden said.

I scanned the crowd for Rimmel. It was going to take me forever to find her tiny ass in this crowded bar.

"We got a table over there." Trent motioned. "Come on."

"Hey," I called. "You seen Rimmel?"

"Rimmel's here?" Trent's eyes widened.

"Supposed to be," I answered, scanning the crowd.

"Oh, she's here," the cheerleader who'd been talking to me earlier injected into the conversation. I glanced at her, surprised. I hadn't realized she was still here.

"Yeah?"

She gave me a smile. "She's popular tonight." I didn't like the glint in her eye.

"What's that supposed to mean?" Didn't these snooty bitches know by now their stupid drama didn't work on me?

"See for yourself." She pointed a finger with a long hot-pink nail glued on the end past the dance floor.

It took me a moment to locate her. She wasn't at all where I thought she'd be.

She was sitting at this huge table full of a bunch of guys and girls. Ivy and Missy were to her left, and she was leaning toward them laughing. She was the smallest person at the table, and the shiny loose waves bouncing around her shoulders drew my eyes like a flare in a night sky.

On her other side sat some guy. He had a beer in his hand but was already clearly wasted. His body language wasn't to my liking.

In fact, it made me want to beat his ass.

Even though Rim was facing away from him toward her friends, he was sitting there clearly open to her attention, welcoming it.

As I watched, a waitress set down a tray of shot glasses beside him.

People cheered.

My teeth ground together when drunk ass reached out his beefy hand and tugged on Rim's perfect hair.

"Ah, hells no," I spat.

"What's going, Rome?" Braeden asked.

I grabbed his neck and steered his head in the direction of the show.

Rimmel made a face when her hair was tugged on and skillfully detracted it from his grip.

He held out a shot glass to her, and she shook her head.

He thrust it at her again, and some of the liquid—was that shit blue?—spilled over his hand and onto her arm.

She frowned and wiped it away, said something, then turned back to her friends.

He tugged her hair again.

When she turned, he gave her a sloppy smile and thrust the shot at her. This time, she took it and set it on the table beside her.

I glanced at Braeden. "He's trying to get my girl drunk."

Braeden nodded. "He's trying to get your girl drunk."

And he touched her hair.

Clearly, this girl needed supervision.

She was oblivious to the effect she had on people.

But I saw…

Thank God I showed up when I did.

CHAPTER SEVENTEEN

RIMMEL

The first sign that you're drunk is telling yourself you aren't.

I was certainly not drunk.

Yet when beer breath tried to give me yet another Smurf Balls—*hehe, I said balls*—I turned it down. Clearly, there was still a little common sense or sobriety left in me.

I was such a lightweight. Those two shots I'd taken before totally made me tipsy. Then I sipped at another before surrendering it to Missy to swallow in one gulp.

I'm not sure what was in that blue potion, but it sure made me giggly. And relaxed. Especially since I was sitting at a table filled with people I didn't know. But they all knew me. It was a strange concept.

I leaned over Missy and looked at Ivy. "You should call me Alice."

Ivy tilted her head and looked at me with interest. After another sip of her beer, she said, "You look like an Alice."

Missy nodded with wide eyes. "You do."

The three of us started giggling.

Beer breath started tugging on my hair again, and I wanted to groan. He was a high-maintenance drinking partner, and I had no idea how to tell him to get lost. I didn't want to be mean.

Suddenly, a low, familiar voice sounded oddly close. "You might want to think twice about putting your hand in my girl's hair again."

I gasped and spun around.

Romeo was towering over the table, angling himself toward me but staring down at beer breath, who immediately removed his hand and began to stutter.

"Hey, number twenty-four. I di-didn't mean nothing. I was just talking to her."

He started to push out of his seat, his drunken movements sloppy. "Here, take my seat."

Poor guy.

I started to giggle.

A smile tugged at Romeo's lips and he waved the guy back down. "Nah, man. Keep your seat. I got one."

The next thing I knew, I was being lifted out of the chair by one arm, and Romeo sat down, fitting me in his lap.

I let my head fall against his chest and gazed up at him, tugging on the brim of his hat. "Hey there, sexy."

His eyes crinkled at the corners with amusement. "Hey, baby."

I puckered up my lips so he would kiss me.

"Why the hell are your lips blue?" he demanded.

I started giggling again. "It was from the balls."

"You better not be talking about the kind of balls I think you're talking about," he growled.

Ivy leaned around Missy and glared at Romeo. "This is girls' night!"

"Then why are there more guys at your table than girls?" he asked, lifting a brow.

Missy grinned.

"He has a point," I told her and rested my cheek against his chest. Then I gasped and jerked upright. "Did I hurt your arm?"

"You're drunk," he muttered.

"It's because beer breath kept giving me balls." I laughed.

He motioned with his thumb. "That beer breath?"

I nodded.

Romeo reached out and grabbed him by his neck and pulled him toward us. "You giving my girl balls?"

"What the fuck!" Braeden roared over my shoulder.

"BBFL," I called out.

Braeden glanced at me with a smile. "Hey, tutor girl." Then he looked back at beer breath and scowled.

"It's a shot, man," he answered Romeo and pointed to the blue drink on the table. "Smurf Balls."

Ivy, Missy, and I started laughing. "He said balls," Missy said.

"For the love of God," Romeo muttered.

"Try it!" I said and held out the shot.

He made a face. "You want me to swallow something called Smurf Balls?"

"It's really tasty," I told him.

Braeden laughed. "Yeah, Rome. Let's see you down the balls."

I sat forward and snatched the other shot out of Missy's hand and held it out to Braeden. "Here, you have some too."

He blanched.

Romeo laughed.

"That's Missy's, Rim," Braeden told me.

"She doesn't mind." I glanced at Missy, and she nodded. I watched her glance over her shoulder at Braeden and gave him a wave.

"Hey, Miss, how you been?" Braeden said.

"I'd be better if you drank the Smurf Balls."

All three of us girls laughed some more.

The guys looked at each other and the shots in their hands.

Really. What was the big deal? It was just Smurf Balls.

I glanced around and noticed everyone at the table watching. I grinned.

"Who thinks they should take the shots?" I yelled.

"Do it!" someone down the table yelled.

Before I knew it, everyone was chanting.

Romeo flashed his perfect white teeth, and my belly jumped a little. "You're lucky I love you."

"Bottoms up, B!" he said.

Both guys held up the blue shots and then tossed them back.

Everyone cheered.

Romeo slammed the shot glass on the table and looked at me. "This is what got you so drunk?" He seemed a little skeptical. "It tastes like fruit punch."

"I told you it was good." I nodded.

"So, Braeden." Ivy snickered. "How'd those balls taste?"

"Well, I got nothing to compare them to, unlike you," he shot back.

"I really don't know what you saw in him," Ivy told Missy, who blushed.

"How the hell did you even get served?" Romeo asked me.

"Beer breath almost knocked me over," I explained, and his eyes narrowed. "But then he said he was sorry and recognized me because of you. They all called me a nerd, which at first I thought was an insult, but then I realized they were saying it nice like."

Romeo held up his hand. "Nice like?"

"Uh-huh." I agreed. "Then they all said I was like the new team mascot for the Wolves, and the next thing I knew, we were drinking Smurf Balls."

"You talk a lot when you're drunk," Braeden said over Romeo's shoulder.

"This guy's been buying your drinks all night?" he pointed at beer breath again.

I shrugged. "I guess so."

He didn't look very happy about that, and it caused some worry to poke through my drunken calm. "Are you mad at me? Did I do something wrong?"

His eyes softened beneath the brim of his hat, and he leaned forward to kiss me softly. "No, baby. You didn't do anything wrong."

He lifted me and stood me on my feet. I swayed a little, and Braeden reached out and pulled me away from the table and into his side. "Girl, you're a hot mess."

"Ladies," Romeo said to Ivy and Missy. "We're going to the Wolves table." He gestured for them to follow.

Then he stood and dug a couple twenties out of his pocket and tossed them on the table in front of beer breath.

"What's this?" he asked, looking up, his eyes totally glassy.

"Reimbursement," Romeo replied, his voice hard.

"For what?"

"Nobody buys drinks for my girl but me." He led us all to the long table near the dance floor where most of the Wolves were sitting. When they saw us coming, they shuffled around so there would be enough seats for the five of us to sit together.

Romeo and Braeden sat next to each other, and then Missy and Ivy slid in, leaving a chair beside Romeo for me. I went to sit down, but he caught me around the waist and pulled me into his lap again. "I think this is a good seat for you," he whispered in my ear.

The little hairs on the back of my neck stood up.

I leaned in to kiss him, but I hit my head on the brim of his hat.

"Ow," I complained.

He reached up and slid it around so it was facing backward. My mouth went dry watching the action. My God, I had no idea Romeo in a hat was so incredibly sexy. The way his blue eyes deepened when he looked at me said he noticed the way I noticed how turned on he made me.

He palmed the back of my neck and pulled me close. His tongue slid across my lips, and I opened so he could sweep inside. The taste of the shot lingered on our tongues and it was like a fruit explosion inside my mouth.

I groaned and sank a little farther into him, but he pulled me back and eased his mouth away. "Later," he promised.

A popular upbeat song came over the club and everyone cheered. Ivy put down her beer. "This is my jam!" she announced. Her and Missy stood up and looked at me expectantly.

"What?"

"We're dancing."

"Have fun," I said and gave them a wave.

"Oh no," Missy said and grabbed my hand. "You're coming too."

"I'm too drunk," I said.

"If you were too drunk, you'd already be out there," Ivy countered.

I glanced at Romeo for help. He grinned. "Go shake it, baby."

"Fine," I snapped. "I will."

The three of us made our way out to the dance floor and found a spot near the edge. Ivy and Missy went right to it; the way they moved made me second-guess myself. I did not dance. Like ever. I was uncoordinated, self-conscious, and awkward.

"Come on!" Ivy said and reached for my hand.

I shook my head. "I don't know how."

"Sure you do!" she said and put both her hands on my hips. I felt myself blush as she moved her hands to the beat, showing my hips where to go.

"You got it." She grinned and pulled back.

The alcohol made me bold, so I kept moving, swaying my hips and tossing my hair around.

Missy laughed, and a guy came up behind Ivy and she started grinding against him.

I stumbled a little watching them. The way their bodies moved together was so erotic that I totally fell out of rhythm.

Next, a really tall guy with super-short dark hair sidled up behind Missy, and she flashed him a smile over her shoulder. He reached out to let his hand hover over her hip, and she spun to face him and nodded.

He grabbed her behind and pulled her right up against his body, and they began swaying together, her dark, sleek hair whipping around.

I never went to any school dances in high school or any of the events Alpha U put on. I'd never actually danced in public before. The one time I tried at home, I fell over and hit my head.

I'd never danced with a guy like that. Hell, I didn't even know people danced like that.

I was standing there feeling really self-conscious and kind of silly. My giggly mood drained away by the second.

Ivy and Missy were totally involved in the guys who picked them up, and I was making a fool of myself standing there watching.

I was just about to turn back for the table when an arm wrapped around me from behind.

CHAPTER EIGHTEEN

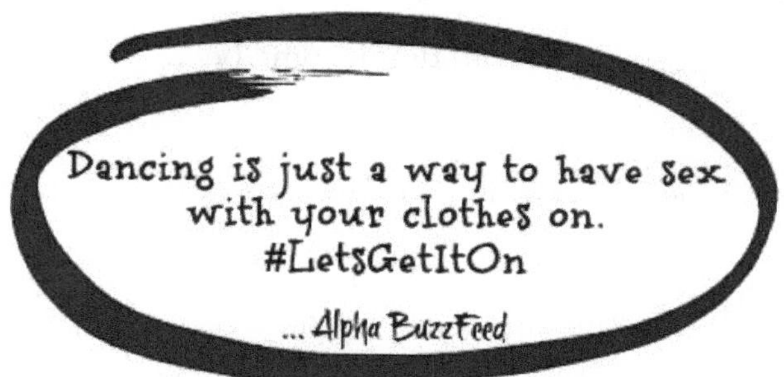

ROMEO

I couldn't help but watch the way Rimmel's small tight ass worked its way out onto the dance floor. Those jeans she had on were giving me a stiffy.

She usually didn't wear tight shit like that, and I really didn't care, but it didn't mean I couldn't admire the view while she was.

The little rips in the front of the legs exposed small patches of her skin, and it made me want to dip my fingers into those tears to feel the silkiness of her skin.

"Dude, that's my sister you're looking at like that," Braeden said in my ear.

I glanced at him and grinned. "She's fucking hot."

He made a face and drank some beer. "Sister," he reminded me.

I looked back at her and grinned. "She's a terrible dancer."

Braeden laughed. "The worst."

I watched as Ivy tried to teach her how to move. She got a little better, but once Ivy pulled away, Rim seemed lost again.

"Hey, she look thinner to you?" Braeden asked.

I gave him a sidelong glance. He shrugged. "Her clothes are tight. I noticed."

Her shirt was tight. It molded to her small frame just as well as the jeans did. I was surprised Ivy managed to get her to wear it. But now that B said something, she did look a little thinner.

I felt like shit for not noticing sooner. I picked up my untouched beer and took a drink. Had I been too preoccupied to notice she wasn't as okay as she let on? Was I missing some of the signs that she was worrying?

"Don't beat yourself up," Braeden said. "She's fine. Maybe she just looks smaller 'cause she ain't drowning in clothes."

"Maybe," I echoed, but I was already wondering if I missed something.

B and I watched as the girls got picked up by some random guys. Rimmel looked more lost than ever.

"You better go show that girl how to dance before someone else volunteers," Braeden said.

Hells no.

I pushed away from the table and made my way toward Rimmel. I could feel her wavering about being where she was. I saw her watching her friends like she had no idea people even danced that way. Clearly, she was out of her element.

Sometimes I forgot how innocent Rimmel really was. Since really learning about her, I got to see her inner strength, her determination. She never took my shit and she was comfortable enough with me that she was no longer timid.

But this wasn't just her and me.

It served as a good reminder for me that even though she was one way with me, deep down she was something else when she was in situations that were foreign to her.

Her innocence was something that drew me to her from the start, and also the way she was so honest with it. She never tried to pretend she was anything other than who she was.

I fucking loved that about her.

And it made me want to shelter her. It made me want to protect that innocence.

I caught her around the waist just as she was about to flee. My arm wrapped around her lower waist, right across her hips, and I pulled her firmly against me.

She gasped and started to pull away, and I chuckled. The sound of my laugh was familiar, and she stopped struggling and peeked over her shoulder around a curtain of dark hair.

"Wanna dance?"

"I'm terrible at dancing."

"I think you just need the right teacher," I whispered in her ear.

She arched against me, and I wished I had use of both my arms. This damn sling was really cramping my style. I used my free arm to keep her pinned against me and slid the fingers of my other hand beneath her shirt so they rested against her bare skin.

Because she was so much shorter than me, I had to bend at the knees and sort of hunch in around her. I brought my face down so it was near the side of her head and the silky smooth strands of her hair flirted with my cheek.

I'd been kind of lazy about shaving lately because of my whole limited mobility, and the scruff of my beard caught in the strands like it was Velcro.

With my body wrapped around hers, I started moving my hips, holding her against me, and practically lifting her off the ground.

"Move with me, babe," I whispered in her ear.

A long exhale moved through her body, and she relaxed into me until she was nearly boneless. My cock hardened as her ass moved against me. Her hand wrapped around the side of my hip and grabbed my ass.

I buried my face in her hair as we moved together, my fingers brushing against her bare skin, and she arched against me farther.

Need and desire swamped me. It hung over us like a cloud. I'd danced like this with lots of girls. I'd practically had sex in the middle of a dance floor. This was sort of tame…

But it had never turned me on more.

The song faded out, and I found myself irritated it didn't go on forever. I wasn't ready to let her go yet.

Instead of another song starting right up, the DJ came on over the mic. "We got football royalty in the house tonight."

A bunch of people howled.

"And it looks like the Alpha and his mate are on the dance floor… this song's for you, guys."

Rimmel tilted her head back and peered up and me from beneath her glasses. "Us?"

Gently, I spun her away so she faced me. I loved the way her hair floated out around her with the little twirl. "Who else?" I growled and pulled her close.

People around us clapped as a slow song about sex started pumping through the club. It was the first slow song I'd heard play all night.

"People are watching," Rimmel whispered.

"Well, let's give 'em something to talk about."

I slid my thigh between her legs and brought her so her chest was against mine. Her thighs tightened around my leg and her fingers curled in the front of my T-shirt. Her body seemed to take over and started to move to the sexy music. I don't know if she realized it or not, but she was dancing just then, and it was sexy as hell.

As she got a little braver, one of her hands slid around my waist and into the back pocket of my jeans. I groaned a little in my throat as she gyrated against my thigh and made a purring sound.

I straightened up a little more, bringing her body with mine as she rocked against me. Her forehead fell against my chest, and she held on. I felt the tension in her body, felt the need and the desire.

I'd never been so fucking turned on in public like this. I could barely see straight. It was taking everything in me not to drag her out of here and throw her in the backseat of my Hellcat.

Couples around us starting dancing and the crowd closed in. Rimmel was breathing a little heavy when she lifted her head. She released me to push the glasses up off her face and on top her head like a headband.

"Whatcha doing?" I asked, leaning in.

"Making everything else around us blurry. All I want to see right now is you."

I took her lips.

I owned them.

If there were ever a doubt in anyone's mind that this girl was solely mine, there wasn't anymore.

Rimmel wrapped her arms around my waist, and once she realized what she did, she began to pull back, to give my side with the sling a little space.

"Don't you dare," I growled and pulled her back. Her arms wound around me again, and I realized I was starved.

I'd been starved for this full-on contact. We'd been so careful of my arm that it limited the way we'd been together.

We were both wound tight. Tighter than I realized. I swept my tongue in her mouth, and the DJ flipped on some kind of light that made the room darker but with flashes of a silver strobe pounding through the room.

It made it harder to pull back.

When I did, she ground against me and looked up with fuzzy eyes. "Romeo," she whispered and swayed against me once more.

"Give it to me, baby."

Her eyes widened because she knew what I wanted.

She glanced around from side to side, glancing at all the people in the room. I grabbed her chin and looked at her. "No. Right here. Just us, remember?"

"I can't."

I brought my leg up a little more, pressing against her throbbing center with even more pressure. Her teeth sank into her lower lip.

I smiled.

"No one will even notice." I leaned into her ear. "But I will. And damn, this makes me so hot."

Her hazel eyes looked up at me with so much trust and love that my heart constricted. Suddenly, I felt guilty, like I was pushing her to do something.

I never wanted to do that.

I'd just been thinking about how much I loved her innocence.

"Hey," I said and swiped at her lower lip with my thumb. "Forget it. Let's just go home. We'll finish this there."

Her teeth sank into the pad of my thumb, and all thought ceased.

Rimmel's lips wrapped around the tip of my thumb and then slid down farther. Her mouth was warm and moist, the pressure she applied gentle. It was a good thing she was practically in my lap because I needed something to hide my raging hard-on.

She rocked against my leg and the music overhead built with perfect tension. The lights were erratic, creating shadows and light every few seconds.

Her silent moan vibrated my thumb and then she released it and wrapped a hand around my neck and buried her face in the hollow between my shoulder and jaw.

We kept dancing, I kept the pressure against her core, and she rocked against me with slow, deliberate movements.

I knew when she was about to come. I felt the change come over her body. The slight sudden tension in her muscles and the way her fingernails dug into the back of my neck.

I pulled her even closer as she came apart in my arms. I knew she was trying to keep it together, to not completely show what was really going on. I held her and kept dancing, even after her body stopped trembling.

Holy shit, she'd just had an orgasm in the middle of a crowded room. I'd practically had sex with her fully dressed.

It made me more determined than ever to get her alone and naked.

The song faded out and an upbeat dance number came on. Rimmel pulled away and gazed up to me.

I kissed her on the tip of her nose, then slid the glasses back on her face.

"Have you had enough girls' night yet?" I asked.

She nodded.

"Thank God. Let's go."

I led her off the floor and back to our table where Ivy and Missy were sitting with the guys. Braeden was out on the dance floor with some hot chick.

"We're going," Rimmel said to her friends as I moved away to say my good-byes to Trent and the guys.

When I was done, I went back to her side and looked down at the girls. "How you getting home tonight?"

"I drove," Ivy said.

Missy laughed.

"You can't drive. You're drunk," I told Ivy.

She shook her head. "They're drunk. I'm not. All I had was a couple shots a few hours ago and this one beer." She motioned to a half-full beer nearby. "I can handle my liquor and those shots weren't strong."

I bent down so I could look at her level in the eyes. She stared back as I searched for any sign she really was drunk and just trying to play it off.

"In a couple hours, I'll be totally sober and able to drag this one"—she gestured to Missy who was doing another shot—"back to the dorm."

She glanced behind me at Rim. "Can Missy use your bed tonight?"

"Of course!"

Ivy met my gaze again.

"No shit?" I asked.

"No shit."

I nodded slowly. I believed her. I think it was the first time we'd been out partying that I hadn't seen her get totally smashed.

Made me wonder why this time was different.

"If you need something. Call."

Something passed behind Ivy's eyes but then was gone. "I will. Thanks."

I held out my fist and she pounded it out. Then I held it out to Missy so she wouldn't feel left out. She tried to pound it out but missed.

Ivy laughed. "Call me!" she yelled to Rimmel.

Rimmel smiled and turned to go. Braeden appeared, and she bounced off his chest. He reached out to steady her.

"We're taking off," I told him. "You coming with us?"

"I'm gonna stay a while," he said and ruffled Rimmel's hair. "I'll give you a chance to put her to bed." He winked and then went on. "Before I crash on the couch."

"That's not necessary," I said, even though I wanted to be alone with her for a while. "I'm the one that drove here."

"I love you," Rimmel told Braeden and leaned in to hug him.

He laughed and wrapped one arm around her. "Yeah. I think it is. Take care of tutor girl before she passes out."

"You need a girlfriend," she told him.

He wrinkled his nose. "Why shackle myself to one when I can graze the crop?"

"Because the right one is better than a bunch. You need someone to love you."

"I thought you loved me?" he said, amused. When he looked up at me, I thought I saw something besides that in his eyes.

I thought I saw a little bit of longing.

"I do. But in a sisterly way. Not the way I love Romeo."

Braeden grinned. "BBFL."

What the fuck did that mean and why did they keep saying that to each other?

It was like a secret handshake no one taught me.

"C'mon, Rim. Let Braeden go get his dance on with the ladies."

I pulled her out of his arm, and she smiled. "I like dancing."

Didn't I know it? I was never gonna forget what our first slow dance was like as long as I lived.

"Grab your stuff," I told her. When she walked off, I turned to B. "You straight?"

"Yeah, it's cool. I'll take a cab or have Trent drop me off."

"You can call me. I'll come pick you up."

We pounded it out, and then I led Rimmel out of the club. Outside was freezing, and I wished I had on more than a T-shirt.

The harsh wind seemed to serve as instant sober for Rimmel, and she perked up as we walked toward the Hellcat.

"You drove here?" she asked, just seeming to realize that.

"Yeah."

"How did you do that with your arm?"

"I just unhook the sling and I'm able to shift. My hand isn't broken."

"But it's movement for your arm!"

"It's limited movement. I'm careful."

She didn't seem too happy with my explanation. "I haven't been driving much, just yesterday and today. My arm feels good. I promise I'm not doing anything that would jeopardize the healing."

She didn't seem too convinced as she climbed into the Hellcat.

As I drove to my place, I noticed she watched me like a hawk, so I took extra care to shift slow and easy.

"See?" I said when I parked in the driveway next to Braeden's truck.

"I still don't see why B didn't drive," she muttered.

"Because I knew I'd want to leave early to be alone with you."

"I missed you today."

I leaned my forehead against hers. "Me too. I'm taking the weekend off from training at the field. I'm gonna stick to you like glue."

"Training going okay?" she asked like she picked up on the fact everything was not okay.

I ran a finger down the center of her nose. "I don't want to talk about football."

"What do you want to talk about?"

"I don't want to talk at all." My voiced dropped low.

She shivered. "Me either."

I knew I'd have to tell her about the NFL come morning, and I would.

But tonight was just for us.

CHAPTER NINETEEN

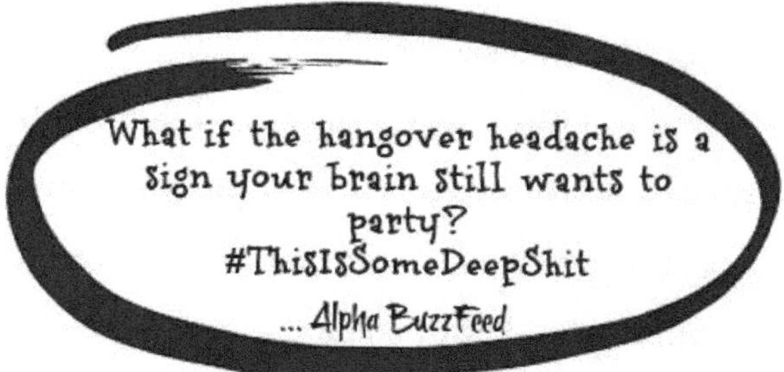

RIMMEL

I woke up slowly, my mind coming to before my body. My cheek was pillowed on Romeo's chest and one leg was thrown over his. Down near my ankle, Murphy was curled up in a ball, purring like a broken lawnmower and creating a warm spot for my foot.

I smiled against Romeo.

If someone had told me a few months ago that this would be my life, I would have recommended they seek help for their crazy.

But this was my life now, and I loved it so much.

It didn't seem to matter how much it was threatened, how much insanity was thrown our way, I always came back to this place of happiness. I always came back to Romeo's arms.

I prayed to God it would always be this way.

Especially now. Especially now that my family unit was being threatened. My mind shied away from the thought, but it wouldn't quite go away. I didn't want to face it, but I knew I was going to have to.

Something was going on with my dad, and it was something I needed to figure out. Beyond everything Valerie said and her folder full of information, my dad was distant. Distracted. And when I told him about being attacked, he apologized like it had been his fault.

I didn't know what it all meant. But it scared me.

Romeo took a deep breath and his hand slid up my spine. I snuggled into him a little closer, pressing my completely bare body along his beneath the sheet.

The electricity between us last night and then again early this morning was mind blowing. I thought perhaps the longer we were together, the more our spark would fade. I always knew I would love Romeo and his touch was all I'd ever want, but I also kind of expected some of that excitement from new love to wane.

But it hadn't.

If anything, it was stronger.

And last night on the dance floor… that had been totally erotic.

I'd had an orgasm right there in center of the club. His body against mine. The pulsing beat of the music.

Writers couldn't even make something like that up in romance books.

Romeo's hand wrapped around my body and lazily explored my breast where it was pushed against him. My nipple responded, and I closed my eyes and let the sensation ripple through me.

"How you feeling this morning?" he asked, pressing a kiss to the top of my head.

"Good," I replied, stretching against him.

"Hangover?"

"Not too bad. I think all that water you made me drink and then the pain reliever you made me take after the second time we made love really helped."

He pulled his fingers through my hair and we lay there in lazy silence for a long while.

"You feel a little thin," he said lightly after a while. "You losing weight?"

"I've just been so busy catching up with classes and trying to fit in time at the shelter that I've missed a couple meals." I felt her grimace against me. "I'm sorry."

"Why you sorry?"

"I know you'd probably prefer someone that wasn't so small."

"I prefer you. Period," Romeo said, his voice final. "But I want you healthy. I don't want you to be so stressed you forget to eat."

"It's just been a lot lately," I confided.

He exhaled. "I know."

Murphy got up from his position near my foot and stretched. Then he walked around the mattress on Romeo's side so he could sit down in front of me and stare.

I laughed. "I think Murphy wants his breakfast."

Romeo chuckled. "How about we feed Murphy, then go out for pancakes?"

"I think you have a deal." A whole day with him sounded like heaven. Ignoring the slight hangover I felt from the Smurf Balls (what was I thinking?), I went out to the kitchen with Murphy on my heels. As soon as he was eating, I went back in the bedroom where Romeo was.

He was standing in the center of the room, completely naked, rubbing a hand over his hair. "I'm pretty sure the restaurant we go to isn't clothing optional." Even as I spoke the words, my eyes traveled over his body. If a man could be perfection, then Romeo was the definition. He was physically unflawed.

Well, technically, he was flawed because his arm was broken, but that didn't count.

I don't think he had an ounce of body fat on him. Every single part of him was solid and sculpted. His abs were totally defined, and when I ran my fingers over them, I could feel every single muscle. He had a long waist and it stretched all the way down into a V-shaped muscle almost like it was creating an arrow to his well-developed manhood. His legs were strong and his thighs were thick. Even his calves were muscular.

He caught me looking, and a slow, devilish smile pulled at his lips. "Enjoying the view?"

I smiled. "Maybe."

He prowled toward me, and my muscles loosened, already anticipating his touch. He came so close we were almost touching, and he dipped his head so our mouths were almost fused. I swayed forward to close the distance, and he pulled back, denying me his lips.

My eyes opened and I glared at him.

He chuckled. "I'm gonna take a shower before we head out."

"Good. You smell."

"Aww, don't be like that, Smalls." The teasing note in his voice didn't go unnoticed.

"Like what?"

"Grouchy because I didn't give you what you wanted."

"Who said I wanted anything?" I sniffed.

He leaned close again, his breath dancing across my lips and the warmth from his large frame radiating against me. “Oh, you want it.”

My tongue slid over my teeth as I stared into his blue, blue eyes. My hand went up to fist in the blond hair at the nape of his neck. I made sure my grip was just a little too tight. “Well, if you won’t give it to me, I guess I’m gonna have to take it.”

I pulled his mouth to mine and took charge of our kiss. I stroked my tongue deep into his mouth and swirled it around with his. He groaned and wrapped his arm around me and pulled me up against his rock-hard body.

Before I pulled away, I nipped at his lower lip and then smiled.

“Damn, Smalls,” he said, breathless.

I swiped at his lower lip with my thumb. “You shouldn’t offer things if you don’t want me to collect.”

“Baby, you can collect anything of mine anytime.”

He released me and stepped back. “I want to take this splint off and the sleeve under it so I can shower without worrying about getting it wet. I'm gonna need some help, though. Think you can help me out?"

"I guess the pancakes can wait."

The shower didn't go exactly as he planned because I wouldn't let him move around too much with his splint off and because I wasn't about to get all my hair wet that I just washed and Ivy styled the night before.

But even with the limitations, by the time the water shut off, both of us were extra clean and Romeo was a happy man.

Once he was dressed with the sleeve, splint, and sling back in place, I went in the bathroom to brush out my hair and apply lotion to my face. I was about to pull the heavy length up into its usual messy bun, but at the last minute, I decided against it. It was still shiny and partially styled from last night. Ivy used enough hairspray that it was no surprise. Since I brushed it out, the curls were a lot looser and it kind of looked like that "beachy" look Ivy said was so in style.

I ran my fingers through it one last time and adjusted the glasses on my nose. Out in the bedroom, I looked around for something to put on, but most of my stuff was back at the dorm. Since I started back to classes, I'd taken most of it back.

"Ugh, I don't have anything to wear," I muttered.

"Wear those jeans you had on last night. With the rips in them," Romeo said.

I glanced around at him. He was staring down at his phone. "You liked those?"

"Hells yeah. They were hot."

I had to admit this pleased me. Yeah, I was the girl who didn't really care and liked sweats over everything else, but I did want Romeo to like looking at me. I made a mental note to rummage through my drawers and find more jeans like this pair.

I pulled them on along with my boots. I grimaced at the black top I was wearing last night lying on the floor. "Can we swing by the dorm? I need something to wear."

"Sure, baby. While you're there, get a bunch of stuff. You can just keep it here."

It was a small thing. Something most people probably wouldn't even think twice about. But for some reason, the idea of moving some of my stuff in here made my heart stumble in beat.

He must have sensed my reaction because he tore his eyes from his phone again. "Rim?"

"You're giving me a drawer?" I asked.

"I should have done it a long time ago."

The look on my face must have given away my feelings. He gave me an odd look. "You keep stuff here all the time."

"In a bag. On the floor. So I can take it with me when I go."

A looked crossed his face, and he tossed his phone on the bed. A string of whispered curse words left his lips as he came forward. "I never thought of it like that before." He shook his head. "I'm sorry."

"Sorry?"

"I keep telling you we're for keeps. I keep telling you you're it for me." He rubbed a hand over his face. "But then I bring you here where you have to live out of a suitcase. I never realized what kind of message that sent."

I shook my head. He was taking it wrong. I never meant to imply that how we'd been together was anything other than wonderful. "I never felt that way."

He made a sound in the back of his throat and stalked across the room toward his dresser. He grasped the handles and pulled out the drawer. I watched as he overturned it and dumped everything out on the floor. T-shirts and socks fell around his feet.

"Romeo!"

Then he did it to another drawer, adding to the mess on the floor.

"There's room in the closet too," he said and dropped the now empty drawer and moved toward the closet. I grabbed his hand. "Please don't make a mess in your closet."

His eyes caught on mine and held. His gaze was intense and unwavering. "Those drawers are yours now. You can take over my bathroom too. Girly creams, hair products, whatever. Bring it on."

I laughed. "I don't have a lot of products."

"Whatever you have, I want to see it next to my stuff. I want to walk in the door and see more of you than just those sexy slippers."

"All this because I couldn't find a shirt to wear," I mused.

"All this because I love you."

"I love you too."

From the bed, his cell made a noise.

He ignored it and twirled the ends of my hair around his fingers. "I almost decked that guy for touching your hair last night."

"What guy?" I asked, wrinkling my nose.

"Beer breath," he muttered. "Seriously. What kind of guy drinks anything called Smurf Balls?"

I laughed. "You and Braeden?"

"Hush, woman." He kissed me quick and grabbed his phone. "Let's go. I'm starving."

On our way out, I thought about something. "Wasn't Braeden supposed to come back here last night?"

His truck was still parked in the driveway.

Romeo grunted. "Yeah, but he ended up with… alternate plans."

I shook my head. "A one-night stand? Really?"

"B's a dog, babe." Romeo said it like it was some travesty and shook his head. "I mean, what can I say?"

I laughed.

"This is him." He held up his phone, which was still going off every few seconds. "We're gonna pick him up on campus and bring him back here."

We stopped beside the Hellcat. "Does he want to eat with us?"

"Probably." He glanced up. "You okay with that?"

I shrugged. "BBFL."

"What the fuck does that mean?"

I told him.

He shook his head. "Only Braeden."

I held out my hand, palm up. Romeo gave me a look.

"Keys." I demanded and lifted my eyebrows.

"You wanna drive?"

"The less you do with your arm, the better."

He started shaking his head.

"Roman Anderson, are you about to sass me?" I said in my best stern tone.

"Sass?" he mocked. "If I do, will you get out your wooden spoon and spank me?"

Only Romeo could turn my attempt at being bossy into a sexual innuendo.

I gave up and dove my hand into the front pocket of his jeans.

He gasped like a drama queen. "Rim! What will the neighbors think?"

I pulled out the keys and waved them in the air victoriously.

He opened the driver's door for me, and as I was getting in, he slapped me on the butt. "Don't forget the books, baby. Can't have you not able to see over the wheel."

I stuck my tongue out at him.

He grinned.

When we were pulling out of the driveway, I asked him where Braeden was on campus so I could stop there before I went to change.

Romeo gave me a slightly proud look. "He's in your building."

Of course he was.

CHAPTER TWENTY

Romeo looked
a little green today
and the way the Hellcat was lurching
around campus its no wonder.
#StayOffTheRoad #NerdCan'tDrive

... Alpha BuzzFeed

ROMEO

I think my tongue might be bleeding.

You know why?

Because I spent the entire drive to campus biting the shit out of it to keep from yelling at Rim as she drove.

To get right to the heart of the matter, my girl was trying to murder my transmission.

But damn, did she try. The way she bit her lower lip and frowned in concentration as we drove (drove = jerked around on the road) was damned cute.

What wasn't cute?

The moans of torture my Hellcat made and the blaring horns of angry drivers at the green light she stalled out in front of.

I almost pissed myself in relief when she pulled into a parking spot near her dorm.

After she cut the engine, she turned to me with a huge smile lighting her face. "I made it!"

"Well." I began and took in her smile and happy eyes. "We didn't die."

She gasped. "That's a terrible thing to say!"

Well, shit.

Then she started laughing. "Oh my God, that was awful! I can't believe you didn't yell at me one time."

I stuck out my tongue. "How bad is it bleeding?"

She leapt forward and kissed my tongue.

"I'll get better!" She bounded out of the car like she was indeed proud of herself for not killing us.

It was cute she thought I was going to suffer through that again.

I apologized to the car before I joined her on the sidewalk.

Upstairs at Rimmel's door, I pulled out my phone and texted B that we were here as she stuck her head in the room to make sure everyone was decent.

She gave me the all clear, and I walked in behind her. Ivy was sitting at her desk, watching a movie on her laptop with a pair of headphones around her neck. She had a mug of coffee in her hands and was still in her pajamas.

"Hey." She gave me a wave, and I hitched my chin at her. "I'm surprised to see you guys."

"I needed some clothes." Rimmel told her, rummaging around in her dresser. Beside her was an open bag that she was throwing some extra clothes into. I imagined her stuff scattered around my place, and it felt right.

A groan rumbled from Rim's side of the room, and I glanced around. Rimmel and Ivy giggled as they pointed toward her bed. All I saw was a pile of blankets and some pillows.

But then it moved.

A dark head peeked out from beneath the covers. "What time is it?" Missy groaned.

"It's after noon," Ivy said.

"Someone had too many Smurf Balls last night," I said.

Missy moaned and grabbed a pillow and pulled it over her head. When she did, a piece of paper slid off the bed and fluttered to the floor.

"You don't look very hung-over," I told Ivy as I bent to pick up the paper.

"I didn't drink after you guys left."

So she'd kept her word and stayed sober. I had to admit I was surprised, and I said as much.

"Romeo," Rimmel scolded me for the honest observation.

Ivy shrugged. "People change."

I glanced at Rimmel and thought about all the ways she changed me. "I can understand that."

"What is that?" Rimmel asked, staring down at the paper in my hand.

I shrugged. "It fell off your bed."

A look passed behind her eyes, and I felt my own narrow.

"I'll take it." She held out her hand.

Yeah. Like I was going to just hand it over after that reaction. I held it up, and she grabbed at it. I held it up out of her reach, and she growled.

I ignored her and looked at the paper.

It was a bill.

From the hospital.

I lowered my arm and pinned her with a look. "Why didn't you tell me about this?"

She snatched it away and tucked it beneath some stuff on her desk. "It just came."

The paper said she was uninsured, even though I know damn well she handed the nurse her insurance card that night.

Is that what she was talking to the snooty bitch at the nurses station about before we left?

"Was that shit not covered by your insurance?" I demanded. She shouldn't have to worry about a hospital bill for treatment she received for being attacked.

It made me want to pound Zach all over again.

There was knock at the door, and Rimmel rushed away to answer it. "Baby sis!" Braeden said the second the door was open. He rushed in and lifted her off her feet. "You need to eat something," he told her.

"You smell like beer!" She wrinkled her nose and pushed away from him.

"What are you doing here?" Ivy asked, rolling her eyes.

"I was in the building. Thought I'd stop by."

Ivy's eyes slid to Rimmel's bed where Missy was and frowned. "Whatever," she said and turned back to her computer.

Rimmel zipped up the bag she'd been packing. "Done." When she straightened, she had a pale-blue sweater in her hands. "I just need to change. Then we can go."

Her eyes slid to Ivy and then back at me. I nodded.

"Hey, we're going out for pancakes. You guys wanna come?"

Ivy spun around and looked at Rimmel. "Is he coming?" She looked at Braeden.

"Girl, you know I'm the highlight of your day." He grinned at her, and she rolled her eyes.

"You guys are like the loudest people on the earth," Missy yelled, pulling the pillow off her head.

"Is that a yes for pancakes?" I asked.

"Is there coffee involved?" Missy groaned.

Rimmel laughed.

Ivy stood up and shooed me and Braeden to the door. "Let us change."

"We ain't got time for that," Braeden said. "You're so high maintenance, if we wait on you, we won't eat 'til tomorrow."

"Should I just wear my pajamas, then?" Ivy asked, her voice dripping with sweet sarcasm.

"You've looked better," Braeden deadpanned.

She launched herself at him, her fist swinging. I caught her and towed her backward.

"Out!" Rimmel ordered. B and I vanished into the hall.

"You're losing your touch with the ladies," I told him, highly amused.

"I might agree. If I thought she was a lady."

I grinned.

A few minutes later, Ivy and Missy came out into the hall. Both of them were dressed down with their hair up in ponytails. Missy was wearing a pair of sunglasses, and Braeden laughed.

"You gotta lay off the sauce, Miss."

"Ha-ha," she muttered.

I pushed open the door and stepped in the room before Rimmel could come out. I wanted to take the last opportunity to be alone with her for a while.

I had answers to get.

She left the ripped-up jeans and boots on but replaced the black shirt she was wearing for a long-sleeved white T-shirt. Over top was a pale-blue sweater with a short hem and a large white heart on the chest. Because the sweater was short, her T-shirt peeked out from beneath it and skimmed her hips.

"Ready?" she asked, picking up her bag.

"Rimmel."

Her shoulders slumped a little. "It's just a bill, Romeo."

"I thought you had insurance."

"I did too," she muttered.

"What?"

Her sigh was heavy. "Apparently, I no longer have a policy."

"How does that even happen?" I wondered.

"According to your mother's file, my father lost his job. My insurance was through him."

I closed the distance between her and wrapped my arm around her.

"I think he's lying to me," she rushed out. "He wouldn't return my calls, but then he did." She looked up at me. "His first words were that my attack was all his fault."

I frowned. That was an odd thing to say.

A voice in my head whispered, *Your mother was right.* "Give me the bill, Rim. I'll take care of it."

She wrenched out of my arms. "Absolutely not."

"Why?"

"Because I'm not your responsibility."

"How are you gonna pay that?" I demanded.

"I'll get a job."

The idea of her getting a job pissed me off. "Because you don't have enough on your plate already?" I shot out. "Just give me the damn bill," I growled.

"No," she growled back.

"If your father isn't going to take care of you, someone has to!" I yelled.

My outburst shocked her and she drew away from me. Behind her glasses, her eyes went wide.

"Rim—" I began. That was a fucked-up thing to say.

Braeden barged in the door. "I heard yelling."

"It's fine," I rumbled.

He didn't leave.

Rimmel faced me, having recovered from the initial sting of my words. "Is that what you think? That I can't take care of myself?"

I started to say something, but she advanced on me. "Maybe you agree with your mother. Maybe you think I'm just with you because of your money?"

"That's fucking ridiculous," I snapped.

She didn't back down. "It is *fucking* ridiculous," she intoned. "And I can take care of myself. This conversation is over."

She dropped the bag of her stuff at my feet like she was going to leave it behind and walked out of the room.

A string of curses filled the air around me. I bent and picked up the bag.

Braeden was staring at me when I walked to the door.

"Women," he muttered. "Too much damn drama."

"Amen." I agreed with him because it was true. Women were full of drama. But Rimmel usually wasn't. And I knew she had a right to be angry. I shouldn't have said what I said, but I was just trying to help her.

Too late I realized it wasn't my help she needed, just my support.

CHAPTER TWENTY-ONE

What time is it?
Pancake Time!
#EveryoneLovesPancakes
#IfYouDontWeCantBeFriends
... Alpha BuzzFeed

RIMMEL

What was supposed to be a relaxed breakfast with me and my boyfriend turned into what I'd like to refer to as the pancake grudge match.

I glared at Romeo.

Ivy glared at Braeden.

And poor Missy glared at the food on everyone's plate like it was trying to make her vomit.

The small pancake house we went to wasn't far from campus, and it was busy despite the non-breakfast hour. It was filled with college students, and more than half of them looked hung-over.

All I could think about was the hospital bill and how stupid it was that I'd gotten so angry.

But he made it sound like I was a child that needed a babysitter.

I didn't.

And I wasn't going to let him treat me like that.

Romeo was a charming devil with eyes that could make any woman forget to be mad, but I was never going to forget to have standards.

And being treated as an equal was one of them.

"Everyone at this table is giving me indigestion," Braeden declared.

"I'm pretty sure that was the Smurf Balls," Missy said.

Everyone laughed and the tension hanging over the table broke.

"Was it just me or did that guy sitting next to Rimmel have the rankest beer breath ever?" Ivy grinned.

I laughed. "Yes! Even drunk I couldn't stand it."

Romeo's hand slipped under the table, found mine, and squeezed. I returned the pressure, and some of the anger I felt toward him lifted. I knew he was only trying to love me the way he knew how, and I couldn't fault him for that. But that still didn't make it okay.

"You gonna eat that?" Braeden said to Missy, who hadn't touched her food at all. She groaned.

He shrugged and stabbed his fork into one of her pancakes and slid it onto his plate.

I hadn't really touched much of my food because I'd been too busy stewing over the argument with Romeo, but watching Braeden eat with such gusto made me hungry.

Okay, and maybe it was because Romeo was holding my hand and things between us didn't seem so drastic.

The conversation turned light and fun, and the five of us relaxed at the table and started acting like a real group of friends. I couldn't help but look around and smile. I'd never had this many friends before. Not real ones.

We were all so different yet still the same.

It was like we had the same basic common threads that would tie us together.

"We should make this a tradition," I announced.

"Glaring at each other over breakfast?" Ivy wondered.

"Watching Missy get drunk on Smurf Balls?" Braeden added.

"Never again," Missy vowed.

"Pancakes," I said like it should have been obvious. "Every weekend. The five of us meet here. For pancakes."

"I like to eat," Braeden said as he stole another pancake off Missy's plate.

"You want me to eat with him on a regular basis?" Ivy raised her eyebrows at me.

"It's what friends do," I said. "They do friend stuff."

Everyone looked at me. I felt self-conscious all of a sudden. Was I the only one who thought all of us were friends?

I glanced up at Romeo. "Right?"

He smiled. "For sure."

"I'll go home and braid us all friendship bracelets," Braeden said in a girly voice.

"I'm in," Missy said. She looked at me and smiled.

"Me too." Ivy agreed.

Romeo nodded, and we all looked at Braeden.

"Let's do this."

I grinned and dove into the rest of my food.

Romeo's phone went off, and he released my hand to reach into his pocket to pull it out.

"I don't know the number," he said before answering it. "This is Roman."

He listened intently for a few minutes and then made a face like he was annoyed. "Look, like I told your reporter the other night—"

His words cut off, and all his attention seemed to sharpen toward the voice on the other end of the line. I glanced at Braeden, who was also watching Romeo.

"He was at my house. He gave me a card."

A few beats of silence.

"James… something," he said.

"I'm sure… Yes."

An angry look crossed his face.

"Is this some elaborate scheme to get an interview?"

Was he talking to a reporter? I wished I could hear the other end of the call!

"Okay, fine… Maybe. When and where?"

A few beats of silence, then Romeo sighed.

"See you then." His voice was clipped, and then he hung up the phone.

"Romeo?" I asked. He was busy staring off into space but made a sound acknowledging me.

"Who was that?"

"A reporter for the *Maryland Tribune*."

"That's like the biggest newspaper in the entire state," Ivy said.

"Isn't that who the reporter from the other night said he was from?" Braeden asked.

"What reporter?" I asked, confused.

Romeo focused his sapphire eyes on me. "He was at the house the other night when I got home from training. He wanted to interview me." Romeo frowned and looked at Braeden. "The guy on the phone said they don't have any reporters named James."

Braeden's eyes narrowed, and an uncomfortable feeling wormed into the pit of my stomach.

"Do you have the card with you?" I asked.

Romeo shook his head. "It's at home."

"Maybe you got the name of the paper that James guy was with wrong. It's probably a misunderstanding," I reasoned.

Romeo draped his arm across my shoulders. "Yeah, that's probably what happened."

But I could tell by the sound of his voice that he didn't believe that.

CHAPTER TWENTY-TWO

An early morning interview? Someone's celebrity status is about to explode.

... Alpha BuzzFeed

ROMEO

I met with the "reporter" who called me at breakfast a few days later. He suggested a coffee shop close to campus, and I decided to go.

I wanted answers.

I didn't like being approached by someone posing as a reporter outside my home, only to be told later that he wasn't a reporter at all.

It was early morning, so most of the tables were empty, but the line was long as students grabbed their morning latte and headed off for a full day of classes.

My first class didn't start for another hour, and I planned to be long gone from this meeting before then. I knew who he was the second he walked in. He seemed a little out of place in a college hot spot, wearing a pair of dress pants and a professional-looking wool coat.

He was probably in his forties with sandy-colored hair and a briefcase in his hand. When he glanced in my direction, I waved, and his eyes lit up like he recognized me and hurried my way.

I stood up and shook his hand when he approached. "Roman Anderson."

"Frank Gurney, *Maryland Tribune*." He had a solid handshake. I liked that.

"Did you want to get a coffee?" I gestured toward the counter. "I'll wait."

He looked at the line and shook his head. "No, that's okay."

I sat back down, and he took the chair across from me. As he was shrugging out of his coat, he glanced down at the half-empty cup in front of me. "Were you waiting long?"

"Nah, I got here early."

He raised his brows. "I wasn't sure you'd show. You didn't seem very interested when we spoke on the phone."

I shrugged. "I wasn't. 'Til you told me the man who approached me outside my house wasn't an employee of your paper."

An uncomfortable look crossed his face. "Did you bring the card you mentioned on the phone?"

I pulled it out and handed it to him. He picked it up and looked over it, frowning as he did.

One of the baristas working behind the counter approached the table. She had a small round tray in her hand. "Romeo?" she asked, a little timid.

"That's me," I said and turned up my smile.

She giggled a little and stepped closer. "I thought you might like a fresh latte?"

"Yeah, that'd be great." I smiled at her and pushed away my cooled, half-empty cup.

She slid the new drink in front of me. "It's the same thing you ordered when you got here." Her cheeks flushed. "I remembered your order."

"You're epic." I reached into my pocket and pulled out some cash. "How much do I owe ya?"

She waved away my offer. "It's on the house."

Mr. Gurney cleared his throat, and the waitress seemed to remember he was there. "Oh! I thought you might like one too. The line's pretty long and you two looked busy." She set the second mug from her tray in front of the reporter.

He looked surprised. "Thank you."

She glanced back at me. "I come to all your games."

I grinned. "That means a lot. The team appreciates your support."

She smiled and shuffled on her feet. "Well, enjoy your coffee."

"If you made it, I'm sure we will." I winked at her before I could stop myself.

Sometimes the charm had a mind of its own.

She giggled and rushed away.

I picked up the new coffee and took a drink. It was exactly what I ordered when I came in earlier.

"Perks of being the local celebrity?" Frank asked with a smile.

I shrugged. "People like football."

He studied me for a long moment. "Maybe. But something tells me the other members of the team could walk in and they wouldn't get personalized free coffee delivery."

I grinned. "Maybe not."

He took a sip of the brew and nodded. "Good taste."

"So?" I gestured to the card lying in front of him. "You know him?"

Frank picked up the card again and read it. Again.

I was getting impatient.

He handed it back to me. "He's not an employee of the *Maryland Tribune*."

"You're sure?" I pressed. "I imagine it's a big paper. Lots of staff."

"The biggest in the state, and yes, the staff is sizeable. But he isn't one of them. I ran a search for all employees named James through our database at work. We do have two men names James on staff, one of them writes obituaries and his last name is Blankenship and the other works in the marketing department and does mostly print ad work."

"This guy said he was a writer."

Frank shook his head as he drank more coffee. "Any idea why someone would pose as a reporter to talk to you?"

"I was gonna ask you if your paper allowed people to go around impersonating their employees."

"I can assure you the *Maryland Tribune* has nothing to do with this."

I measured him with a long stare. He didn't flinch or crack under pressure. I exhaled. *Fuck*. I believed him.

"Look, you're a hot topic lately. Your huge win at the championship, being named MVP of the game. Your stats alone from last season were making records, and all the interest from the NFL makes you a good story."

"Not to mention the fact that I broke my arm in an unrelated sports injury and the NFL is gonna drop me before I even sign."

Frank's eyes widened with surprise. It was too real looking to not be genuine. "The NFL is dropping you?"

The reporter the other night already knew this… said it was public knowledge. So why didn't Frank?

"It's not official yet," I hedged.

He glanced at my arm, which was on display in its sling. "You and your girlfriend were attacked. Is that how you were injured?"

"That's right." I agreed. It didn't surprise me that he knew that. The police had been called and Zach had been taken into custody. That was definitely a matter of record. The details, though, those remained confidential as far as I knew.

"I gotta tell you. You have a hell of a story. Human interest but also sports related. I'd love to interview you, write up a feature article for the paper."

"You mean this conversation hasn't been on the record?" I arched an eyebrow.

He shook his head. "No. I admit I called because I want to write the story. But this meeting was because I was curious about the card you were given and because I wanted to set the record straight that we were not involved."

"So everything we said was off the record?"

"Yes."

That was good. I didn't want anyone knowing that someone who was lying was sniffing around me and Rim.

But in the meantime…

I checked my watch. "I've got like thirty minutes before class. Is that enough time for an interview?"

"You'll do it?"

I grinned. "Sure, why the hell not?"

Maybe it would satisfy anyone else who was more curious than they should be about me.

In no time, he produced a notepad, pen, and a small recording device. "You mind?" he gestured toward the recorder.

"Not at all."

He started firing questions at me like I fired the football down the field. But I was a professional; I could take a pass just as well as I could throw one.

I dialed up the charm and settled back into my seat. I put on my easygoing smile and enjoyed the ride.

But beneath it all, I wasn't all cool and calm.

Beneath the confident player who was determined to bounce back from an injury was a man with one constant question hammering at the edge of my mind.

If James Darling wasn't a reporter, then who the hell was he?

CHAPTER TWENTY-THREE

#Exclusive
The #BuzzBoss has learned the sentencing for the campus #Hater is today. Will it be jail or a straight jacket?
... Alpha BuzzFeed

RIMMEL

I stood outside the courtroom with trepidation in my limbs.

I knew this day was coming, I'd even prepared for it.

But how did a person prepare for facing someone who taunted and attacked you for months only to have it escalate with being tied up, strung up, and sprayed down with a water hose?

It didn't matter we'd gotten an extra week before the hearing. It didn't matter that Zach was going to be punished for everything he did.

The damage was done.

The bruises on my body were almost healed, the rope burns faded, but the deepest marks were inside, where the judge wouldn't be able to see.

I still dreamed about it sometimes. Of hanging there above the ground, bound and helpless. I still felt the twinge in my heart when I first turned on the shower or when the water rushed too fast in my face.

And sometimes when I'm sitting in class or at the library studying, I remember what Romeo looked like when he was plummeting to the ground. I was haunted by that first bleak look in his eyes when he admitted his arm was broken.

I didn't know how to look at Zach and not feel all the intense fear and emotion I did on that night. The best I could hope for was this would give me some kind of closure, some kind of peace.

Romeo broke away from the quiet conversation he was having a short distance away with Tony. Valerie was here too, standing by the wide courtroom doors, looking stunning in a dove-gray pantsuit and a light-pink shell beneath.

"Hey, baby," Romeo said, wrapping his hand around my back and pulling me in so he could kiss my forehead.

I grabbed onto the lapel of his suit jacket and swallowed.

"I don't want to see him."

"I wish you didn't have to."

He tucked a strand of hair behind my ear and leaned down to whisper. "But on the bright side, his jaw is wired shut so he won't be able to say a word."

"That is good news." I smiled.

"Dad says this will be over fast. After this, Zach will be out of our lives completely."

I nodded and changed the subject. "Any word from the NFL?"

Romeo's eyes dimmed a bit. "Not a word."

It had been an entire week since the two pro teams withdrew their offer. Romeo and his father were still waiting on a call back to tell him if he was being dropped from the NFL completely.

"If I could have taken that break for you, I would have," I whispered.

"I never want you hurting because of me," Romeo whispered and stroked a hand down the side of my head.

My hair was straight and sleek today. I wore it down, and it seemed to inspire petting from Romeo every few minutes.

I would have to remember to wear it like this more often.

I caught his mother watching us and for once didn't look away immediately.

Truth was I wasn't so blatantly angry with her anymore.

Don't get me wrong. I was still totally upset and I really didn't want to be around her, but some of the heat from my anger had faded.

I told myself it wasn't because I was starting to think she might be right.

That thought caused my eyes to jerk away from her. Mad or not, every time I looked at her, all I saw was her accusation.

She must have taken my momentary stare as an invitation (which it so was not) and walked over our way. Her suede heels clicked over the polished marble floor in the hall, and she stopped beside Romeo.

"Are you two ready for this morning?"

"Dad prepped us," Romeo replied, his fingers laced with mine.

"Rimmel," Valerie said, and I couldn't not acknowledge her. My mother ingrained too much respect for others in me.

Before she died, that is.

Or maybe she was killed.

"Yes, Mrs. Anderson?" I said politely.

"I know you've been dealing with a lot lately." She began and my hand tightened around Romeo's. "I haven't wanted to burden you—"

I snorted.

She looked put out but then continued. "But the fundraiser for the shelter is the end of next week. I really would like to get your final approval on all the preparations and arrangements."

Of course. The fundraiser. Michelle at the shelter wouldn't stop blabbing about it. She was so beyond excited that our little shelter was going to be represented so elegantly.

And even though I was totally pissy toward Valerie, I was excited too. The fundraiser hadn't even happened yet and already we were getting sizable donations. A local paper even came and took pictures and did a feature.

It resulted in three animals getting adopted to loving homes.

It had been everything I'd dreamed of and more.

I just wished Valerie hadn't helped make it such a success. It was hard to be thankful and bitter at the same time.

"I apologize, I haven't been very helpful the past few weeks," I replied. "I and everyone at the shelter are so incredibly grateful for this event. It's already helped us tremendously."

Valerie smiled.

"When would you like to meet to finalize everything?" I asked.

"How about this evening? I have all the paperwork and things at the house. Perhaps you and Roman would like to have dinner with Tony and me? We can go over it all then."

"Mom," Romeo said, his voice holding restrained warning. "We can't."

Her face fell a little, and I squeezed his hand. "Actually, dinner sounds fine."

Both mother and son looked at me with surprise.

"Rim, you don't have to do this," Romeo said in my ear. "Mom can drop the papers off at my place and you can look over them."

For once, Valerie kept her mouth shut. I counted that as progress.

"No, dinner is fine. That way, if I have questions, she can answer them. It will make the process shorter and make the event better."

"I agree," Valerie said.

"Of course you do," Romeo muttered.

The large wooden door to the judge's chamber opened up, and a man stepped out and said something to Tony, then stepped back inside, leaving the door open.

"It's time," Tony called.

Nerves bunched in my stomach and my heart began to beat harder.

"I'll be right beside you the entire time," Romeo said.

I nodded.

Why wasn't he nervous like me?

The judge's chamber was a large open room with dark wood paneling, heavy drapes, and a huge commanding desk in the center. A man in a black robe sat behind the desk, and off to the left was Robert, Zach's dad, sitting in a forward-facing chair. He was dressed impeccably in a black suit and didn't look back at us once.

Romeo shifted so his body blocked most of mine and his large frame blocked whoever was sitting beside Robert. I tried to calm my nerves as we walked toward our side of the room.

Tony took the first seat on our side and Valerie sat behind him. Romeo guided me with a hand on my back to the chair beside his father, and he sat down on the opposite side of me.

I couldn't sit down until I got it over with.

With Romeo finally not blocking me, I looked to the other side of the room.

My eyes went directly to Zach.

He was staring at me.

Chills raced down my spine and I felt my hands tremble. I hated the way he made me feel, but I was powerless against it.

And, my God…

Zach looked terrible.

The clean-cut, boy band ex-fraternity resident was no more. Instead, his hair was disheveled, dull, and in need of a trim. It fell over his forehead like it felt lost without his hair gel. His skin was pale like it hadn't seen the sun in weeks (which, okay, it hadn't) and his cheekbones were more pronounced than before.

His jaw was wired shut and his lips looked chapped. He was wearing a suit, but it didn't seem to fit quite right. It was too large in the shoulders and hung off his frame like he'd been sick.

I almost felt pity for him.

Almost.

Because the second I looked into his eyes, it all came rushing back.

Despite the glassy, sedated look he fronted, I saw deeper.

Clearly, he was on medication—medication he probably needed—but as I looked deep into his eyes, I knew the meds weren't enough. There was still something inside him that was broken and twisted.

I don't know if Zach had always been this way or if something in recent months or years had caused this change, but as I looked at him right then, his eyes drilling into mine, I knew Zach had snapped.

I also knew right then that his dad would most definitely argue an insanity plea and he would win with it.

Even me, the victim, couldn't argue.

Zach was clearly unstable, and I genuinely hoped he got some help.

Behind the walls of a padded cell, that is.

As I stared, his lips pulled into a droopy restrained smile. It cut me to my core.

Romeo's warm hand wrapped around mine, and he tugged me down into the seat beside him and safely back into reality.

True to Tony's word, the hearing went rather quickly. Zach's lawyer/father did all the talking, and the couple short glances I stole in his direction left me wondering if he was even listening to anything that was being said.

Aside from that moment of clarity that I saw in the depths of his eyes when we first walked in, it seemed that Zach was somewhere else, somewhere all alone in the confines of his mind.

I was called upon to tell my side of the story, and as I did, I felt Romeo listening with restrained anger as I recalled details I hadn't told him before.

When I was finished, I wanted to sag back in my chair and cry. I felt like I'd had to relive it all over again. But I held myself up straight and kept my focus ahead on the judge.

At one point, he glanced at me, and I thought I saw a bit of respect in his eyes.

That's when I knew it was all going to be okay.

That's when I knew Zach was going to be held accountable and Romeo and I would be safe from him.

Romeo also spoke, and surprisingly, one of the students who helped Zach string me up testified too. He told everyone that Zach threatened him if he didn't help, and so he did it because he wasn't sure if he told anyone would believe him.

In the end, the judgment was handed down.

Zach was sentenced to involuntary admittance into a renowned psychiatric facility upstate. The psychiatrist who testified to the fact that Zach did indeed suffer from several forms of anxiety and a potential personality disorder among a few other confidential things would be taking over his care at the hospital.

His minimum stay at the facility would be one year. After the year was filled, there would be another hearing (that Romeo and me did not have to be at) to determine if he was well enough to be released into outpatient treatment.

Oh, and Zach's family was being held responsible for all hospital and doctor expenses that resulted in his attack against Romeo and me.

When the judge added that little bit on, I glanced at Romeo.

He smiled smugly and I knew, *I knew*, he made sure his father went after that so I wouldn't have to get a job and pay that bill.

It was a relief to not have that bill hanging over my head, but what Romeo didn't realize was I still had to support myself. If my father really was out of work and in debt (I wasn't quite ready to admit this yet), then it was time for me to step up to the plate and support myself.

I could.

I would.

And Romeo would just have to get over it.

When the hearing was over, we all stood to exit the courtroom. There were two large men dressed in white uniforms waiting in the wings to take Zach off to the facility.

His father didn't glance at us one time as we walked past. Maybe he was still angry about what "Romeo did to his son" or maybe he was ashamed.

As we were passing, Zach bolted to his feet. His sudden movement scared me, and I stumbled back. I threw my arm out and caught myself on the table Robert had been using for his files.

A sound tore from Zach's throat, muffled and deep from being trapped in his mouth, and he half leapt across the table and grabbed my arm.

I shrieked as he yanked me hard and towed my body across the tabletop toward him.

CHAPTER TWENTY-FOUR

Do what is right.
Not what is easy.
#ButWhatIfWhatsRightIsEasy?
... Alpha BuzzFeed

ROMEO

Oh *hells* no.

CHAPTER TWENTY-FIVE

#ComebackQuarterback
What's a quarterback do when his right arm is out of commision?
He throws left handed.
#24IsUnstoppable

... Alpha BuzzFeed

RIMMEL

I didn't get very far across the table.

While Robert stood there in shock at his son's beastly behavior, the judge started banging his gavel and yelling, "Order in my court!"

What the hell he thought that would do I have no idea.

Romeo burst into action, the only one who seemed to have some sense that this was coming.

Or maybe (yeah, probably) Romeo was just always on guard when it came to me.

At this moment in time, I had to be grateful for his overprotective streak. Romeo dashed forward and wrapped his single arm around me and lifted. It was as if I weighed nothing more than a pebble the way he picked me up and tucked me sideways beneath his arm.

Zach didn't want to let go of my arm, so I was sort of trapped in limbo, tucked against Romeo yet still being held by Zach.

Romeo let out a string of *very* unprofessional curse words and spun so his body—his broken arm—was used as a battering ram against Zach's arm.

He was weak from injury and medication, and his body buckled immediately. He sagged back as the guards and orderlies rushed forward. His hands were cuffed and restrained by one of the men wearing white.

Not that he needed restrained. He was back to looking empty and glassy eyed.

Romeo stood me on my feet, breathing hard. He reached up and ripped the sling off, giving his broken arm more freedom of movement.

Then he swept me against his chest, both arms clamped around me.

I didn't stop the little whimper that escaped me or the need I felt to bury my face in his chest.

Would Zach never stop?

And holy momma did it feel good to be wrapped up in Romeo again. It had been weeks since I felt both his arms hold me.

It was incredible to be enclosed by him.

Once a little of the shock wore off, I pulled back. "Your arm." I worried.

"It's fine," he murmured and pulled me back into his chest.

"Get him the hell out of here!" Romeo roared over my head.

Everything and everyone seemed to bolt into action. Zach was carted away; the orderlies and guards went with him. Robert left in a fluster, and Valerie and Tony came forward to see if we were all right.

"Ms. Hudson." A deep voice came from behind Romeo. "This is highly uncommon. Are you hurt?"

It was the judge. I took another moment to catch my breath and pulled back from Romeo. He didn't go far. He stood so close to me that I could feel every breath he took.

"I'm not hurt, just a little surprised."

"I think we all were surprised," he responded.

"Are you sure a year in this hospital is going to be enough?" Tony worried. "He is clearly very unstable."

"Well, the year is the minimum. He will be reevaluated and watched very closely. If he is still even slightly unstable, he will be kept in."

From behind, Romeo's arms curled around my waist. I leaned into him.

"If that's everything," Tony spoke up. "I think these two need some time to breathe."

"Of course." The judge inclined his head. But before he turned, he looked at me and Romeo. "Please accept my apologies. I do not tolerate these kind of outbursts in my courtroom, and I will be sure it doesn't happen again."

"I doubt that will stop her nightmares tonight," Romeo said, his voice hard.

I gasped. "Romeo!"

Oh my word, he was a rude!

As we walked out of the room, Valerie lectured him beneath her breath on his harsh words.

Out in the hall, Romeo shoved a hand through his hair. "Are we done here?"

The sling he'd been wearing was dangling from his suit sleeve; any second it would become an adornment to the floor.

Beneath the jacket, he was wearing his splint and the sleeve beneath it. At least he had that support, but his healing had been going so well the last few weeks. I really didn't want him to screw it up now.

I moved forward and untangled the fabric from his arm.

"Yes, we're done. That was the last time you will have to look at or deal with Zachary," Tony said.

"Let's go," Romeo said and took my hand.

I turned toward Tony. "Thank you," I said sincerely.

He smiled.

"Don't forget dinner tonight!" Valerie called after us as we went down the hall toward the elevator.

When it dinged open, Romeo pulled me inside and hit the 'close door' button about ten times.

"Hey." I reached out and grabbed his hand as the doors slid closed. "Calm down."

He moved fast, wrapped his arm around my waist, and pushed me gently up against the wall of the small space. His mouth was on mine before the elevator jerked to a start. He kissed me with a ferocity that made it impossible to catch my breath.

Both his hands grasped my hips and he lifted me off the ground. My legs went around his waist and my ankles locked around this back.

I was wearing a skirt and the buckle on his dress pants pressed against the soft fabric of my panties between my legs. I melted into the wall even as I arched against him.

I had no idea the advantages of wearing a skirt. Maybe I should wear one more often.

His mouth was like a giant eraser to my chalkboard. Everything inside me was wiped blank, and all that remained was his mouth.

His hands.

And the way he was moving between my legs.

I felt the elevator jolt to a stop, but I scarcely paid attention. I ate in as much of him as I could, completely taken over by his raw and sudden need.

A loud clearing of a throat had Romeo jerking away. He glanced over his shoulder and then back at me, blinking to clear the fog wrapping around us.

"Sorry about that," he said, his voice was deep and gruff. He set me on my feet and pulled me out of the open elevator door and past the man standing there in shock.

"What was that?" My words were breathless as we walked through the parking garage toward the Hellcat.

"That guy makes me insane," he ground out. "All I could think about in there was pounding him again, making it twice as worse this time."

"But you didn't."

We approached the Hellcat, and he spun around to face me. "No. I didn't. Because really, what would it have solved? But the anger and the visual of his hands on you." He shook his head like he was trying to rid the image. "I had to do something with all that pent-up frustration."

His eyes started to boil with desire again.

"And there's only one other feeling that could match the intensity of my loathing for that guy."

"What's that?" I whispered.

He grabbed me again and pinned me against the side of the car. "My love for you. My desire for you. It's the one thing in this entire universe that can push me to the very brink but also bring me back."

He trailed a finger down the side of my cheek. "It's over, baby. Maybe now the nightmares will stop."

My eyes snapped to his. "You know about the nightmares?"

He nodded and lowered his face to mine. "Of course I know."

"But I never told you."

"You didn't have too." He pressed a gentle kiss to my forehead.

"You gonna put this back on yet?" I held the sling up between us.

"I promise you my arm is fine. I went to the specialist at the beginning of the week, remember? I went to a physical therapist as well. Light, ordinary everyday movement is fine. I don't have to wear that sling as much anymore. It was mainly to stabilize the injury when it first happened and to help with the swelling."

"I know." I protested. "But I just want you to be careful."

He cupped my face in both his hands. My eyes slid closed. It had been a while since he'd been able to do that. "I will be." He murmured and kissed me slow and sweet. It was such a contrast to the way he went at me in the elevator, but it was just as devastating.

My knees started to shake, and I reached up and gripped his wrists (lightly). "Can we go?"

He chuckled. "We have all afternoon until dinner tonight."

It was a rarity to have most of the day to ourselves during the week. But because of the hearing, the dean excused us from classes today so we could be in court.

"Well, maybe you could leave that sling off… just for a little while longer. I sort of missed being held by you."

"Your wish is my command."

I leaned up on my toes and kissed him again. "Anything I want?"

"Mm-hmm."

"I want to drive home."

He went from very accommodating to alarmed in two seconds flat. "You wanna what?"

I held out my hands for the keys. "Too much driving is bad for your arm."

"It's fine." He groaned.

"It will make me feel better."

"But the poor Cat will suffer," he muttered.

"What did you just say to me?" I gasped and pressed a hand to my chest. "I thought you said I was a good driver!"

I almost laughed out loud at the look on his face. I'd have to remember to act like that more often when I wanted to throw him off his game.

"Fine." He relented and walked around to open the driver's side door. After I piled my books on the seat and climbed in, he leaned down in the door. "Try not to rip out the engine, huh?"

I rolled my eyes, and as I did, something caught my attention off to the side. "Hey," I asked. "What is that?" I pointed to what looked like a piece of paper under the windshield wiper.

Romeo straightened and snagged the sheet off the glass and looked down at it. "It's a newspaper article." He glanced up. "One of the ones written about me."

Since he did the interview with the *Maryland Tribune* several other papers called for an interview. He'd always had a sort of celebrity status since I'd known him, but usually it was limited to campus and the people who knew him.

But since the championship, the NFL offers and the drama with Zach Romeo had become even more popular.

"I don't think I've seen this one yet," I said and pulled it out of his hands to look down.

The article was half a page and featured him smiling widely with his blue eyes and blond hair on full display. The heading of the article read:

"WILL HE BE THE COMEBACK QUARTERBACK?"

Beneath the article, there was a smaller picture of him on the field, wearing sweats and in motion of throwing the ball with his left hand.

He'd been training the left side of his body for a while now, and I knew he was getting better and learning more control.

"What do they mean the comeback quarterback?" I asked.

He scoffed. "Because the NFL dropped me, but I'm still on the field training every day, determined to keep up my skill and fitness. They're saying if I get drafted next year, I'll be the 'comeback quarterback.'"

"You know," I said. "We don't know that the NFL has totally dropped you."

"They've been silent for too long." I heard the disappointment and finality in his voice, and my chest constricted.

"Well, they're a bunch of big dummies."

He laughed. After he jogged around the car and climbed in the passenger seat, I looked up from the paper. "Wonder how this got on your dash?"

He shrugged. "Someone probably recognized my car and put it there." He turned the paper so he could look at it. "This article just ran today. Maybe they thought they were the first to show it to me."

"Maybe," I echoed, but still, it just seemed odd.

He took the paper and tossed it into the backseat. "Remember, be gentle with my Hellcat."

I grinned and started up the car.

CHAPTER TWENTY-SIX

ROMEO

"Why did you have to agree to dinner with my parents?"

Her throaty laugh made the fact we had to get out of bed even worse.

"I figured it would be safer that way," Rimmel said, running her fingers across my bare abs.

"What do you mean?"

Her fingers kept caressing me, flirting along my body. Her touch was light, and even though I'd already had her twice, I felt a deep stirring in my chest.

But it wasn't for more sex. It wasn't from the insatiable desire she made me feel.

It was because she owned me.

I loved her with every cell in my body.

"I figured it would be easier to be in the same room with your mother to go over the details for the event if you and Tony were there too."

I palmed her bare hip. It shouldn't be this way. She shouldn't feel like she needed a buffer when she was in the same room as my mother.

Before I met Rim, I never really thought much about what my future relationships might be like or how my parents would be with my forever girl.

But even if I had thought about it, it would never have been like this.

I always just sort of assumed everyone would get along. And I wished we did. Not just for me, but for Rimmel. She needed more family and she deserved the love and security a big family could offer.

Instead, she got me and Braeden.

We were damn good, but sometimes I worried we wouldn't be enough.

"I really wish things were different," I told her.

She snuggled a little closer. "Part of me can't even be upset anymore because your mom loves you. She loves you so much."

"Yeah, but that's no excuse for the ways she's acted."

"No, I guess not."

"Rim?" I asked after a few long moments.

"Rome?"

I smiled despite the question I wanted to ask. "What'd you do with that file my mom gave you?"

Her body tensed just a little, and I stroked her back to hopefully display I meant no harm in asking, but honestly, this was a topic I couldn't avoid forever.

"You mean the one on my dad?"

"Yeah."

"It's in my bag." She tossed out her arm toward where her bag lay across the room.

"You carry it around with you?" I asked, surprised.

"I didn't know what to do with it. It's not the kind of thing you sit out on your desk or hide under a pillow."

"Like a hospital bill," I quipped.

She poked me in the ribs. "You totally orchestrated that as part of the sentence against Zach."

I shrugged. "I just suggested to my dad, *our lawyer,* that it didn't seem fair you had to pay a bill for care Zach was responsible for making you get."

"Thank you." The sincerity in her voice was a relief. I was kind of afraid she was mad.

"Anything for my girl."

"I haven't read it all." She rushed out the words.

"The police report?" I asked.

I felt her nod against me. "I just can't… It's sick to me. How could I live in a world where my father killed my mother?"

Her words cracked and broke something inside me. I sat up and leaned against the headboard so I could look down at her.

She looked so vulnerable lying in bed with the white sheets tangled around her and hair falling across her cheek. "Baby, what if that's not the story? What if all this fear you're holding on to because you're scared is worse than the actual truth."

"But your mother said…" Her voice faded away as a tear tracked down her cheek. She dashed it away quickly, like she was afraid to cry too.

"I love my mother, but she's a drama queen, Rim," I said point blank. "She does a lot of good in the community and has dedicated herself to her family, but she took it too far."

"I don't know." Rimmel pushed herself up and tucked the sheet around her, hiding most of her hot-ass nakedness from my eyes.

"She got that file, barely had time to digest it, and then got a call we were attacked and in the ER. She was beside herself with worry, rushed into the room, and said some shit that was really stupid."

"You believe her," Rimmel said, her voice quiet and a little bit in awe.

I wasn't going to lie to her. Not even about something that could cause problems between us. I leaned forward, grasped her face, and stared straight into her eyes. "This isn't me choosing a side. If I were forced to choose, it would be you, Rimmel. I'd pick you over anything, anyone in this world."

"But?"

I exhaled and released her face. "But my mother's PI wouldn't have been able to find something if there wasn't something to find."

She glanced down at her lap.

"Mom is a lot of things, but creating an entire document of false information—especially the type of information it is—she's just not that cruel, baby."

Rimmel's long, thick hair was hung over her shoulders, and when she looked down, it created a curtain and hid her face from me. I couldn't see her reaction to my words, but her silence cut like a knife.

"I think," she said, her voice almost too quiet to hear, "one of the reasons I'm so upset with your mother is because part of me believes her." Even her quiet tone couldn't hide the pure, unfiltered anguish those words made her feel.

Her shoulders started to shake and a sob ripped out of her throat.

"Ah, shit," I swore and pulled her into my lap.

She cried and cried. Everything she had bottled up inside her since that night at the field seemed to pour out of her until her voice turned hoarse and there was literally no tears left for her to cry.

I couldn't remember the last time I cried. Hell, maybe I never had. But the sounds of her sobs and the feeling of her small body quaking under the pressure she felt made me feel wrung out inside as if I too had sat here and sobbed.

I didn't say anything because there was nothing to say. She knew I loved her, and telling her in that moment sort of seemed wrong. Like I was acting like my love was enough to make everything else okay.

The truth was it wasn't.

There was nothing at all that could make this okay.

So I lay there, both arms tight around her, as she clung to me and cried.

When her body finally stopped trembling, her voice sounded like sandpaper in the silence of the room. "I am so incredibly sorry."

"I'm not. You've been holding that in way too long. We've got to deal with this, Rim. Pretending it isn't in the room with you every single second of every single day is madness."

No wonder she'd lost weight. She was living in silent torture. And I let her. I'd been focused on my arm, my training, and all my doctor's appointments. We'd been prepping for Zach's hearing and going to classes. When she was with me, we escaped into our own little reality, only coming out when we really had to.

"This thing with Zach is over. He's locked away. Your scholarship is back, and as smart as you are, I know you're caught up with classes."

She nodded against me.

"My arm's healing. In just a couple weeks, this cast will be off. I'll keep training and stay here with the Wolves. Everything is calming down now, sweetheart. It's time we tackle this."

"I know," she whispered against me.

"I'm gonna call over to the house and cancel dinner."

"No!" she said and pushed off my chest. Her face was red and blotchy. I reached out and brushed all the hair out of her face. "Just because my personal life is a disaster does not mean the shelter has to suffer."

"Mom can handle the event."

"But I want to. This is something I'm passionate about. You know how much I love the shelter and all those animals. I can deal with this and put on an amazing fundraiser for the shelter."

"I'll help," I said.

"Aren't you busy with everything you have going on?"

"It's off season. I'm nursing an injury. A little time off wouldn't hurt me. Besides, you need me."

"I do need you," she whispered and averted her gaze.

It was the first time she'd ever said that out loud. A surge of the instinct to protect her rose up inside me like a tidal wave and pushed out everything else. "You got me. No matter what," I vowed.

She smiled and it lit up her entire face. "I'm just gonna go get ready for dinner."

"Gimme some sugar." I tugged her close.

She giggled and pressed close. Her lips tasted salty from all the tears.

I watched her move around the room, pulling out clothes in the drawers she'd taken over, and then shut herself in the bathroom. I got up and pulled on some jeans, a T-shirt, and grudgingly pulled the sling back into place.

I couldn't wait to be rid of the stupid thing.

Rimmel came out of the bathroom dressed in a pair of black yoga pants and my Alpha U hoodie. Her hair was in a ponytail high on her head, and her face was washed clean so it looked less blotchy.

"I like seeing you with my name on your back."

She blew a kiss to me across the room. "I know I should probably dress a little nicer for dinner, but I don't feel like it. Besides, your mother needs to get used to me the way I am. I'm not changing."

"Woman, you're perfect. Don't you forget it."

Rimmel went out into the kitchen to feed Murphy. She was talking to him like he was totally listening, and her voice filled the house. I left the bed all rumpled because I liked seeing the evidence of the sex we just had.

And because I planned to mess it up again after dinner.

Rimmel called to me from the front door after she had her in depth talk with Murphy. Before I left the bedroom, I stopped in the doorway and looked back. The messy blankets, her clothes on the bed and floor. From this angle, I could see her brush on the bathroom counter along with some lotions and lip balm.

I smiled.

I didn't know just how right it would feel to have her here with me.

Rimmel was it for me.

She was my forever.

CHAPTER TWENTY-SEVEN

RIMMEL

Romeo was right.

I couldn't keep pretending.

One way or another, I needed to know the truth.

CHAPTER TWENTY-EIGHT

#NoticeToTheFaculty
Students today spend more time on homework than ever in recorded history.
#GiveUsABreak #HomeworkSucks
... Alpha BuzzFeed

ROMEO

Mom was alone in the kitchen when we walked in. She had a glass of red wine at her elbow and soft jazz playing through the surround sound. Her eyes widened a fraction in surprise like she thought we weren't going to show. I probably wouldn't have if Rimmel hadn't insisted.

"Roman." She smiled and pushed off the barstool. "How are you?"

When she came forward to hug me, I didn't stop her and I one-arm hugged her back. I was angry with her still, but she was my mother and I loved her. "Thanks for having us for dinner, Mom."

"You're welcome anytime. You know that," she said, pulling back, her eyes still trained on my face. "I still keep the fridge stocked for you."

I felt a pang of guilt because I hadn't come over here to raid the fridge or just shoot the shit with her since that night on the field. I knew sometimes she got lonely due to my dad's demanding work schedule.

"How is your arm?" She glanced down at the sling and splint. "You've been seeing your doctors?"

"Yeah, I have. They say it looks good and they think after some PT, I'll be good as new."

Her eyes swelled with tears. "I'm so glad to hear that. I've been worried."

I looked away. I couldn't stand to see that look on her face anymore. I didn't want to feel guilty for being mad at something she did.

"Rimmel," she said, finally taking her attention off me. "Thank you for coming." I saw her look over

Rimmel's casual appearance, and I knew she must be dying to say something considering the formal way she was dressed in a skirt, heels, and jacket, but to her credit, she said nothing at all.

"Of course. Anything I can do to help with the event."

"Where's Dad?" I asked.

"Holed up in his office. He's been in there since we got home from court. Said he was working on something that couldn't wait."

"Is he going to join us for dinner?" Rim asked.

"Oh yes," Mom answered.

The tension in the room was palpable, and now that the pleasantries were over, conversation felt forced.

Mom cleared her throat. "Dinner is ready. It's in the dining room. Why don't you two go ahead in, and I'll just get your father?"

I led Rim into the dining room and we sat on the long bench on one side of the table. The tabletop was filled with covered dishes, and I started poking around to see what we were eating. My stomach growled loudly as I snooped.

"Must look good," Rimmel giggled.

"Prime rib, twice baked potatoes, salad, and roasted vegetables," I said appreciatively. "If they don't come in here fast, I'm gonna start eating without them."

Rimmel smacked me in the stomach and laughed.

My parents entered, and after we exchanged the usual greetings with Dad, they sat down and Mom starting passing food around.

I piled my plate until you couldn't see it at all. I'd missed my mother's cooking, and I planned to load up.

Rimmel took about a quarter of what I did, and I used my fork to stab another piece of meat off the serving platter and dragged it over to drop on her plate.

She gave me a bewildered look, and I grunted between bites. "That'll put some meat on your bones."

"Honestly, Roman," Mom said, but the fondness in her tone couldn't be ignored.

"I have news," Dad announced before everyone had even taken their first bite.

Except me. I was plowing through my plate like an award-winning sumo wrestler. This shit was good.

"You're going to choke!" Rimmel scolded me.

"Poor thing. He's clearly starved." Mom tsked.

"It's going to surprise the hell out of you!" Dad went on, totally ignoring the ladies.

"What is it?" I asked, lowering my fork. Lately, all the "news" we'd been getting had been terrible and one more thing to overcome.

I glanced at Rimmel, who'd set her fork down beside her plate. I'd just now managed to get her to unload most of what she'd been carrying around for weeks. I wasn't sure she could handle anymore.

"Maybe we should talk about this after dinner," I said. "In your office."

He waved away my concern. "This isn't something that can wait. Besides, this is the best news you're going to get all year."

"Well, just tell us already, Anthony!" Mom said expectantly.

"The NFL called."

My fork clattered against my plate. My first thought was they finally delivered the final nail in the coffin of my pro career. But Dad said it was good news. He wouldn't consider that good.

So what the hell else could it be?

"Actually," he amended, "the owner of the Maryland Knights called me.

"Ron Gamble called *you*?" I echoed. He was one of (if not *the*) richest men in the entire state. He had his hands in a ton of businesses and was very active in not just community, but statewide affairs. He was also a huge football fan.

So much so that he owned Maryland's pro football team, the Maryland Knights.

"All the press you've been getting, the interviews, the full front page spread the *Maryland Tribune* ran… it's grabbed his attention."

"Why would he care about all the drama going on in my life?" I muttered.

"Because everyone else cares," Dad pointed out. "You've become quite popular, son, and not just at Alpha U."

I guess I'd realized that. I just hadn't focused on it. I'd been too busy living my life and being with Rimmel.

"What did he want?" Mom asked, exasperated.

"The Maryland Knights has made an offer, Roman. They want you on the team."

Mom gasped, and Rimmel leapt forward and threw her arms around my neck. "I knew they wouldn't just let you go!" she squealed.

I chuckled because her excitement was so damn cute. And it was also infectious. But I wasn't about to get excited.

Yet.

"Why?" I asked bluntly.

Rimmel made a noise and drew back. "Because you're an awesome player."

"I was. But now I'm broken." I looked at Dad, waiting for an explanation. I wanted to be thrilled shitless about this. I wanted to believe I hadn't lost my shot at a pro career because of one stupid injury.

But I wanted the facts first.

"I think that's why they want you." Dad began, then held up his hand to hold back any of our comments. "Of course, that isn't the only reason. Your record speaks for itself."

"They weren't interested before," I stated.

"Well, they didn't have an offer on the table for you. But then you broke your arm and half the college camped in the waiting room. People waited with baited breath to see how you were. And when you came out with an injury that could end your career, you didn't let it. You reassured everyone in the hospital, anyone who came up to on the street or campus, that you were fine. But it wasn't that you just said it." Dad paused.

"He lived it," Rimmel finished.

Dad nodded. "Exactly. The second the swelling went down you were back on the field. Even with limited abilities you didn't stop. You've taught yourself how to throw with your left arm."

"I don't throw as well as with my right arm," I added.

"You will. It's only a matter of time," Dad said like that was just a detail. "Local papers, statewide papers have run stories on you. You were the hero who became the underdog. You gave up your pro career to protect your girlfriend from a… an unstable man." Dad glanced at Rimmel. "And the people love her too."

I felt astonishment radiating off her, and I half smiled, taking in her expression.

"The clip of her about to leap on the field when she thought you were hurt went viral, son. The images of you running across the field and leaning over the railing toward her are everywhere. People identify with you two. They're rooting for you."

"So he wants me because I'm good publicity," I said, annoyed. I wanted to earn my spot. I wanted to be pro because I deserved it, not because I looked good on the front page of a newspaper.

"Ron Gamble has enough money to buy publicity, son." Dad frowned. "I really thought you would be more excited about this. I already reviewed the contract. I thought it was going to be a done deal."

I blew out a breath and pushed away from the table to stand. "I am excited. But I'm not a spokesperson. I'm a quarterback."

"He knows that. The team knows that. I talked to the head coach of the Knights just a few minutes ago. I told him your condition. The minute you give the okay, I'll have your doctors send over your file. Training camp starts in July. As a rookie, you'll report early with the rest of the newer players. The more seasoned players will join the rest of you a few weeks after."

I nodded because I knew how that worked.

"That gives you more than four months to prepare and go to physical therapy."

"And if I can't play?" I asked.

"Then you'll basically be a glorified spokesperson. You can do endorsement stuff for the team. Sign autographs, and when your contract is up, then you'll go your own way."

"How long is the contract?"

"One season."

So it really was a test run. It really was them putting their faith in me that I would be able to be the "comeback quarterback" and, of course, bring them good press in the process.

"It was made very clear that if you perform well on the field and your injury isn't a problem, you will be given a renewed contract—next time for more than one season."

It was all right here. Everything I wanted was being dangled in front of me.

Only it was better.

My last two offers were from teams across the country. I was going to have to move, for at least part of the year. I wouldn't see Rim very much or Braeden or my family. Maryland was home. I'd grown up here. I'd never lived anywhere else. I was open to the opportunity to move, and I knew I likely would some day because of football.

But now I didn't have to.

Now I could stay in my home state. I would be able to see my family more often and visit campus whenever I could. I'd be representing the state that loved me and a state I loved.

In all honesty, the Knights wasn't the best NFL team out there. But the head coach had a solid reputation for being fair, and so did Ron Gamble. I was willing to put in the work to help make the Knights better, and it seemed they were willing to give me a chance.

"You read the contract?" I asked Dad.

In my voice, Rimmel heard what I hadn't said, and she started bouncing around in her seat.

"I did. The first one they sent over I made a few changes and sent back. They approved, and now it's waiting for you to read it over and sign it."

"They're going to let me play, right? Not just sign autographs."

"I doubt you'll be a starter like you're used to here. But if you're able to play physically, then they will give you a chance."

I could do a lot with a chance.

I had my foot in the door of the NFL. All I needed to do was step through and prove I should be there.

I glanced at Rimmel. She nodded.

I grinned, and my parents jumped up from the table. Before they could rush me, Rimmel held up her hand. "Wait!"

Everyone stared at her.

She glanced at me. "What color is the team?"

I laughed out loud. "Does it matter?"

She wrinkled her nose. "Well, I am going to be wearing a lot of it."

I grinned. "The Knights are purple and orange-y red."

"I like purple!" Rimmel said enthusiastically.

"Well then." I took in everyone in the room. "I guess it's a deal."

Rimmel launched herself at me, and I caught her with one arm. She kissed my cheek and laughed.

Dad held out his hand and we shook. "Congratulations, son. I'm so damn proud of you."

"Thanks, Dad," I said around Rimmel's animated hug.

Mom hovered close by with a smile on her face and tears in her eyes. Rimmel seemed to notice and moved back.

"Oh, Roman," she said. "You're just everything a mother could ask for. And then some. I'm proud of you."

I held out my arm and folded her into a hug. She sniffled against my shirt and returned the hug with great force. When she pulled back, she wiped at her eyes.

"This calls for a celebration!" she said. "I have some champagne just waiting for the right moment, and this is definitely it."

After dinner, Mom and Rimmel sat at the table and went over all the last-minute details of the fundraiser for the shelter. I planned to sit in the room with them, but she beamed at me proudly and shooed me and Dad into his office so we could go over the contract.

"Feel free to take it home, read it through. I'll answer any questions you have," Dad said when he handed me the papers. The Knights symbol was on the cover page. It was a large shield with a sword.

It was pretty badass, and I grinned.

"You read this, right? The whole thing?" I asked.

"Son, I have read that backward and forward. No way would I let you sign something that was in any way a bad deal."

I knew that. I knew it all the way to my soul. "I don't need to read it, then." I grabbed a pen out of the cup on his desk. "I trust you as a lawyer, a manager, and as my father."

He seemed taken aback by my words. "That means a lot."

"It's the truth."

I flipped to the very last page and scrawled my signature across the line.

At that moment, Rimmel burst in the room with her cell in camera mode. "We need to document this!"

Dad came around the desk and we stood together as I held up the contract with my name signed across the bottom.

It was my dream come true.

"I think I need to get myself some Knight memorabilia up on the walls," Dad mused.

"And I need to go shopping for Knight T-shirts and hoodies!" Rimmel said.

"Thank goodness I look good in purple," my mother said as she entered the room.

I'd never felt so lucky in my entire life. My dream job, my dream girl, and a whole family of support.

Oh, and Zach was locked away.

That was pretty fucking awesome.

"Here you go." I handed the signed paperwork to my father.

"I'll send this over immediately." He took the papers. "I'm sure they'll be in contact. They will likely want to meet. There will be press. It's going to be a busy time."

I was ready. So ready.

"There's chocolate cake and coffee in the kitchen," Mom said.

I draped my arm across Rim's shoulders as we started for the door.

"Oh, Roman?" my father called out.

I turned back.

"Don't you at least want to know what you're getting paid?"

Funny, the money part hadn't even crossed my mind. Hell, I'd probably play for them for free. 'Course, money didn't hurt.

"How much?" I knew it wouldn't be much. I was a rookie and I was injured.

"Including your salary and signing bonus, it comes out to just over one million."

Shock rippled through the room.

I cleared my throat. "Come again?"

"I told you they understood your value."

"A million dollars?" I said, trying it out on my tongue. Maybe I'd heard him wrong.

"Did you think I'd let you sign for anything less?" Dad grinned.

"That's a lot of money," Rimmel whispered.

Hell yeah, it was.

"That's your starting salary, son," Dad said. "Next season, I'll really go after the big bucks."

"Let me get through training camp and this season first," I mused.

Rimmel smiled up at me.

Yeah, I was definitely the luckiest guy in the world right now.

CHAPTER TWENTY-NINE

RIMMEL

When the news broke about Romeo's new status as a Maryland Knight the remaining tickets for the shelter fundraiser flew out the door.

Romeo couldn't go anywhere without being stopped or photographed. It was pure insanity, but he played it cool, when I knew deep down he loved every single second of it.

I was so incredibly proud of him and so grateful to the Knights for looking past his injury and seeing what I knew he was going to do.

And the cherry on top of this delicious good news sundae was he was staying in Maryland. I knew he'd have to travel and fly around to games, but at least his home base would be where I was.

The week of the fundraiser went by in a blur. Last-minute preparations were endless, and Michelle and I worked around the clock to make sure everything was perfect. Valerie also helped, for which I was grateful.

My personal feelings aside, she knew how to put on a successful event. And with just an hour before it started, I already knew it was going to be a sensation.

I'd even gone shopping.

It wasn't that bad.

Okay, I hate shopping.

But I loved the girls' day Missy, Ivy, and me made out of it. Ivy drove and the three of us went to a huge mall about an hour away to look for gowns to wear to the fundraiser. Because it had become such a high-profile event (especially with the new Knights quarterback in attendance), I needed to look the best I could. This went beyond having dinner with Romeo's parents for the first time or showing up at Zach's court hearing.

This was for the animals.

And besides, it was a black tie event. Nothing I owned even resembled black tie affair.

Thank goodness Ivy and Missy were into fashion. Between the two of them, all three of us walked out of the mall with gorgeous dresses and matching shoes.

Yes, I got a pair of heels.

No, I wasn't entirely confident I wouldn't fall on my ass.

After shopping, we stopped somewhere for dinner and talked about boys, movies, and nail polish trends.

It wasn't my normal everyday conversation, but it was awesome.

I loved Romeo more than anything, but sometimes just being with your girlfriends has a way of making a girl feel lighter and more carefree.

I got ready for the event at the dorm because Ivy was doing my hair and makeup. Missy got ready with us too. Both of them looked so pretty. I knew when I looked in the mirror, I would be the odd one out.

But I didn't have to be as stunning as them. I just wanted to look beautiful.

Ivy was wearing an emerald gown that skimmed over her body and hit the floor with grace. The jewel tone actually made her blue eyes turn more of a jade, and despite the way she looked in the dress, it was her eyes that held your attention. It had a plunging neckline but wasn't trashy, and she wore a matte gold rope chain that tied in a knot near the end. Of course, she was wearing a pair of sky-high gold strappy heels, and her hair was done up in some elaborate twist with curls spilling out of the top.

Missy's gown was white. She was the only person I knew that could make a white gown look even whiter. Her olive skin looked permanently kissed by the sun, and her long dark hair was a beautiful contrast against the light fabric. She wore her hair in a loose side braid that hung over the bare shoulder of her toga-style dress.

Her shoes were also sky high in a cobalt blue that she matched up with cobalt earrings and a bracelet.

As Ivy was spraying another round of hairspray (seriously, I think more was on the walls than on my head), I groaned. “Are you done yet?”

“Man, you’re nervous tonight,” Ivy quipped and set aside the can.

“I can’t help it. This is important.”

“It’s going to go great,” Missy said. Then she looked at Ivy. “Let her look at herself already. She’s probably scared you did something crazy to her.”

“She knows better!” Ivy patted my shoulder. “You’re done.”

I got up from the chair and the silky fabric around my legs swished and swayed as I walked to the mirror.

My gown was all black. I hadn’t wanted anything flashy or too attention-grabbing like Missy and Ivy had on. Of course, Ivy would never allow it to just be plain.

I stepped up to the mirror and looked at my reflection.

I was beautiful.

My gown was modest but still sexy with a high-waisted black skirt that wasn’t too full, but wasn’t fitted like Ivy’s. The top was black lace with a skin-colored lining and had lace cap sleeves with a high neckline. I was a small person, thin without many curves, but this gown gave the illusion of more shape than I had.

Ivy parted my hair down the center and then braided it back on each side, tied the ends in some sort of bow, and pinned it all at the base of my head. The top was full yet sleek and there were a few wispy curls against my neck and around my face.

Knowing my aversion to makeup, she used a light hand but did something a little more smoky and dramatic with my eyes. She finished off the look with pale-peach lips.

I smiled and turned slightly to check out how I looked from behind. It was a backless dress, with the lace stopping at my shoulder blades to expose the creamy paleness of my back.

"You need to put the heels on before you trip over the hem." Missy laughed.

I laughed and reached for the black heels that were half the height of my friends'. Still, when I stepped into them, I felt like I was on stilts because I was so used to wearing boots and sneakers.

"Did I do good?" Ivy asked.

I felt like I was in a dream, like the reflection in the mirror was surreal. "Yes," I said and reached out and hugged her.

She returned my embrace just as there was a loud, obnoxious knock at the door.

"Ten to one that's Braeden," Ivy muttered in my ear before pulling back.

"I'll get it," Missy said.

"Day-um, girl." Braeden's voice boomed through the room. "You look hot."

Missy giggled, and Ivy gave me a look that said Missy better not get any ideas about picking up where she'd left off with Braeden.

I secretly agreed. It took Missy a while to get over the fact that Braeden really hadn't wanted any more than fun with her. But lately she'd been happier and more open to the idea of other guys.

"You better be on your best behavior tonight," I called out to him.

Braeden pushed open the door the rest of the way so he and Romeo could step into the room beside Missy.

"I'm wounded you think I need a lesson in manners." He placed a hand over his heart.

I snorted.

"What the hell are you wearing?" Braeden shouted, startling everyone. It was like he was just noticing I wasn't wearing my usual sweats and hoodie. "Rome, you better get your girl. She thinks she's going out in that."

I gasped and glanced down at myself. "What's wrong with it?"

Romeo stepped around the bed and the people crowding the room and swept his eyes over me. The blue in his irises deepened to navy. "You know everyone's going to be staring at you tonight," he murmured.

I tilted my head to the side. "In a good way? Or a bad way?"

He smiled.

"In a *that girl is half naked* kind of way!" Braeden interjected.

Romeo rolled his eyes.

"Naked!" I burst out. "I'm completely covered!"

"You can see through the lace," he argued and hit Romeo on the shoulder.

Romeo glanced at him. "You're on your own, B."

He gave Romeo a look like he was from Mars. "You're gonna let her wear that?"

"I think she looks beautiful," he said, his eyes never leaving me.

My cheeks heated and a warm feeling spread through my chest. "Good way?"

"Best way," Romeo corrected.

"You two are seriously making us all sick!" Ivy groaned. "Let's go before we're late."

Braeden was still looking at me, and I laughed. "The top is lined, Braeden. With fabric. I assure you there is nothing on display."

"Well, I was trying not to look," he muttered. "I mean, damn. Next time buy a dress with black lining or some shit. You about gave your BBFL a heart attack when I thought I was seeing your—"

Romeo grabbed him by the front of his jacket. "What?" he growled.

"Her lady bits," Braeden whispered, completely appalled, but it was so loud everyone heard it.

Every one of us burst out laughing.

Even Romeo. "Dude, you are not right."

Braeden ran his hands over the front of his black suit jacket to smooth out the fabric. He looked really good in a pair of jet-black dress pants, black dress shoes, a matching jacket, and a silk dark-green tie.

"You look good, Braeden," I told him. "Your tie matches Ivy's gown."

He slid a glance at her and grimaced. "I hope no one thinks we're together."

I swear if looks could kill, Braeden wouldn't be breathing.

"Please." She sniffed. "Everyone knows I would never."

"Let's go," Missy groaned and opened the door and walked out into the hall. Braeden and Ivy followed.

Romeo offered me his arm. "Heels, huh?" he asked, amused.

I made a face. "Seriously. I might fall and kill myself."

"I'd never let that happen." He winked.

He looked like he just stepped off the pages of *GQ*, standing there with his wide shoulders, tapered waist, and long, strong legs. He was wearing a navy-colored suit in a material that begged to be touched. His dress shirt was the color of steel and his tie was a shade of brilliant blue that totally matched his eyes.

His blond hair was combed back, but it still managed to fall over his forehead, giving him a rakish appearance. He wasn't wearing the sling on his arm, but I knew he had the splint on beneath his coat. He barely wore the sling these days, unless I badgered him into putting it on.

"If this event was for anyone other than the animals, I would totally skip just to be alone with you," I murmured, desire clear in my voice.

He leaned down and kissed my ear. "Oh, baby. We still have later."

I shivered with the delicious promise.

It was a short drive to the location of the event. We settled on a large, opulent hotel with a grand ballroom and a large capacity for guests. We were hosting a sit down dinner for which people paid a hundred dollars a plate.

I was shocked when Valerie suggested that price, but she insisted it was worth it and people would pay it. Since the event sold out, she proved herself right.

I didn't have to pay for my plate, and neither did Ivy, Missy, Braeden, or Romeo. Valerie said it had been taken care of.

That translated to she paid for us. I didn't argue. I didn't have the energy. I simply just didn't care.

Besides, the majority of the money went to the shelter.

People were arriving as we were, and the wide double doors to the ballroom were thrown open, giving a clear view to the room inside.

The carpet was a dark onyx, which you would think would be impossible to keep clean because every little speck of anything would show up like a star in the night sky.

But no. This carpet was so clean it was almost off-putting to step on. Nothing, not even a spec of lint or dust, dared to tarnish its opulent design. In the center of the room, a dance floor had been arranged because after the dinner, the speakers, and hopefully the large donations, there would be music and entertainment.

Around the perimeter of the room, large round tables were placed in a sweeping pattern so as not to disrupt any kind of flow in the space and to ensure everyone had a view of the large platform near the dance floor.

All the tables were draped in pale gold, with a shimmering netting material over to make everything glisten under the lights.

The center of the tables were adorned with photographs in large glittering frames. Valerie had wanted to place flower arrangements there, but I wanted something more personal. She gave in, and now each table held a small grouping of animals that had come through the shelter and found loving homes.

There were also photos of the animals that stayed there with us now, ones that needed good homes.

All around the room were large easels with more photos, drawn-up plans for a remodel and modernization of the shelter, and pictures of the people who donated their time to the animals.

There was also more in-depth literature printed out in small brochures that gave in detail what the shelter was in need for, yearly costs to run the place, and what the average daily needs were for a place like ours to thrive.

There was a sign-up sheet for volunteer hours, literature on animal care and grooming, and of course, there were various tables set up all around that were there solely for the purpose of taking donations.

Our goal for tonight was to raise a minimum of twenty thousand dollars. I wasn't sure we could do it, but we'd already made a good chunk off the tickets. Somehow, Valerie had gotten the hotel to donate the room so we didn't have to pay a hefty rental fee.

We did have to pay a fee for the dinner, but apparently, Valerie got it at a heavily discounted rate.

I had to admit, when the woman set her mind to something, it was as good as done.

Even when it was something like digging up secrets on my father.

Once we showed Ivy, Missy, and Braeden the table we were all sharing, Romeo and I went to the entrance where Valerie greeted people as they came in. Michelle (the shelter owner) was there as well, and she was beaming with excitement at the prospects for tonight.

I was nervous to greet people, but I did it anyway. I smiled and laughed and shook a million hands. Romeo never left my side. When someone (like the press) tried to talk to him about the Knights or his training, he deftly turned the subject back to the reason we were all here.

There was a lot of media present, including the reporter that interviewed Romeo for the *Maryland Tribune* and a couple local television stations doing pieces for a human-interest story.

There was a brief cocktail hour while guests were arriving, and I barely had time to breathe, but it flew by so fast I was surprised when Valerie touched my arm and whispered it was time to start the presentation.

Butterflies swirled inside my belly because I was going to be doing a little bit of speaking. Mostly just telling everyone my part in the shelter, some of our goals, and introducing Michelle who would also be speaking.

We were about to close the ballroom doors when some of the press in the hall started snapping pictures and a whirl of excitement filtered through the room.

"Mr. Gamble!" one of the reporters called out. "What brings you here tonight?"

Romeo whipped around and stared out into the hallway as Ron Gamble, owner of the Maryland Knights, stepped into sight.

He was wearing a tuxedo with a wide white silk tie. His hair was graying at the sides and temples, and he had a solid build. He probably wasn't even six feet tall, but the man had an undeniable presence.

I would almost call it arrogance if it weren't for the kindness I saw in his eyes.

• • •

He paused and turned to the reporter who yelled out his question. "I'm supporting a good cause."

When he turned back around, his dark eyes went right to Romeo. He smiled widely and held out his arms. "Roman Anderson, your reputation precedes you."

Romeo grinned. "As does yours."

He laughed and held out a hand, his left one, for Romeo to shake. "I've been wanting to welcome you to the team since you signed but haven't been able to break away." He glanced at me, and I smiled warmly. "But then I heard about this worthy cause and figured I'd use it as an opportunity."

"We're glad to have you, Mr. Gamble."

He waved away Romeo's words. "Call me Ron."

To my surprise, he turned to me. "You must be Rimmel."

I felt my eyes widen. He knew my name?

Ron chuckled. "Oh yes, I know who you are. I hope you'll join us at all the games you can. I'd ask you to sit in my private box, but that would only deny the public your face. The camera sure loves you."

I blushed probably ten shades of red. "Of course I'll be there."

"Good. Good." He nodded. "I'll look forward to speaking with you later on this evening," he said to Romeo. "I'll just go find my seat."

"I'd be happy to escort you," Valerie said, stepping forward.

"Well, I'm certainly not going to say no to that offer."

"Mr. Gamble," I rushed out, stopping him before he could go.

"Ron to you too, sweetheart," he said.

I nodded. "Ron. I… I just wanted to tell you what a smart man I think you are."

He threw back his head and laughed. "I'm sure some wouldn't agree with you."

I smiled. "You know what they say about opinions…" I let my voice trail away.

He chuckled. "I do."

Valerie was looking at me like I had five heads, sitting here talking to the most powerful man in the state like this.

I lifted my chin and stepped forward. "Romeo is the best player you're ever going to have. Even injured." Then I hurried to add, "But he won't be injured for long."

Behind me, Romeo laughed beneath his breath.

Ron watched me with clear amusement in his eyes. I wanted to kick myself. I wasn't trying to be amusing. I was trying to be sincere.

And someone had to thank the man for what he'd done for Romeo. Valerie wouldn't, because I knew she probably thought it was beyond polite to bring this kind of thing up.

And Romeo would never because he was humble. Well, in some ways.

(In other ways, he had a giant head.)

That left me.

"I know you're taking a chance on him, and I want to thank you for that. He works hard, harder than anyone I know. He's going to be your team's good luck charm. I just know it."

Romeo stepped forward and placed his palm on the small of my back. I wondered if that was his way of telling me to shut it.

"I like you," Ron said. "Honest. Sincere. Most people are afraid to talk to me like I'm a regular human."

Romeo's hand moved from the small of my back to curve around my hip. Ron watched us and then shook his head. "Football royalty," he mused. "That's exactly what you two are on the path to becoming."

"I hope you enjoy the evening," I said. I really wasn't sure what you said when someone predicted you'd be royalty.

"I will." Valerie started to lead him away, but he looked back over his shoulder.

"And it's not really a chance I'm taking on this one." He hitched his thumb at Romeo. "It's a sure thing. I would know. I only ever bet on sure things." He winked. "They don't call me Gamble for nothing."

When he walked away, I looked up at Romeo. "I think that went well."

He chuckled, his voice rich and low. Tiny goose bumps ran down my arms. "Maybe I should fire Dad and hire you to manage my deals."

I snorted. "Are you kidding? That could have gone horribly wrong. Thank goodness he has a sense of humor."

As Michelle and Valerie gathered up front, I murmured, "I need to get up there."

I started forward and got maybe two steps. Then my ankle turned on those god-awful (and painful!) heels.

My last thought before I tripped and fell into a heap on the perfect carpet was if this fall didn't kill me (which unfortunately it wouldn't), then embarrassment surely would.

CHAPTER THIRTY

ROMEO

The girl couldn't walk in heels.

She could barely stand in them.

Right before she totally busted her ass, I rushed forward and caught her.

Her breath whooshed out of her lungs and her eyes were closed tightly like she was anticipating the jolt against the floor.

"I got you," I said.

Her eyes opened as I swung her up in my arms.

"Your arm!" she gasped and tried to leap down.

I chuckled, aware of every eye in the place on us. "You better hold still before you hurt it worse."

She gasped and went rigid.

Okay, that was mean, but damn was she cute. And I wasn't putting her down.

"I think I better escort you to the stage. Can't have you injuring yourself or anyone else with those potential weapons of mass destruction on your feet."

Rimmel grimaced, and I carried her with ease around the tables, across the dance floor, and up to the stage where Mom and Michelle were waiting.

"I'm so embarrassed," she muttered.

Up on the platform, I turned so everyone could see me carrying her and I grinned out at the crowd. I heard some muffled laughter in the back, which only egged me on.

"Kick off your shoes," I told her.

"What? No. Put me down."

"Kick them off or I'll make you talk while I hold you."

"You're going to pay for this later," she muttered and kicked off her heels. They landed nearby with an audible thud.

I stood Rim on her own two feet and then stepped up to the waiting microphone. "She just can't walk in heels."

Everyone laughed and a few people applauded.

I happened to see Mom seated Ron Gamble at our table between my father and me. He was smiling and nodding at something Dad was saying while watching me.

Figuring I embarrassed Rim enough, I left her to it and took my seat at the table. Braeden gave me a *this is the shit* look when I sat down, and I knew he was talking about Ron Gamble.

I was surprised too, but I would roll with it.

Rimmel spoke briefly, but it was the most passionate speech I'd ever heard someone give about animals. After she went, Michelle went into more detail, and then a short video of the shelter played on a large screen.

When that was over, dinner was served, and then a live band Mom somehow scored started playing, rounding out the night.

The lines at the donation tables never vanished.

Rimmel beamed and mingled with people like she was a pro. She was the frickin' light of the entire night. Everyone gravitated toward her. She was infectious. She infected people with her warmth and light. She was absolutely the kind of person that made others remember how good she made them feel, long after they walked away.

I didn't talk too much football with Ron because this wasn't a football event. I wasn't going to degrade all the work Rimmel and my mother put into this fundraiser by turning it into a show about me. Besides, it was sort of nice to have a break. All the press, interviews, and phone calls lately were a lot. I was glad to have a break.

Plus, my instincts were telling me Ron wasn't here to check me out for football. He just wanted to know what kind of teammate he'd brought into the fold. Quarterbacks were important pieces in the game. They could make or break a season. And there was a lot more to a good quarterback than just the way he threw.

Ron knew that. I knew it.

And I hoped the way I acted tonight gave him even more confidence in me.

When a slow song played through the room, I took the chance to pull Rim out onto the floor. I'd been sharing her with everyone all night, and I wanted some one-on-one time.

"People's eyes follow you around the room," I told her, pulling her close.

"You're being a drama queen," she said rationally.

"I don't like it." I ignored her words completely. I was *not* a drama queen.

"My eyes are always on you."

"As they should be." She laughed. Seconds later, her cheek rested against my chest. "Donations are pouring in. It's going to be so good for the animals."

"I've been to a lot of events my mother has chaired, so I can say with full authority that this is the best one."

"Really?"

"Mmm." I was distracted by the feel of her against me and the memory of what happened the last time we were on a dance floor together.

But my happy memory was interrupted when Rim's body tensed beneath my hold. "Rim?"

"You know how you said everyone's eyes were on me tonight?" she asked. Whatever was in her voice put me on red alert. I forced myself to remain relaxed, at least outwardly anyway.

"Yeah."

"Well, I don't want to sound paranoid or anything," she began, "but that man over there has been staring at me all night. It's kind of creeping me out."

"What man?" I was no longer able to hold my relaxed posture. All my muscles tensed.

"Maybe I'm just imagining things," she muttered.

Rimmel wasn't the kind of girl who cried wolf. She was the kind of girl that didn't even ask for help after the wolf chewed off half her arm. If she was saying someone was making her uncomfortable, then it was because there was a creep in this room.

"Where?" My eyes scanned the area.

"Over there by the entrance and to the right. He's wearing a black suit and no tie."

Casually, I rotated us in a circle as we danced. I found him right away. Not because he stuck out in a crowd. Not because he was particularly interesting.

I knew him.

Clear memories of the night he approached my Hellcat outside my parents' house flashed vividly through my mind. It was the man who told me he was a reporter, but he wasn't.

"Romeo?" she whispered.

"You said he's been staring at you?"

"Yeah, but not the direct kind of stare. More like watching me. He was never far behind when I was speaking with people throughout the night. At first, I didn't notice. It was only like a creepy feeling. But once I caught him looking..."

"Go sit with B," I told her.

"Why?"

"Just go."

She caught my hand. "Don't cause a scene. Just forget it."

"I know him."

"Oh." She dropped my arm. "Maybe he just wanted to say hi to you, then."

"Probably." I kissed her head and tried to tamp down some of the suspicion bubbling inside me. "Go sit with B."

As I spoke, I looked back to where he was standing. He smiled.

Braeden was coming toward the dance floor with a woman on his arm. I gave him a pointed look, then glanced at Rim. He dropped the woman he was walking with and started toward us.

I glanced back at the man.

He was gone.

Oh hells no.

I rushed off and pushed through the doors, knowing this was the way he'd come. Out in the hall, he was leaning against a far wall.

"Who the hell are you?" I demanded.

"Roman," he said like we were old buddies. "You never called for the interview."

"You aren't a reporter."

"Sure I am."

"The *Maryland Tribune* has never even heard of you."

"Probably a good thing I quit, then."

I wanted to punch the smirk off his face. "Quit playing games. Who are you?"

"Speaking of games. Congratulations on your big contract with the Knights."

I glared at him in stony silence.

"A million is a pretty nice payday."

"How do you know how much I'm getting paid?" I asked low. As far as I knew, the personal details of my contract hadn't been released.

He shrugged. "I'm a reporter. I do research. The article I read a while back was my favorite. Catchy headline. 'The comeback quarterback.'"

"Were you the one who left that paper on my windshield?" I stepped closer, threatening.

Who was this fool? What the hell did he want?

The look in his eyes told me he was exactly the one who left it.

"I wonder," he mused. "How much of that money would you give up to protect that girl you just can't keep your eyes off. I think her name is… Rimmel?"

At my sides, my fists clenched. "The last guy who threatened her ended up with some broken bones, a wired jaw, and is currently sitting in a straightjacket in the loony bin."

"Threat?" He raised his eyebrows. "That wasn't a threat."

I heard the door to the ballroom open and the music grew a little louder.

The man pushed off the wall, but I didn't back up. He nearly collided with my chest. *Let him. Give me one solitary reason to knock him out.*

He had to look up when he spoke because I was taller. "I don't threaten. I merely give warnings."

I drew my fist back.

"Rome!" Braeden shouted from behind. He rushed up behind me, and the man smiled.

"Think about it," he said.

And then he just walked away. Right out the exit and into the night.

Braeden turned to me. "What the fuck was that about?"

I stared after him. "I don't know…"

Finally, I glanced at my friend. "But I'm sure as hell gonna find out."

CHAPTER THIRTY-ONE

#LateNightMusings
When you wait for the waiter at a restaurant, aren't you a waiter?

... Alpha BuzzFeed

RIMMEL

Romeo was on edge.

It wasn't anything he said. It was what he *didn't* say.

When he and Braeden came back in the ballroom, both of them seemed distracted and sort of pissed off. But by the time they made it to the table, they were all smiles again.

I questioned Romeo about the man. He told me it was one of the reporters who interviewed him for a story, and I'd been right; he just wanted to say hi. I must not have seemed totally convinced, and Romeo finally admitted he'd wanted to talk football and when Romeo refused, things got heated.

Braeden backed up the story.

Notice I said *story*. Something inside me just wouldn't let me believe it was truth.

Still, I let it go. The last thing I was going to do was make an issue out of something in the middle of a crowded room.

The rest of the event went by in a blur. I couldn't believe the response the shelter was getting, and I caught Michelle crying in the bathroom more than once because she was so happy.

By the end of the night, I was exhausted but also proud. Even through everything, Valerie and I managed to work together and put on an amazing event.

When the cleaning crew entered to start breaking down everything, I thought I might faint from relief. Maybe it was the exhaustion that caused me to do what I did.

Or maybe I did it because it was the right thing.

I thanked Valerie. It was a sincere thank you, and not on behalf of the shelter or Michelle. It was on behalf of myself. Even after our relationship basically went to hell in a hand basket, she still helped. She still honored her commitment.

Valerie didn't appear surprised that I would thank her. But she did seem touched at the true gratefulness behind my words.

It wasn't until Romeo and I were alone that I really started to think again about what happened earlier that night.

"Romeo?" I asked as I hung up my gown in his closet.

"Yeah, baby?"

"Are you telling me everything about earlier?"

He answered my question with one of his own. "Have you seen that man, the reporter, around before tonight?"

"No." I glanced over my shoulder.

"Think about it, Rim." He rubbed a hand over his head. "School, the shelter, on the street… anywhere."

"Nom I haven't." I turned around. "What's this about?"

Did Romeo think that guy was stalking us?

He shortened the distance between us and caressed my cheek with the backs of his fingers. "Nothing. I just don't want those reporters bothering you. Some of them can be relentless."

In the bathroom, I washed off my makeup and took down my hair. The only thing I was wearing was an old T-shirt of Romeo's, and I was surprised when he didn't come in the bathroom to "brush his teeth" while I was getting ready for bed.

Brush his teeth = stare at my butt while I bent over the sink to wash my face.

When I was done with my routine, I clicked off the light and stepped into the bedroom. He was typing something on his phone, and then I heard the little sound for a text message being sent.

"Who ya talking to?" I walked over to where he was sitting on the side of the bed.

"Who cares?" he asked and tossed the phone down beside him before reaching for me.

I climbed into his lap and he kissed me, but then he pulled back and pressed my head against his shoulder and wrapped his arms around me.

An odd feeling of foreboding passed through me.

I peeked down at his still illuminated phone screen.

…her dad

Those were the only two words I caught before the screen went dark.

"Hey," he whispered. I lifted my head. "I love you."

"I love you, too."

He kissed me softly, slowly and deep.

I forgot all about the words on his phone and what they could mean and gave in to the way he tasted and felt. We made love just like he kissed.

Slow.

Thorough.

Deep.

The emotion that swirled about the room was so intense it was at times hard to breathe.

When at last I lay curled up in his arms, the text came back to haunt me. He'd been texting Braeden. Whose father was he talking about?

Mine?

And why now? Why tonight?

I thought about the reporter and how something seemed to weigh on the man beside me.

I don't know how long I lay there going through endless possibilities, but in the end, I just didn't know.

I didn't like not knowing.

I liked to be informed.

While I wasn't one hundred percent sure Romeo had been texting about me and my father, I was willing to bet on it.

Carefully, I climbed out of bed and padded into the other room. My bag lay on the floor by the couch where I'd dropped it when we came in.

I reached inside and my hand closed around the file folder I kept there. I carried it to the couch and flipped on a small lamp on the table beside me. Murphy leapt onto the cushions and curled up in my lap.

I took comfort in his warm, reassuring body as I opened to the first page inside.

And then I started to read.

CHAPTER THIRTY-TWO

I drank some Red Bull, but it didn't give me wings.
#FalseAdvertising
#IFeelBetrayed
... Alpha BuzzFeed

ROMEO

I reached for her and she wasn't there.

The mattress beside me was empty. The sheets on her side had long gone cold.

I sat up and looked toward the bathroom, but the door was open and the room was dark. I glanced at the clock. It was early, but the sun was up.

After tossing off the covers and pulling on a pair of boxer briefs, I went in search of my girl. I found her at the living room window, looking out into the yard.

Her back was turned, but the tension that radiated off her body indicated something was wrong. When I reached her, I wrapped my arms around her waist and pulled her against me. Her fingers gripped the mug of coffee in her hand so tight they were colorless.

I followed her gaze out the window to the partially snow-covered ground.

She was staring at the pool.

"Penny for your thoughts," I whispered.

"My mother didn't drown."

Suddenly, my insides felt like the ground outside. Frozen, cold and hard. I knew just by the air in the room, by the way she stood, and waking up to find her gone, whatever was wrong wasn't good.

But this…

This was something that went beyond that.

I brushed the hair back away from her face and tightened my arms around her, offering some kind of shelter from the storm raging inside.

"You read the file."

Her head bobbed up and down. "I couldn't sleep."

I closed my eyes. I guess the false sense of security I tried to belay last night hadn't been received.

Fuck. I was sick of this. Of her sheltering me. Of me sheltering her. I was sick of people coming at us, the past threatening our future.

"I—"

She made a noise to cut me off. "I know, Romeo. Just let me get this out."

I was afraid her mug was going to shatter and slice her hands. I pried it away and set it aside. The second I wrapped my arms back around her, she covered my arms with her hands.

"They lied to me."

"Who?"

"Everyone. My dad, my grandparents. The police. It seems everyone knew what was in that file but me."

"What's in the file, Rim?"

"According to the coroner's report, my mother was dead before she hit the pool. There was no water in her lungs to suggest she drowned. She died from blunt force trauma to the head. They say the hit likely killed her instantly."

The catch in her voice made my throat constrict.

"I keep sitting here thinking I'm glad." Her words were tortured, like she felt guilty for her own feelings. "All these years I'd thought she suffered. I thought she'd fallen, hit her head, and slipped into the water. I thought she knew what was happening. The nightmares, Romeo, the nightmares that haunted me, water claiming her life, the burning sensation in her lungs, the way the world started to blur out inch by inch…"

I made a noise in the back of my throat. My God, she tortured herself with these thoughts? It was unbearable to hear once, let alone have it on repeat in the back of her mind.

"I'm glad she died instantly. I'm glad it was over before it began. It means she didn't suffer."

"That doesn't make you a bad person, baby. It makes you compassionate."

"That isn't all the file said," she intoned. Her voice was alarming, flat. "Her death wasn't ruled an accident.

That's what I'd been told. It's still marked as unresolved."

"What? Why?" I asked, even though a sick, knowing feeling wrapped around my heart and started to squeeze.

My mother was right.

"Apparently, the police launched a full-on investigation. They questioned everyone, including my father. It's on record that when she died, we were in fact in heavy debt. I think there was suspicion that my father killed her himself, but they didn't have any evidence to support an arrest. My mother didn't have any life insurance. Her death didn't solve any financial hardships. In fact, it only posed more. Her memorial service and the need for childcare all would cost more money that my father simply didn't have."

"Did they report on why the family was so in debt?"

I lifted a hand and swiped a tear off her cheek. "They said it was gross mismanagement of funds coupled with a slow construction season."

I didn't say anything, so she continued. "Plus, my dad had an alibi for the approximate time of death. He was at work. His entire crew and the clients he was working for were with him that day. There was no way he was home to do it."

"That's a good thing." I squeezed her. It meant her father wasn't what my mother implied.

"But it still wasn't ruled an accident. According to the report, the trauma was caused by blunt force, the kind that couldn't happen from slipping and hitting her head."

"So they think she was murdered?"

"They don't know. They couldn't find any evidence to support the theory beyond her head injury. My mother was well loved. Everyone they interviewed only said good things."

"Maybe it was a home invasion," I suggested.

"Nothing was taken from the house and there were no signs of a struggle. There was no suspicious DNA on her body. No fibers, hair, or skin. Of course, because she was in the pool, it could have been washed away."

"And they checked out your father?" How far had they dug around? What about his supposed gambling problem? Wouldn't that raise a red flag?

"He was the main suspect for months. They questioned him at length. All those times I thought he had to work late, all the nights I spent with Gran… he was at the police station, being questioned and accused."

"But he didn't do it. They let him go."

"And my mother is dead and no one knows why." Rimmel turned in the circle of my arms and looked up at me. Her eyes were bloodshot and rimmed red. Her lower lip was swollen from where she chewed it. "Why didn't they tell me this? Why did they lie to me all these years?"

"The same reason I didn't tell you the truth about that reporter last night. The same reason you kept me away from my phone the night of the big game. They were protecting you."

"But it's my right to know!"

"I agree. But you were eleven. You were devastated and likely in shock from the way you found her. Why fill your head with theories and suspicion? It would have only confused you more."

She buried her head against my chest and cried.

I held her and stared out at the pool. I wondered if we'd ever know what really happened to her mom.

When she'd gotten out most of her tears, she pulled back. "I'm not eleven anymore, and I can handle the truth."

I smiled. "You're one tough cookie."

"I'm gonna call my dad. I'm gonna make him tell me in his words what really happened."

I nodded.

"But first, you need to tell me about last night."

I pulled back and ran a hand through my hair. "That was the guy who was outside the house a while back, the guy who said he was with the *Maryland Tribune*."

She frowned. "Why was he there?"

"He threatened me," I said point blank. "He threatened us."

No way was I going to say it was really just her he threatened. Besides, any threat against her *was* a threat against me.

"What!"

"I'm pretty sure he left that article on my windshield at the courthouse. I think he's been watching us."

"Why do you think that?"

"Because he knew shit, Rim. He knew how much I'm getting paid to play."

"But you kept that confidential."

"Exactly."

"I saw your text last night. The one to Braeden. The one that said 'her father.' Were you talking about me? What does my father have to do with this?"

I exhaled in frustration. The last thing I wanted to do was cast more doubt over her father, especially after everything she just read in the file. But the truth was the truth.

"I know the cops didn't uncover any gambling years ago, but, babe, it's the only thing that makes sense. Your loss of insurance, your father's job. People sniffing around you and me, talking to me about money and how much I'd pay to protect you."

She sucked in a breath.

"I think he's mixed up with some bad people."

Part of me hoped she would yell at me, tell me how insane I was and that she couldn't believe I'd say such things about her father. I hoped to hell I was wrong about what I was thinking.

She didn't yell.

She didn't tell me I was insane.

She didn't tell me I was wrong.

"There's information in the file that proves his gambling."

A curse dropped from my lips.

"It's recent. Not from years ago when Mom died. The PI followed him around. There's pictures of him going in to a known underground gambling club." Rimmel looked me straight in the eye. "Your mother was right."

CHAPTER THIRTY-THREE

RIMMEL

The phone rang and rang.

I called three times in a row.

He didn't pick up. Not once.

I didn't bother leaving a voicemail. He'd see I called. Besides, what would I say?

Hey, Dad, it's Rimmel. I know you were suspected of killing Mom. I know you're in gambling debt. And did I mention someone is threatening my boyfriend?

That would go down as the worst voicemail in the history of voicemails.

Romeo watched with a veiled look in his eyes as I growled at the phone and punched the END CALL button once again.

"What kind of father ignores his only daughter?" I demanded.

Romeo pressed his lips together and said nothing. I saw the anger in the depths of his eyes. I saw the distaste. He was holding himself back from saying nasty things about the only parent I had left.

It made me beyond angry that he was in this position at all.

Now I kind of understood how he must have felt standing between his mother and me.

I called up a different number on the screen and hit SEND.

She answered on the second ring. "Rimmel! I'm so thrilled to hear from you!"

"Hi, Gran," I said. Just the sound of her voice, the sound of home, sent a wave of homesickness through me. Tears burned my eyes, but I blinked them back. I'd cried enough.

"How are you?"

"I've been better."

There was a brief pause on the line. "Oh, honey, what's wrong?"

"I've read the police report on Mom's death." I dropped the words like a bomb. There was no gentle way to say this.

A charged, lengthy silence filled the space between us.

"How?" she whispered.

"Does it really matter?" I asked, trying to hold in my anger. This wasn't my grandmother's fault. Well, okay, it kind of was, because she'd known about this too. She lied too.

"No. I suppose not."

"Why did you lie? Why did you tell me it was a horrible accident when the police have it listed as unresolved? *What happened to my mother*?"

"Oh, honey." The catch in her voice said it all.

Everything I read was true.

"I have a right to know."

"We were trying to shield you. You'd been through so much."

"I'm not a little girl anymore. And this is affecting my life."

"What? How?" Her voice was completely alarmed. "Have you called your father?"

"Yes. Many times. He won't return my calls. I had to leave him a message that I was attacked and in the ER, and only then did he call me back."

"Oh my God!" she gasped. "Honey, are you hurt? What happened?"

"It was a few weeks ago, Gran. I'm fine."

"Weeks ago?" she murmured. "He didn't say anything."

"So he's talking to you, then?"

Silence.

So he wasn't.

"I know about the gambling," I said.

She sucked in a breath.

"I assume you do as well."

"This isn't a conversation we should have over the phone." Her voice was sad and strained.

"Fine. I'll fly to Florida. I'll be there soon."

"At least let me send you money for the plane ticket."

I agreed because I spent most of what I had on my gown for the fundraiser. I was seriously going to have to get a job when all this was over. It was up to me to take care of myself.

"Thank you," I said when she promised to transfer the money into my account, plus a little extra for food.

"You know your grandfather and I love you. So much. We've only ever wanted what's best for you."

It hurt to hear those words because I believed them. And because I loved them too.

But I was still upset they let me live a lie.

When I disconnected the call, I tossed my phone onto the couch and looked at Romeo.

"I'm coming with you."

"You don't have to."

"I know."

I nodded. I wanted him to come. I needed him. What if I went to Florida only to realize it no longer felt like home?

In that moment, I hated lies. I hated liars and half-truths. I hated what lies could do to people.

I glanced out the window again and then back at Romeo.

Without a word, I walked past him and out the front door.

He yelled my name, but I didn't stop. I kept going. There was something I had to do.

CHAPTER THIRTY-FOUR

#DidYouKnow?
Early morning sex has been proven to be more effective than coffee.
#YouAreWelcome
... Alpha BuzzFeed

ROMEO

Where the hell was she going!?

One minute she was looking torn and hurt, and the next she looked like a barefoot warrior ready to roll some heads.

It was hot as hell.

But it was also scary.

The front door waivered against the winter wind as I rushed after her. I cursed against the biting, frigid air and my lack of shirt, but I didn't turn back.

Rimmel was halfway across the yard, wearing nothing but one of my T-shirts and a pair of sweatpants I was surprised stayed up on her.

She wasn't even wearing socks.

"Rimmel!" I roared. "You're gonna freeze to death!"

She kept going, right up to the main house back door.

My steps faltered.

She was going to my parents?

What the fuck for?

I started running because in her current mood, if she were going after my mother, then fireworks would likely fly.

"Rimmel," I called again, rushing inside after her. She was about to turn the corner, but she stopped and held out her hand to me.

I wrapped my hand around hers, and she continued going without a word.

Mom was sitting at the small table in the kitchen, a mug of tea at her elbow and a bunch of paperwork spread out in front of her.

She looked up when we walked in. The smile died on her lips. She knew this wasn't some kind of pleasant visit. She glanced at me, and I shook my head.

I didn't know what Rimmel was doing, but I wasn't going to stop her. Whatever was going on in her heart and her mind needed resolved. If whatever she needed to say would help her, then my mother was going to have to withstand her wrath.

"Rimmel?" Mom asked, giving her full attention to my girlfriend.

"Thank you," Rimmel said, shocking the shit out of my mother and me.

"You were just as responsible for the success of the event as I," Mom said, gesturing to all the papers in front of her.

"I'm not talking about last night," Rimmel said, withdrawing her hand from mine.

"Then…?"

"Thank you for telling me the truth. For not just covering up what you found and letting me continue to live a lie."

For once in her life, my mother was struck silent. She twisted the platinum chain hanging around her neck on her finger.

"I know you didn't do it for me. You did it more or less to chase me away. You did it for Romeo. But even still, I'm grateful. I know I wasn't before, but now I…" Her voice cracked, and I stepped toward her.

She shook her head, telling me to let her stand on her own.

"Now I see things differently. So thank you."

My mother got up and rushed around the table toward my girl. "Oh, honey, I'm so very sorry."

She hugged Rimmel without hesitation. Rimmel stood stock still, not returning the embrace or pushing it away.

"I shouldn't have done it that way. I should have been more caring. You've done nothing but love my son and support him. You've stood by him even when his entire future was at stake. I know I don't deserve your forgiveness, but maybe someday you'll offer it. Please know that I accept you wholeheartedly into this family and as part of my son's life. I truly hope someday we'll have a close relationship."

And Rimmel called me a drama queen?

Um. I don't think so.

After a few seconds ticked by and my mother fell silent, Rimmel moved. She lifted her arms and hugged my mother back.

"We're flying to Florida," I informed her when she pulled back from Rim.

She touched Rimmel's arm. "I hope it brings you the peace you need."

Back at my place, I grabbed my hoodie off the bed and pulled it over Rimmel's head.

"Spring break is next week. But I can't wait that long to go," she said.

"I'll call the dean. He freaking owes you after everything that's happened with your scholarship and with Zach. I'll get him to excuse us from classes."

She squeezed my hand before she moved away. "I'm gonna pack."

I'd always been curious about where Rimmel came from.

I guess now I was going to see.

CHAPTER THIRTY-FIVE

RIMMEL

I still hated flying.

It was more tolerable because Romeo was beside me, but it was never something I would ever like.

"I'm not looking forward to all the plane rides to your away games," I said when we finally stepped out of the airport.

"You're gonna come to my away games?" He grinned.

"As many as I can."

"Something tells me that will make Ron Gamble very happy."

"I only care about making *you* happy." I couldn't keep the worried note from creeping up behind my words. How was Romeo going to be happy with me if things like this kept happening to us?

From day one, Romeo and I had been hit with obstacles at every turn.

He was worth it. One hundred percent. But how much more could he take?

How much more could I take?

"Don't do that," he murmured, pulling me around on the sidewalk.

"Do what?"

"Worry." He pressed a kiss to my nose. "After this is over, it's smooth sailing through the rest of our lives."

I wanted to believe that.

"C'mon, let's get a cab," I said and walked toward the cab line.

"Hells no." He grabbed my hand and tugged me away. "We don't ride in cabs. We ride in style."

I laughed. "And what kind of style is that? The bus?"

He made a face. "I'm renting a car."

"What? That's too much money."

"I can afford it. I'm a pro football player." He winked at me with a sly smile.

"Better get a convertible. Your big head won't fit in a regular car."

He threw his *big* head back and laughed.

I loved the sound of that. I loved the sound of *him*.

I tilted my head to the side and just stared. "You know, you could be a garbage man on the street with not a penny to your name and I would still love you more than anything, right?"

He grabbed me beneath my armpits and lifted me until my feet dangled above the ground.

"Your arm," I reminded him.

"This is good exercise for it."

His eyes did that thing again. The thing where they saw only me, took in only me. The love he had for me literally turned tangible right there on the sidewalk.

Right there out in the open. I felt people staring, but I couldn't break away from him.

I didn't want to.

"You got something against garbage men?" he finally asked.

I giggled. "Of course not."

The lopsided smile he bestowed upon me caught my breath. And I'm pretty sure the woman standing nearby dropped her bag and stumbled.

"I fucking love you," he growled.

"I fucking love you." I tried to growl the words like him, but it sounded pathetic. And that word… it wasn't my favorite. But he sure liked it.

"You sound like a baby kitten." He sat me down and tucked his arm around me. "C'mon, Smalls. Let's get a ride."

Romeo rented the nicest car on the lot (big surprise there). It was a red convertible and an automatic. I was more excited about it not being a stick shift than I was about it being a convertible.

Not that he would let me drive. But at least this way he wouldn't be using his arm.

As we pulled out of the rental lot, I texted Braeden to let him know we made it safely. And then I texted Valerie the same.

I wasn't sure what our relationship would be like in the future, but I no longer carried any anger or even resentment toward her. I knew she didn't, either. I'd like to think someday we would at least be friends. But honestly, I hoped for more than that.

I laughed out loud when Braeden texted back. Romeo gave me a puzzled look, and I held out the phone to show him.

It was a picture of B dressed in a super heavy coat, a hat, and gloves that he plastered with snow. His last accessory was the large frown on his face.

"I take it he's still pissed we didn't let him come." Romeo grinned.

"Yes, and he's trying to make me feel bad because we're in sunny Florida with no snow."

Romeo laughed, probably because he knew Braeden's pathetic attempt was actually working. I did feel bad he wasn't here. But honestly, I didn't want him to have a front row seat for my messed-up family. My relationship with him was close and untouched by family drama. I wanted it to stay that way.

"You know," Romeo said. "Next week is spring break."

"Yeah, I'm gonna have to spend it catching up on what we miss this week."

Romeo made a rude noise. "We could just stay here, get a place on the beach." He slid a glance my way. "You like the beach? Or does the ocean—"

"Scare me?" I finished.

He nodded.

"I like the beach."

He grinned and held out his fist. I bumped mine against it.

"But I don't swim in the water."

"That's cool," he said. "You on the sand in a bikini is good enough for me."

I rolled my eyes.

"Text B back. Tell him to fly in. We'll pick him up at the airport next week and hang at the beach."

"You seriously want to go stay at the beach?" I asked, surprised. The idea was so… spontaneous.

"Why the hell not? We need a break. Some sun, sand, waves… that's my kind of party. Besides, in a few months, I'm gonna have to leave. Training camp starts, getting ready for the season, the press, the games."

Romeo reached across the seats and grabbed my hand. "I want time alone with you before that happens. I want a whole week with you, drama free."

I wanted that too. Now that he'd planted the idea, I wanted it more than anything.

"We won't be alone if Braeden is with us," I pointed out.

"We'll find plenty of time to be alone." He wagged his eyebrows.

"What about Ivy? And Missy?"

"Invite them too."

"Really?"

"Whatever you want, baby." He kissed the back of my hand.

Excitement filled me. I'd never really had a vacation before. Yeah, my grandparents took me to Sea World and Disney a lot when I was growing up. And I remember we went on a trip to the Keys when my mom was still here. But I'd never had any kind of spring break trips with my friends. I never had any slumber parties in high school. And I'd never stayed at the beach.

But as much as I wanted to go, I didn't have the money to help pay for something like that.

"Don't worry about the money." Romeo groaned, reading my mind.

He interrupted our conversation to ask me which way to turn on the highway. Once I told him, he turned and glanced back at me.

"I want to do this. I can afford it. Let me."

"You haven't gotten paid yet, have you? Don't you have to wait 'til training camp?"

He shrugged. "I can afford this without my NFL pay, baby."

I bit my lip, and he grinned. He knew I was caving.

"Text Braeden," he said. "We'll get on the net later and book a place to stay."

"What if everything is booked?" I worried. It was spring break after all.

"We'll find something," he promised.

I texted Braeden, and he sent me back a picture of him in a pair of sunglasses and holding a bottle of suntan lotion.

He was crazy.

Ivy squealed so loud I had to pull the phone away from my ear. She was supposed to be going home to visit family, but she vowed she would get out of it and change her ticket to come to Florida instead.

Missy agreed but seemed a little less thrilled than Ivy.

"She didn't want to come?" Romeo asked when I hung up.

"She did. I think she's just kind of on the fence about being around Braeden."

"Understandable."

After a few quiet moments, Romeo pulled out his phone and hit a button.

"Driving while talking?" I lectured him.

He hit the speakerphone button and the ringing of the line filled the car.

"Hey, man." Trent's voice came on the line.

"Spring break. Florida. The beach. You in?"

"Seriously, man?"

"Yep. I got the place. You just need the plane ticket."

"Hells yeah," Trent replied instantly.

"Sweet," Romeo said. "Hey, B is coming too. You guys should try and get the same flight."

"Will do."

"Awesome. See you next week at the airport."

When the call was over, he gave me a knowing look.

"Are you trying to set up Missy and Trent?"

"Just evening out the numbers. Can't be outnumbered by a bunch of women," he quipped.

He was totally trying to set up Trent and Missy.

"I'm not sure if that's going to work," I said.

He shrugged. "Well, at least with Trent around, she'll see there are more guys in the sea than just Braeden."

I glanced out the windshield and realized we were almost to my dad's. "Turn here," I instructed.

A few minutes later, we turned into a modest neighborhood with mature palm trees, sidewalks, and houses that weren't new, but not quite old.

Most homes here looked the same. They all had vinyl siding with varying colors. The driveways were concrete, and the yards were fairly simple because the heat made it difficult to have large, full flowerbeds. Almost all the houses had pools in the backyard. Pools were pretty much a staple in Florida. If you didn't have an in-ground, then you almost always had an above-ground one.

Except of course for my house.

My house had an empty space where a pool used to be.

"It's this one," I said. My lighthearted mood evaporated as I gestured to the next street, the street I'd grown up on.

Romeo didn't say anything as he turned and slowed the car to snail's pace.

"It's up here on the left," I said. "Third one down."

Romeo pulled up to the curb of a two-story white home. It seemed smaller now that I was older, less grand and maybe a little worn.

"This one?" he asked.

I nodded, and he cut the engine.

My father's truck was sitting in the driveway. It was a late model, and it too looked a little worn.

"So," I said to Romeo. "This is my house. This is where I grew up."

And as I stared up at the place I'd once loved, an unwanted thought taunted the recesses of my mind.

This is also where your mother died.

CHAPTER THIRTY-SIX

#Buzz on campus is that our resident hottie took his #Nerd off to Florida...
#ItsNotSpringBreakYet
#EarlyVacayOrSomethingMore
... Alpha BuzzFeed

ROMEO

Her nervous energy filled the car. Just the way she stared out the window at the house made me want to wrap my arm around her and drive away.

This was hard for her. I understood why. I just wished it didn't have to be this way.

But wishes were for stars and birthday candles.

This shit was real life.

I stared at the home Rimmel had spent the majority of her life in. It was small compared to my parents' home. It explained the awe I'd seen in her eyes when she'd been inside the first time.

It was a white home with a large window to the left of the front door. The door itself was painted a shade of yellow that I knew had probably once been more vibrant. On either side of the door was a white column that held up a small roof to keep the rain off the entrance.

There wasn't much landscaping, a few large bushes and a palm tree farther out in the yard. I'd bet it was once more kept, but when her mother died, everything changed.

On the right lower side of the house was a one-car garage with a white-painted garage door. Above it was another pair of windows.

There wasn't much detail to the place. It was simple and straightforward, kind of like the girl sitting beside me.

"Think he's home?" I asked.

"His truck is here." She shrugged and reached for the door handle.

"I'll get our bags," I told her.

She came back into the car and touched my arm. "No, don't. I don't know what's going to happen…" Her voice trailed away.

I touched her face. "We'll do whatever you're comfortable with. If you want to go, you say the word, give me a look—whatever. You let me know and we go."

"I'm really glad you're here," she whispered.

"Me too, baby." I kissed her before she got out of the car.

I waited at the end of the driveway, and we walked up the concrete together. Her dad drove a late model Ford pickup. I could respect that.

At the top of the drive, we followed the path that led up to the small porch and front door.

Rimmel hesitated before pulling her key out of her bag and inserting it in the lock. Seconds later, she pulled it back out and glanced over her shoulder. "It's already open."

She dropped the keys back into her bag and pushed open the door. We stepped into a two-story entryway with a small side table and round mirror on the wall. There was mail—weeks worth—piled on top of the table. The floor was tiled, an off-white shade of ceramic with matching grout. The flooring stretched out through the entry, past the stairs, which were to the left, and straight ahead and into one great room that appeared to be the kitchen and living room in one.

Rimmel hung her bag on the wooden post at the bottom of the stairs. "Dad?" she called out.

The walls were painted a neutral beige and the room should have been bright, if the blinds covering the large windows at the back of the home had been open.

We walked farther in. The kitchen was to the right with a large island separating it from the living room. It was a standard kitchen with laminate countertops made to look like granite, white cabinets, and a tiled backsplash.

On the other side of the kitchen near a set of French doors that led to the back was a small dining table.

There was a man sitting there with his head in his hand and a mug off to his side.

Rimmel saw him the same time I did, and her footsteps halted. She stood there like she was unsure what to do, like finding him just sitting alone in a darkened room wasn't normal.

"Dad?"

He rubbed a hand down his face and then dropped his arms and looked up.

"I've been expecting you."

"Gran called you?"

He chuckled. "Oh did she ever."

Rimmel hesitated again, and frustration lit me up. What the hell kind of greeting was this? If he knew she was coming, did he have to be sitting there like this… so morose and morbid?

My heart hurt for her in that moment. It literally ached right there beneath my ribs. Is this how she grew up? Is this how he'd always been?

If so, this went a long, long way in explaining how it was she was so desperate for affection at the age of thirteen that she gave her virginity to some guy down the block.

I wondered if he still lived there. Maybe I'd go beat his punk ass.

"I tried to call," Rimmel said, shaking out of her momentary surprise and moving past the island to open up the blinds on the door and windows. "But you never answer your phone anymore."

"I've been busy," he responded, but we all knew it was a lie.

Sunlight filtered in the room and with it a clearer view of the man sitting a few feet away.

He was probably in his late forties and had dark hair peppered with gray. His skin was weather worn like he spent a lot of time in the Florida sun, which given he worked as a contractor most of his life, I would say it was an accurate assumption.

He wasn't a huge man, but he wasn't slight either. I'd estimate him to be around five foot ten standing and maybe one seventy. Like the house, he appeared as though he'd seen better days, with scruff darkening his jaw, uncombed hair that needed washed, and tired bloodshot eyes.

His flannel shirt was rumpled and I hoped to God he was wearing pants.

"Why are you sitting here in the dark?" Rimmel asked and glanced into the kitchen. She wrinkled her nose. "When's the last time you cleaned?"

"You didn't come here to ask me about my housekeeping skills," he replied and reached for the mug near his elbow. He picked it up and took a slow sip.

Our eyes met over the rim of the cup.

After he swallowed down what was inside, he leisurely lowered the glass. "You the boyfriend?"

"Dad, this is Romeo. And yes, he's my boyfriend. Romeo, this is my dad, Brock." Rimmel motioned for me to come forward.

"Nice to meet you, Mr. Hudson," I said and held out my hand across the table.

He looked at it but didn't offer his. "What the hell kind of name is Romeo?"

"What the hell are you doing sitting in your house in the dark in the middle of the day?" I replied.

I shouldn't have said it. But I wasn't about to let him think I would be pushed around. Or that I would let him push Rimmel around.

"We need to talk, Dad," Rimmel said and pulled out a chair at the table.

Her father looked at me pointedly.

I looked back.

Rimmel sighed. "He's staying. Romeo knows everything anyway."

"And just what is everything?" Brock looked away from me and focused on his daughter. I sat down beside her.

I wondered how long it would take her to notice he was drunk.

"I read the police report, Dad. I know Mom's death is listed as unresolved. I know you were a suspect in the case."

"Then you know they had no evidence that I did anything."

"I'm not here to accuse you," Rimmel said. "I'm here because I want the truth. All of it."

"Your mother was my entire life. When she died, I might as well have died too." He stared at Rim. "I would have killed myself before I would ever kill her."

Did he not hear what he just said? Did he not know what she would read between those lines? He basically just told her she hadn't been enough.

"Rim," I said softly. "Maybe we should let your dad get some sleep and come back, talk then."

"I'm fine," he argued.

Rimmel wrinkled her nose when his alcohol-laced breath wafted out. "Are you drinking?"

She grabbed his cup and sniffed it, then pulled it away like it offended her senses.

"It's been a long day."

"Have you been to bed at all?" she pressed.

"How could I sleep when I knew you were coming here to question me?" he bit back.

She recoiled, and I barely held on to my temper. This guy was a piece of work. I never in a million years expected this when we pulled up to the house.

Rimmel pushed away from the table and snatched his mug. She dumped the contents down the sink.

"I was drinking that!" he protested.

"I'll make you some coffee."

He pushed away from the table and stood. Because her back was turned, she didn't notice how he stumbled a bit.

Thank God he was wearing pants.

"You can't just come home and start bossing me around." He walked into the kitchen and pulled a bottle of bourbon out of the cabinet.

"When did you start drinking?" she asked and snatched the bottle off the counter before he could get a glass. "When you lost your job?"

"I've had a rough couple months."

"I was just home for the holidays. You weren't like this then."

He averted his gaze.

"Or was that just a lie too? You'd go off every day like you were leaving for work, but instead, you'd go to some underground place and gamble away all your money."

"How did you find all this stuff out?" His eyes narrowed. "Those records were buried. What I do when I'm alone is private." He glanced at me. "This your doing? You trying to turn my daughter against me?"

"You're doing a fine job of that all on your own."

"Romeo," Rimmel said, a note of warning in her tone.

I clenched my jaw.

Brock looked back at Rimmel as she finished putting on a pot of coffee to brew. "Is that it, then? You my judge and jury? You here to tell me you never want to see me again?"

"Of course not," she said wearily. "I just want to know the truth." She pinned him with a gaze. "What really happened to Mom?"

"Someone killed her, but it wasn't me."

"Do you know who did it?"

He averted his gaze again.

Rimmel pressed. "Do you know why?"

My entire body went on alert. The tension in the room was rising like a balloon filling with helium. He wasn't in any shape to have this conversation. It was painfully clear to me that he never put the past behind him. He was a haunted man.

The lies he told, the lies he *lived*… they broke him.

The rich scent of coffee filled the room, but he reached for the bottle Rimmel set aside. He grabbed it up, uncapped it, and took a swig directly from the bottle.

"Just tell me," Rimmel pleaded. "*Please.*"

He took another swig and then suddenly chucked it across the room. It made a whipping sound through the air and then hit against the wall and shattered, glass and booze going everywhere.

I jerked out of my chair and rushed to where Rimmel stood. His sudden movements had caused her to throw her hands up over her head. Quickly, I positioned myself in front of her, shielding her with my own body.

"It's my fault!" Brock yelled like he didn't even realize what he'd done. "Is that what you want to hear?"

Rimmel's hand fisted in the back of my shirt.

"I might not have bashed in her head and shoved her in that pool, but I'm the one who killed your mother."

Rimmel gasped at his harsh, graphic language.

"I'm the one who killed her."

CHAPTER THIRTY-SEVEN

#BadPickUpLineAlert
If you were a Transformer
you'd be Optimus Fine.
#ButSeriouslyDontSayThis
... Alpha BuzzFeed

RIMMEL

I couldn't stop shaking.

I don't know who that was in there, sitting at the table in the dark, drinking, but that man wasn't my father.

I didn't let him see how upset I was, because it felt like I was letting a stranger see my vulnerable side.

But Romeo knew.

The second Dad busted that bottle, Romeo stepped in. I knew by the set of his jaw and the tension in his body there was no way I would talk him down.

I admit I didn't even try.

I needed a breather.

So when Romeo told me to wait outside, I did. I took my bag and walked out. I didn't even dare a glance back.

I stood there chewing my nails and listening intently for shouts or breaking glass. But none came.

A few minutes after I stepped out, Romeo did the same.

"What happened?" I rushed out.

"Nothing. I told him to sleep it off and call when he was sober."

"The coffee pot." I worried, thinking I shouldn't leave it on if he was going to be sleeping off the booze.

"I shut it off," Romeo said gently and placed his palm on the small of my back to steer me toward the car.

When the engine was running and the AC was cooling down the interior, I looked at him. "I'm so incredibly embarrassed."

Romeo pulled me across the seats and into his lap. "You have nothing to be embarrassed for."

A broken laugh ripped from my throat. "Are you kidding? He was a complete drunken mess. And he was rude to you."

"I can take it."

"I've never seen him like that before," I whispered. "He wasn't like that growing up. He's a good man. He never raised his voice to me and he never got drunk like that."

"Guilt will drive anyone to their breaking point," Romeo murmured and stroked his hand down my arm.

"You think that's what it was? Guilt?"

"I don't know him," Romeo said rather diplomatically.

I laughed. "No, you don't. Which is why maybe your opinion would be more astute than mine."

"Astute," he mused. "Now that's a college word."

I poked him in the ribs and smiled. Only Romeo could find a way to lighten my mood even just a fraction.

He exhaled and leaned his head against the back of the seat. "I think your father probably carries the guilt of your mother's death every day. He might not have killed her, but he feels responsible. He held it together as long as he could, most likely for your sake. But when you went away to college…"

"No one was here for him to focus on," I finished.

It made so much sense.

And it was incredibly sad.

"Where you want to go from here?" he asked.

"I want to go to my grandparents' house. Gran will tell me everything my father couldn't."

"Want to drive over there like this?" He wiggled his hips beneath my butt.

"I think I'll pass," I said and crawled over into the passenger seat.

"Can't blame a guy for trying."

I shook my head, and he pulled away from curb. A few minutes later, we passed by the house of the boy who took my virginity. Since that day, every time I passed that house, a sick, regretful feeling filled me.

But today, I didn't dwell on it. I looked away. It was in the past and I wasn't about to let one more thing from back then ruin my present.

Gran opened the front door of her house the second we pulled in the driveway. When she stepped out onto the porch and waved, a feeling of love swept over me.

"Gran!" I said and rushed across the driveway and into the grass. She met me halfway and swept me up in a welcoming hug.

"Look at you!" she said, holding me at arm's length. "Have you lost weight? Are those the jeans we picked out together? They look wonderful. So stylish. And your T-shirt, so you."

I laughed. The T-shirt was plain white, but it wasn't so large I was swimming in it. It was more fitted. And in my effort to make it a little more stylish, I chose one with a small embellishment. Off to the side, it had a yellow pocket.

"It's good to see you," I said and hugged her again.

"How was your flight?" she asked.

"Terrifying."

She laughed. I heard Romeo approaching from behind, and Gran pulled away. "And who is this handsome devil?"

Romeo unpacked his megawatt charm-dripping smile. "Ma'am, I'm Roman Anderson. I'm dating your granddaughter."

"I don't know who's luckier. Her or you," Gran teased.

"Definitely me." He winked.

She giggled like a schoolgirl, and I felt my mouth drop open.

"Come along," Gran said. "I have some freshly brewed sweet iced tea with your name on it."

Romeo offered her his arm, and she took it. The pair went ahead, leaving me to stare after them. He held open the front door for both of us, and when I walked past he grinned.

"Where's Grandpa?" I asked, taking in the familiar home.

It hadn't changed since I was a child. It was neat and tidy with a basic layout and basic furnishings. My grandparents weren't fussy people, and they hardly ever bought anything new. My grandpa always said, "If it ain't broke, don't fix it," and according to him, their home wasn't broken.

"Golfing," she called from the kitchen. Romeo was looking at all the photographs lining a shelf. He picked up one of me when I was maybe four. I had pigtails, glasses, and a missing tooth.

"Who's this brat?" he asked with a grin.

"Ha-ha."

Gran bustled in with three glasses of iced tea and a plate of cookies. She looked as she always did, full of energy and youth despite her age. Her hair was gray, but she kept it highlighted so it was a platinum shade and not dull. It was a pixie cut and she styled it so it stuck out in a messy, modern way. Gran was taller than me, probably around five foot five, and had a thin frame. Her eyes were blue, and she always wore nice, matching outfits, even at home.

Basically, we were opposites.

But we loved each other.

"We weren't sure when you were coming, and you know how he is about getting in his games." She set the tray on a wooden coffee table and handed a glass of tea to Romeo.

"It's fine," I said. "I'll see him later." In truth, I was relieved. One less person to have to try and get the truth out of.

"Have you been home yet?" Gran asked, getting right to it.

"Unfortunately."

"Oh, honey. I'm so sorry you had to see him that way." She patted my hand, and I glanced at Romeo. His thoughts clearly mirrored my own.

She knew what kind of state he was in. It made me wonder how often he was like this.

"He was beyond conversation," I told her. "He was drunk."

She nodded, a sad look written on her face. "We've tried to help him. I'm afraid we've probably only made him worse."

"How's that?" I asked.

Romeo picked up a cookie and shoved the whole thing in his mouth. Gran smiled. But when she refocused on me, the smile was gone.

"Your father has a gambling problem. It's been an ongoing addiction since he was a teenager."

The gambling wasn't a surprise to me. But the fact that it started so long ago was.

"He started betting in high school, nothing really major, just boy stuff. Sports, cards, races. When his father and I found out, we put a stop to it. We got him therapy, and he got better. He stayed that way for many years. He met your mother." She smiled softly. "Fell in love, and they got married. They were so young and happy. And when they found out you were on the way, well, life was just perfect."

"So what happened?" I asked. How could a life so perfect go so horribly wrong?

"Life, I suppose. They had you, bought a house, took on a car payment. Your mother stayed home to be with you—something they both agreed on—but I think the sole responsibility to take care of everything and everyone financially started to strain him. He worked hard, long hours. To help blow off steam, he started playing cards with a few of his work friends on the weekends. Poker mostly. I think that's when it started again."

"He didn't go back to therapy?" I asked.

"No one knew what he was doing, and he couldn't admit he had a problem. Then one day they got a letter in the mail about the missed house payments, and your mother was beside herself. When she called, I knew right away what must be going on."

"So what happened?" Romeo asked and spread his arms across the back of the couch. I leaned just a little closer to him.

"We confronted him, of course. He admitted he'd been using all the household money on cards and bets. Your mother was so upset, and that hurt him. He promised to get help."

"But he's still gambling," I said. Clearly, he didn't get help.

"He did stop. At the time. He went to meetings for addiction and got a sponsor he could call. Your mother loved him and she forgave him. We offered to help them as much as we could. Grandpa and I paid the mortgage up so it was current and helped out with a few other overdue bills. The last thing we wanted was for them to lose their home."

"I don't understand," I said. "What does any of that have to do with my mother's death?"

"Because it went beyond the mortgage and utilities. He'd run up a debt of over fifty thousand dollars. He didn't tell anyone that. He was afraid it would push your mother too far and she'd leave him. So despite the help we'd given them, by that point, he was in far too deep to just walk away."

"So he had loan sharks after him," Romeo surmised, his voice tight.

I could only imagine what he must think of my family and, by extension, me. This went beyond a nosey, meddling mother. These were deep-rooted problems… problems that likely caused my mother's death.

"Yes," Gran said. "Look, I don't know all the details. To be honest, I didn't want to know. When your mother died…" Her eyes took on a faraway and sorrowful look. "The details of those, those men just didn't seem important. Maybe revenge should have been my focus or maybe even justice, but this family was too broken."

She looked at me with a regretful frown, and I swallowed thickly.

"You were just a little girl. I don't know how much you remember from that time, but I remember exactly the way you looked when I walked into the house that day. It still haunts me." Gran's eyes shifted over to Romeo. "Her clothes were all stained with pink and her eyes were so hollow it scared me."

"Gran," I whispered. I didn't want to hear about how I looked that day. Sometimes I still felt the panic and shock vividly.

Her eyes met mine. "I didn't do the right thing back then. All I could think about was protecting you and keeping together what family you had left."

"So you lied to the police," Romeo said.

"Not really. They knew about the gambling and that we helped pay up the house. And we didn't know—not when we were questioned—that your mother was killed as retribution for the money he couldn't pay back."

And there it was.

The truth.

It stood out there in the open like a single blooming flower in a barren field. It wasn't something I could overlook, something I could just forget I heard.

My father was responsible for her death. She paid *his* debt… with *her* life.

How terrified she must have been that day. I would never know what exactly happened, but I imagined the men broke into the home, or maybe she let them in, thinking they weren't there to do her harm. And then they killed her.

"Did Dad know right away what happened to her?"

"I think he did. But I think it took a while to admit it to himself, but he couldn't deny it for very long because he was paid a visit by the men who killed her."

Romeo's body jerked. "He saw them?"

"I don't know if it was the same men. But they worked for the man who Brock owed money to. They told him the debt was considered paid in full and if he told anyone anything, they would come back for Rimmel."

I gasped.

"He let them get away with that?" Romeo growled.

"We all did," Gran said. The shame in her tone made me feel sorry for her. "It was a terrible situation, and when the police came up with no leads, no connection to the money he owed to the bookies, we never said a word."

"So her death was listed as unresolved. My mother never got justice for what was done to her."

"They would have put your father in jail, honey. You would have been left with no parents at all. How could I be responsible for you losing the only parent you had left?"

I shook my head. It was all so unreal. To think all this went on while I was lost in a bubble of grief over my mother.

I was the only one who truly grieved for her.

Everyone else was running around trying to cover it up.

"So he kept his freedom, his life, his reputation, and was absolved of all debt," I said, angry. "And Mom. She lost everything."

"He's paid a price, Rimmel. Every day, every minute, for the rest of his life."

"It's not enough," I said and pushed off the couch. I paced, completely agitated.

"I'm not saying what he did, what any of us did back then, was right. It wasn't. But there was no right thing. Our focus shifted to you. To making sure you had a stable, safe environment with as little change as humanly possible."

"But everything was changed!" I yelled. "For years I've been terrified of pools, of drowning. I've been tormented by nightmares and the memory of finding her floating facedown. I felt alone and ignored by Dad because he spent so much time working. He might have still lived with me, but he wasn't present. I've lived half my life thinking what happened to Mom was a horrible accident, but it wasn't. It could have been prevented."

"Rim," Romeo said and moved across the room toward me.

I didn't want to be comforted. I wanted to yell and be angry.

"When I got into Alpha U, I was secretly thrilled. I tried not to show just how happy I was, because I was afraid it would hurt Dad's feelings. But I wanted out. I wanted away from that house, from the memories. And now I know it was my leaving that started all this up again. Maybe if I had stayed, he wouldn't be drowning himself with liquor and gambling again."

"None of this is your fault," Romeo and Gran said at the same time.

A sob bubbled up in my chest, but I used my anger to push it down.

"How bad has it gotten?" I asked, turning to stare out the window. Romeo stayed close, close enough that I could feel the heat off his frame, but he didn't touch me. "How badly in debt is he?"

"I don't know," she replied. "He's upset with us because we told him we wouldn't give him any more money, that we wouldn't bail him out this time. We can't keep making excuses for our son. We can't keep protecting him this way."

"Well, he owes enough that men are following us," Romeo said.

"What!" Gran said and jumped to her feet.

"They see an easy payday because I just signed with the NFL."

Gran was beside herself, asking questions, and I heard the sound of Romeo's voice answering, but I stopped listening.

I was so utterly exhausted. My mind was spinning, and the hurt I felt threatened to strangle me. After a few moments, my anger got the better of me. "Are you going to lie for Dad again when they come after me?"

Gran gasped. "Don't talk like that!"

The words hurt to say, but they always say the truth hurts. My body seemed to drain all at once. I looked at Romeo and he held out his arm. I fell against his chest with a sigh.

"I'll call your grandfather. Sit down. We'll work this out. No more lies."

"I can't," I whispered and pulled back. "I need to think. I need some distance."

Romeo wrapped his arm around me. "We're going to get a hotel."

"You can stay here," Gran offered.

"I think it's better if we don't," Romeo said, and I could have kissed him. He went and grabbed my bag from beside the couch and moved back to my side. "We'll call when we get settled."

Gran's eyes were seconds from spilling a bucket of unshed tears. I couldn't be here when they finally spilled over.

"Rimmel," she called out when we opened the door.

I turned back, and she rushed forward and wrapped me in a hug. I shut my eyes against the emotions pummeling me.

"Everything I did was to protect you. Please remember that. I love you," she whispered.

I pulled away and walked outside.

I was aware of her watching us the entire way to the car and as Romeo backed out of the driveway. When he drove far enough that the house was out of sight, he glanced at me.

"Where to?"

I stared out the window, barely seeing the bright sunshine or the clear blue sky.

"Anywhere but here."

CHAPTER THIRTY-EIGHT

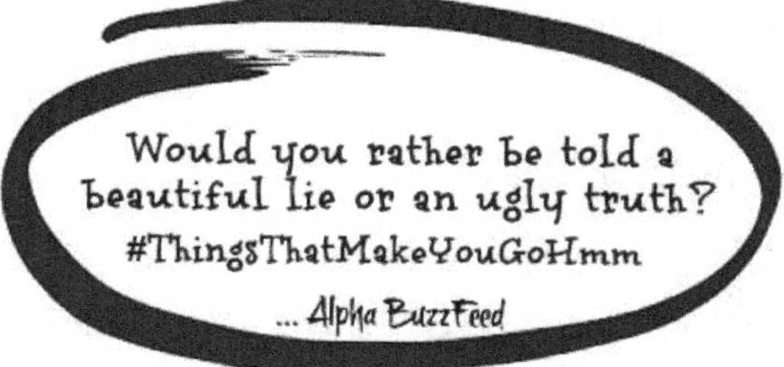

ROMEO

Rimmel now had answers.

Probably more information than she even wanted.

Part of me was beyond livid that my mother set all this in motion.

And the other part of me was glad she finally knew the truth.

I drove to a local hotel, one of the nicer ones we passed. Rimmel sat in a chair in the lobby, looking small and fragile, as I booked us a room at the front desk.

The lady tried to hit on me. Usually, I would deftly avoid it with charm and they wouldn't even notice I was rebuffing their attempts.

Not today.

For the first time ever, the attention I attracted seemed like a bother. I knew that woman saw Rimmel sitting there. We'd walked in the hotel together. I don't know what it was about Rim (her size maybe) that made people think they could overlook her or in some way shove her aside, but it was seriously starting to burn my ass.

When she handed me the keycard and tried to slip me her number, I snapped.

I leaned over the counter like I was going to take it. A glint came into the woman's eyes, and I smiled. "Put that away before you embarrass yourself," I said low. "That girl sitting over there—you know the one who looks like she's had better days?"

The woman's eyes slid to Rim and back.

I nodded. "Yeah, her. Even on her worse day, which is not today, she would still be one hundred times more than you will ever be."

The woman's blue eyes widened and her mouth dropped open slightly.

"Careful," I murmured and pushed off the counter. "You're gonna catch a fly."

I sauntered away, and even though I'd just acted like an ass, I felt a little bit lighter. I was so angry inside that releasing even a little steam was a relief.

No, it wasn't that blonde's fault, but she was the unlucky person I laid eyes on first.

"C'mon, baby," I said quietly when I reached Rimmel. She was resting her chin in her palm and staring down at her lap. She hadn't even heard my exchange with the receptionist.

I wrapped my hand around her upper arm and helped her up before grabbing our bags and reaching for her hand.

"This place has room service. I got a menu. How about a movie, some food, and a hot shower?" I asked once we were in the elevator.

"Replace the food with your arms and you have a deal."

"My arms are a given," I said and wrapped them around her just to prove my point. Her sigh tightened me up inside for so many reasons.

I was her soft place to fall.

I was her strength in that moment.

I was her comfort.

And the sound she just made totally made me semi-hard.

The elevator dinged, and I told my cock to take a chill pill as I led her down the quiet hallway. The carpet was dark green with flowers all over it, which I thought was terrible, but it was clean and plush so I would just overlook the pattern and color.

Along the white-painted walls were sconces every few feet that reflected soft lighting up the walls and out into the corridor. The doors were all very dark hardwood with gold plaques in the center displaying the room numbers.

When we reached the door, I held it open, and Rimmel stepped in before me. We entered a small sitting area, with a small kitchenette to our right. To the left were a couch, small chair, and a television sitting on a large stand. Against the far wall was a window with standard hotel drapes drawn against the sun.

Thank God the carpet wasn't the same in here as it was in the hall. Instead, it was a neutral color that reminded me of sand. The walls were painted white, and the couch matched the carpet. But everywhere else around the room were pops of blue and teal, giving the room a beachy flare.

Rimmel went over and opened up the curtains. From here, I saw the top of a palm tree swaying in the breeze.

Near the kitchenette was the door that led into the bedroom with a king-size bed. It was done in the same colors as the sitting area, with its own flat screen facing the bed.

The bathroom was off the bedroom, and it was nice, with wooden cabinetry, light-colored granite, a single sink, and a tiled shower with a glass door.

"This place okay?" I asked Rim after she wandered around checking everything out.

"You could have gone somewhere less nice," she said. "I wouldn't have cared."

I would have.

After everything I saw and heard today, I wanted more than ever to protect and spoil her. I knew she'd never allow the spoiling, so I had to get it in while I could. And while she was too upset to call me on it.

"I think I'm going to take a shower," she said. "You mind?"

I shook my head. "I'm gonna order some room service. I'm starving."

"'Kay."

"What do you want to eat?"

"I'm not hungry."

"You're right. Steak does sound good."

A ghost of a smile haunted her face. I grinned and walked to her. When she didn't look up, I tilted her chin with the back of my hand. "When you're ready to talk, we'll talk."

"I don't want to talk."

Maybe she didn't now. But she would.

"You heard everything I heard," she burst out. "Talk about a screwed-up family. I don't know how to feel. Angry or grateful!"

"Grateful?" I echoed surprised.

"Grateful that they shielded me from it all for as long as they did. I was so messed up for years after Mom died. I gave my virginity to someone who didn't even like me."

My back teeth slammed together. Just the thought of that pervert who took advantage of her made me want to hit something.

Her hazel eyes, which were a warm honey tone at the moment, stared up at me wide and bleak. "Can you imagine what I would have done if I'd known everything else that was going on back then?"

"I honestly believe you would have found your way to the girl you are right now no matter what," I whispered.

She leaned her head against my chest and groaned. "How do I forgive him for this?"

Up until that point, I'd been rubbing her back, but her words made me pause. I knew she meant her father, and the truth was I wasn't sure she could. Or should.

"I don't know," I finally answered.

I know I'd just met the man, but my dislike went all the way to my core. I knew he was sick, he had an addiction, but because I never dealt with anything like that before, I couldn't understand it.

How could a man go so far down the wrong path that it cost his wife her life?

And even more, how then could he sweep the truth under the rug and not get her the justice she deserved?

Yeah, it was done for the sake of love for Rimmel… but that just wasn't a good enough excuse for me. Maybe because I was standing here right now holding her as her heart shattered over everything he'd done.

Rimmel looked up, her eyes watery. "What if I can't forgive him, Romeo?"

Rimmel's capacity for forgiveness and trust went beyond anyone I'd ever known. And I told her that.

She snorted. "Are you kidding? I've been so suspicious of people my whole life I never let anyone in."

"Until me." My chest swelled a little with pride.

"I didn't want to let you in either."

I tucked a strand of hair behind her ear. "But you did. And then you let in Braeden. And Missy and Ivy. I even think some part of you has forgiven my mother."

She started to roll her eyes and make an excuse, but I caught her chin and shook my head. "You let us all in, and, baby, when you let people in, you do it all the way. You can't help it. It's just the way you are."

"But this is different."

"You're right. It is. I don't know if you will ever be able to forgive him, but I do know it's nothing you need to worry about right now."

She pulled in a deep breath and stood back. "I love you."

Those three words never failed to pull at my chest. "I love you, too."

I watched her close herself in the bathroom with her bag full of toiletries, and only when I heard the spray of the shower did I blow out a frustrated breath.

I was fucking pissed.

Turns out my asshole moment at the front desk hadn't help dispel any of my anger.

Like at all.

I felt like a pot of boiling water, bubbling and steaming so hard the lid was threatening to blow right off.

I hadn't expected all this when we boarded the plane. I expected her dad to own up to making some mistakes, to having a gambling problem, and launch into a whole thing about how he felt guilty for his wife's death.

I really didn't expect him to actually be guilty.

Sure, he wasn't the one who physically killed her. But he might as well have.

And Rimmel had to live with that. She had to live with the lies she'd been fed at such a young age. What totally blew my mind more than anything else was that her grandmother vowed they did everything to protect

Rimmel, but in their attempt to protect her, they essentially left her floundering through life in the dark.

So what did she do?

She made some mistakes, some very costly mistakes.

And then she retreated into herself. She retreated into a place where she just wanted to be invisible.

But last semester, things changed for her. And they changed for me. She came out of her shell but stayed true to the person she wanted to be.

And now here they are once again, throwing her back into the dark.

I wouldn't have it. Rimmel would not exist in a world of secrets and lies. Rimmel was light and truth. Her family hadn't protected her.

But I would.

I stalked across the room and pulled out my cell and shot a quick text to Braeden.

I MIGHT NEED U EARLY

His reply was instant.

JUST SAY THE WORD

He didn't even know everything that was going on, yet he would be here. *That* was family. *That* was what it was to be there for one another.

After I ordered room service, I connected my laptop to the hotel Wi-Fi and searched around for a place to rent for spring break. It took a couple tries to find something that was available, and it ended up being a much bigger house than we needed, but I booked it anyway.

We needed a vacation. A getaway from all the damn drama.

The shower shut off, but Rimmel didn't come out right away. I listened for any sounds of muffled crying but didn't hear any, but it didn't really make me less angry.

Unable to sit any longer, I got up and prowled around the room. I watched the people out the window and turned on the TV in the sitting room to some old movie. When the bathroom door opened, I was in the other room, staring out at the palm trees.

"Romeo?" Her voice was soft, almost like a whisper.

She was standing in the doorway of the bedroom, with nothing but a towel wrapped around her body. Her hair was brushed out and fell down her back like a dark waterfall, making my fingers itch to run through its softness.

"You're angry," she said. "I can feel it vibrating off you and filling up the room."

I felt bad that she knew how pissed I was, but energy didn't lie, and I could only hold it in so long. "Yeah." I acknowledged the truth.

"Is it me you're angry with?" The hesitation and the nerves that laced her words had me spinning around from the window.

I closed the distance between us swiftly and took her by the shoulders. "Why would I be mad at you?"

"For dragging you into this mess. If it wasn't for me, you wouldn't have greedy, dangerous bookies following you around, snooping around in your career and threatening to ruin everything you've had to work so hard for."

I threw back my head and laughed. "You think this is about my career?"

"It's already been almost ruined once because of me. If this got out, blackmail, gambling, and God knows what else, you'd be thrown out of the NFL."

"You're right. I am pissed." I paced away from her.

I heard her swallow even from across the room.

"I'm pissed that *you* are being threatened. I'm pissed that no one—not even your own father—had enough guts to stand up for you. To fight for *you*."

"But—" She began.

"Don't you get it yet?" I cut her off. My words came out more harshly than I intended. But the emotion was so clogged up inside me there was no other way to speak at that point. "You're my once in a lifetime. Not football. Not the NFL. Not money. *You.* I could—I would—walk away from everything and anything. But not from you."

I surged across the room and took her face in my hands.

"Never from you," I whispered.

"Romeo."

I fused our mouths together, never breaking contact for even a second, the friction of our lips creating electricity that skittered down my spine and tingled the balls of my feet. Rimmel surrendered to my touch and to the sensation throbbing between us, and her hands wrapped around my wrists, clinging to me.

Suddenly, all that anger eating me up inside turned to stark, white-hot passion, the kind neither one of us could deny. Her skin was still supple and damp from the shower as my hands left her face and slipped over her shoulders.

The towel around her was tied in a small knot just above her breasts. My fingers grasped it, desperate to pull it free.

But I stopped.

I tore my mouth away and looked into her eyes. "Tell me yes, baby."

"Yes."

I flung the towel onto the floor and tugged her hips to bring her up against my body. My cock was already so hard it hurt, and I pushed my hips into her as we kissed.

Her hands were deft as they slid up beneath the hem of my T-shirt and caressed my stomach. I felt my muscles jerk in response because my skin was so sensitized in that moment I was afraid if she kept touching me, I'd cream in my jeans.

I pulled back, and her heaving chest only drew my eyes down to her puckered nipples as they begged for my attention.

I palmed the back of my T-shirt and ripped it over my head and let it join her towel. I managed to get the button on my jeans undone before she came at me, and I lifted her until her legs were wrapped around my waist. I spun and pinned her back against the wall. As if her body knew exactly what I would do next, she arched back and my mouth descended on one of her breasts.

I sucked the silky flesh into my mouth as a groan vibrated my throat. Rimmel dug her hands in my hair and held my head at her breast while I kissed and sucked until she was rocking her core against my stomach.

When she couldn't take it anymore, Rimmel yanked my hair so my head came up, and her teeth caught my lower lip. I pulled away from the wall and carried her to the bed where I laid her across the middle.

The little vixen didn't stay where I put her, though, and she sprung back up and reached for the waistband of my jeans. I helped her pull them off, and she licked her lips when my rock-hard cock was finally free.

I meant to push her back on the bed and take her deep and hard. But she had other ideas. Her hand gripped the length of my shaft and pumped it. Once. Twice. Then she lay out on her belly, propped up on her elbows, and took me deep into her mouth. The tip of my cock hit the back of her throat, and she purred. The vibration was sort of like a momentary trip to heaven, and I moaned.

I glanced down as she began to work my rod, and all I could see was her luscious bare ass on full display. I admired the way her narrow waist tapered into softly curved hips and gave way to her small, rounded ass. There wasn't a blemish on her creamy skin, and I started to reach out to palm one of those cheeks, but she did this thing with her tongue…

My eyes rolled back in my head.

She must have known I was about to come because she released my cock and pressed it up against my belly as she gently sucked and kissed my balls.

I grabbed the back of her head and guided her around until she'd licked and kissed every inch. Just as she was about to take my throbbing length into her mouth again, I pulled back, denying her.

She looked up at me, her face still dangerously close to my swollen head. Moving fast, I leapt on the bed, straddling her naked body, and let the underside of my hard length rub against her back as I massaged her shoulders.

Her body went pliant under my touch, and I moved down so I was kneading her bare ass cheeks and parting her thighs so I could see her wet and ready center.

Her bud was already swollen and glistening, calling out my name. I flicked a finger over it, and she shuddered. So I did it again and again. Reflexively, her thighs jumped apart farther with every tease until I was able to fit myself between them and dive in.

She gasped when my mouth hit her from this angle. I'd never done this to her from behind. But judging by the way she raised her little ass up in the air and pushed it toward me, I would say she liked it.

I tasted her and sucked her anxious clit until her knees were shaking and she couldn't hold her hips up any farther. I pulled back and flipped her over. Rimmel's cheeks were flushed, her lips swollen, and her hair fell over the end of the bed and trailed toward the floor.

"Romeo, please," she murmured and wiggled her hips.

I plunged into her without warning, taking her hard and deep just as I craved. The total possession I felt in that moment was unparalleled to anything I'd ever known.

I rested my weight on my good forearm and elbow and used my free hand to caress her cheek. We touched from chest to toe as I rocked myself into her again and again.

I knew when she was close because her head tilted back and her chest arched into mine. I buried my face in her neck as I pounded in her one last time.

We fell together. Both of us lost in the same world of sheer bliss. I don't know how long it lasted, only that it was so complete time didn't matter.

My heart was still pounding when I forced myself off her so she would be able to breathe and collapsed on the mattress right beside her.

"I needed that." She sighed.

I laughed. "That right there was some good shit."

"Amen," she replied, and I laughed again.

There was a loud knock at the door, and the person on the other side yelled, "Room service!"

I'd forgotten about the food.

"Hang on!" I yelled and jumped up to grab a pair of basketball shorts out of my bag and pull them on.

Rimmel giggled and ran into the bathroom to hide.

"Get your sexy, naked ass out here, woman!" I yelled when the waiter was gone.

She came out wearing her glasses and one of my T-shirts. It wasn't naked, but it sure as hell would do.

"Dig in," I told her, giving her a ride-by kiss on my way to wash up. When I was done, I inhaled my steak, potatoes, and salad. Then I ate some shrimp.

Rimmel ate, but not as much as I wanted. But I kept my mouth shut, because me badgering her to eat wouldn't make her feel any better.

I discovered she ate more when I fed her peeled shrimp right from my fingers.

She was spoiled.

When she was finished eating, she went for the coffee maker in the kitchenette, and soon the bold scent of brewing coffee filled the room.

"You feeling better?" I ran my fingers through her hair when she plopped into my lap.

She nodded. "Are you?"

"How could I not be?" I gave her one of my best smiles.

"Can we just stay here the rest of the night? Coffee and TV in the bedroom?" Her voice was wistful.

"Sounds like a plan to me."

Neither of us moved. The coffee was still brewing, so there was no point in getting up until it was done and she could pour a cup.

"I'm going to the police."

Her words were a bomb to the sex and steak-infused good mood I had going on. "You're going to turn your father in?"

"It's the only way." Her voice was sort of flat, so it was hard to know what she was feeling.

"The only way for what?"

She sat back and looked at me. "To make sure this doesn't hurt you."

I swore. "I told you not to worry about me."

"Me not worrying about you is like you not worrying about me."

"Don't you sass me, Smalls," I warned.

"If I go to the police and tell them everything, they can find the man who's been following you and who threatened me. They can shut that whole ring of whatever it is down."

"And what about your dad?" I asked gently. "He isn't innocent in all this."

Her teeth sank into her lower lip. "I know. He's probably going to get in trouble. A lot of it. But maybe he'll get some help too. Maybe finally owning up to all his mistakes will help him heal."

"And what about you?" I picked up her hand and pressed a kiss to the back.

"What about me?"

"How will you feel knowing you're the reason your dad's in prison?"

"I'm not the reason. His actions are the reason. His consequence is me trying to set everything right."

I smiled. "You're one smart cookie."

"No." She sighed. "I'm not. I just don't want anyone else getting hurt. Especially you."

Her fierce need to protect me never failed to surprise me, even though I felt the same about her. Being on the receiving end of that kind of love was something I never thought I'd experience. "As long as you're okay, I will be too."

She dragged in a deep breath and nodded. "I'll call them." She started to get up, but I pulled her back down.

"If you want to call the police, I won't stop you. Hell, I personally think it's a good idea."

"But?"

"But sleep on it first. You may feel differently in the morning." *And if you decide not to do it, I will understand. I won't make you choose between your father and me.*

She tilted her head to the side and stared at me. "Okay. First thing in the morning."

"Good. Now go get your caffeine so I can get you in bed."

She smiled a lighter smile than I'd seen her wear for quite a while. "Just knowing there's a solution to all of this, a light at the end of the tunnel, makes me feel a lot better. The police will know what to do. It's their job."

I watched her bound into the kitchenette toward the coffee. I didn't tell her I didn't think it was going to be that easy. I let her have any small amount of peace she could.

But me?

I knew it was going to be a hell of a lot harder than she realized.

CHAPTER THIRTY-NINE

#We'reScrewed
A home intrusion occurs every thirteen seconds.

... Alpha BuzzFeed

RIMMEL

The coffee didn't keep me awake.

The last thing I remembered was snuggling close to Romeo in the center of the king-sized bed, cradling the warm mug, and laying my cheek against him.

He turned on a movie, but I couldn't tell you the title. I was too lost in my own head, with my own thoughts, and the comfort I was drawing from the man so close beside me.

In a strange way, his anger made me feel better.

Not that I wanted him to be so twisted up inside, but because no one had ever been angry like that on my behalf.

Not my father.

Not my grandparents.

My mother would be, but she wasn't here.

When his vivid blue eyes focused on me and I heard the ferocity with which he said he would fight for me and was angry *for me*, the life I thought was crumbling around my feet suddenly didn't seem so desolate.

I knew Romeo couldn't be my crutch. I knew I needed to find other ways to get through all this than just by leaning on him. And I would. I was strong. Stronger than I ever realized. But it sure did help that I wasn't alone.

When I awoke, the room was dark, the TV was off, and there wasn't a hint of light in the cracks beneath the curtain.

The mug of coffee was gone, and I assumed Romeo took it before I could dump it everywhere, because the bed was dry and so were we.

His breathing was steady; his heartbeat was sure and strong beneath my ear. I pushed in a little closer against him and shut my eyes so sleep could claim me once more before reality intruded on the drowsy comfort I enjoyed.

But it wasn't my thoughts that intruded.

It was a sound.

I listened intently, trying to figure out where it was coming from and what exactly it was. It was sort of like a scuffle or a muffled scrape.

But then it stopped.

I lay there listening intently for a few minutes, and when no other sound came, I told myself I was being silly. It was likely the person in the room beside us entering or exiting their room.

Hotels were bound to have noises, and none of them would sound familiar to me.

It made perfect, logical sense.

So why did I suddenly feel so creepy?

It was like the day I'd been in the dorm bathroom and thought I was alone… but I hadn't been.

The thought was just too disturbing, and I opened my eyes.

The darkness was intruded upon by a sliver of soft light. I lifted my head very slightly to look out into the sitting room. A beam of golden light from the dim hallway stretched across the carpeting. It was there and gone so fast I wondered if I was seeing things.

By the way adrenaline surged through my bloodstream and my heart rate galloped against my ribs, I knew that it wasn't my imagination. It was real.

Someone was in this room.

Someone who hadn't come to bring us tea and cookies.

I swallowed and slid my hand around Romeo's waist and tried to signal him awake by tapping against his side. I was afraid to call out his name and alert whoever was in here that I wasn't asleep.

But time wasn't on my side, and I lay there desperately trying to think up some amazing plan to outsmart this person.

I patted Romeo again, harder and more fiercely than before.

I felt him jerk awake, and I squeezed his side.

"What's the matter?" he asked, and I cringed.

So much for being quiet. And so much for an amazingly smart plan.

There was a much less muffled noise—okay, it was downright loud—and Romeo understood immediately why I woke him.

"What the—" He began, the sleepy quality to his voice evaporating instantly.

But he didn't finish his sentence.

At the same moment, two men rushed into the room. A hand wrapped around my bare ankle, the one I'd thrown over the top of the comforter in my sleep.

(Side note: if this wasn't a lesson as to why you should always sleep with the covers up to your ears, then I don't know what was.)

Everything happened at once.

I shrieked, and Romeo lurched up.

A light flicked on.

I was yanked out of Romeo's arms, out of the comfort of the bed, and was roughly dragged down the mattress until there was no bed left at all.

At the last second, I grappled for the blankets, the edge of the mattress, anything that would keep me from being pulled any farther.

But it was useless. My hands came up empty, and with one last great tug, I was pulled completely off the bed and plummeted toward the floor.

It wasn't a far fall.

But that didn't mean it didn't still hurt.

I landed like the most ungraceful swan that ever lived. Like someone who just performed the greatest belly flop in the history of belly flops.

I would have hit my face if I hadn't reflexively brought up my arms to protect it. I was glad I wasn't wearing my glasses, because those might have cut my face with such a hit.

"Rimmel!" Romeo roared as I flipped onto my back and kicked at the man who was still gripping my ankle.

My foot finally connected with something soft, and the man cursed and loosened his grip enough that I could pull away.

Romeo seemed to materialize from above me, literally launching himself off the bed like a battering ram. He hit the man who pulled me off the bed, and the pair collided, both going down in a heap.

Romeo pulled back his fist to pummel the man he landed on and got in a few solid hits before the second man pulled him off his partner.

But Romeo didn't stay down.

He jumped to his feet and went at the second man as the one who grabbed me cradled his injured face.

Romeo was trained like an athlete—he was an athlete. And his football skills kicked in. He went in low and caught the man around the hips, and the force behind his hit sent the two men out into the sitting room, out of sight.

Panic like no other clawed at me when Romeo moved out of the room. I wasn't scared for me. I was scared for him. I had no idea who these men were or what they wanted.

They could have a gun.

He could be shot.

The thought sent me scrambling up off the floor as I ignored the pain that radiated through my body. I didn't have time for pain.

I ran forward, but the man on the floor caught me around the knees. I started swinging my fists downward to do some damage of my own, but it didn't seem to work.

Before any damage could be done at all (except to my pride), he stood and dragged my body back against his.

I felt the cold, sharp edge of a blade press against my throat, and my struggling stopped.

"I oughtta fricken slice you right now," he growled in my ear.

Out in the other room, the sounds of furniture overturning and the breaking of glass were more alarming than the knife at my throat.

"Go ahead," I challenged and lifted my chin for even more access to my throat. Inside, I was screaming at myself for being so crazy. But outwardly, someone else was taking over. Someone who was going to call this guy's bluff. "Do it. Something tells me if you do, you won't get whatever you came here for."

He didn't say anything, but he didn't let go. He towed me out into the other room, keeping the knife against my flesh.

The room was a mess from what I could see. The lamp in the corner had fallen over and busted. The only light we had was from the bedroom. The cushions on the couch were all over the room, the coffee table was on its side, and Romeo was on top of the intruder and in motion to deliver another punch.

"Let him up or I'm gonna make this one here a shish kebob," the man holding me called out.

I felt ridiculous and weak in that moment. Here Romeo was kicking ass, and I was standing there with a knife to my throat. If I hadn't been so easy to get ahold of, Romeo probably could have knocked out one guy and came for the other.

I was nothing but a liability. I prayed to God it didn't get us killed.

Romeo dropped his arm and looked over his shoulder. When he saw the position I was in, his eyes narrowed. "Get your hands off her."

"Up," the man holding me ordered.

The man beneath Romeo started struggling to get up, and a muscle clenched in his jaw. Even though I saw the desire to punch and fight, Romeo stood up, angling his body so he had his back to no one.

The man on the floor got up. He had a busted lip and a cut on his cheek. As soon as he stood, he plowed his fist into Romeo's midsection.

I screamed, and Romeo bent a little from the force of the hit.

Screw the knife. I started fighting, kicking my legs and pinching the man who held me with my hands.

"Hold still, bitch."

"Fuck you!" I yelled and struggled harder.

The knife pierced my skin, and I yelped. The warm feeling of blood oozing down my neck alarmed me.

"Oh fuck no!" Romeo roared and lunged at us. The man who punched him grabbed ahold of him and towed him back.

"I wouldn't if I were you." The distinct sound of a gun being drawn changed the dynamic of the entire room. "This gun will make that knife wound look like a scratch," he intoned.

"You have a gun?" Romeo spat. "Why the fuck didn't you pull it out when I was pounding you?"

"Because we need you alive," he replied. "For now. But her? Her life isn't as important at the moment."

So now I had a gun and a knife pointed at me.

Oh, fun times.

Romeo held up his hands in surrender. His face was dark with anger, but I also saw defeat. He wouldn't do anything that would put me in danger. Including saving himself.

"Stop pointing that at her," he said roughly.

The man with the gun glanced at him with a smirk. "You giving me orders?"

"I'm assuming if you don't want me dead, that means you want something from me. I can tell you right the fuck now you won't get shit, not even a conversation, while you're pointing a gun at my girl."

The gunman considered that and then swung the barrel and pointed it at Romeo.

"No!" I cried. "Point it back over here."

The man laughed. "Ah, young love. So willing to die for the other."

"Keep it here," Romeo said, his voice level. He patted his chest. "Right here."

When the gun didn't move away from him, he glanced over. "Drop the knife."

"No," the man holding me said.

"Drop. It." Romeo growled.

He laughed.

The man with the gun sighed. "Just put it away. I think we have their attention."

"Whatever you say," he replied, and the knife against my throat was pulled away.

I jerked away from him. He didn't grab me again, but he did step up so close that I could feel his body against mine.

I shuddered because it was so disgusting.

"What do you want?" Romeo asked and inched closer to me.

The gunman noticed and demanded he stop.

"So much for being a reporter," Romeo said.

I gasped. I hadn't realized it at first with everything going on and the fact I wasn't wearing my glasses, but the man with the gun was the same man I saw at the shelter fundraiser and the same man Romeo said was posing as a reporter.

"I report things," he defended. "I've been reporting what you've been up to for weeks."

"To who?" Romeo asked.

He shrugged. "My boss."

"Who's your boss?"

"That's on a need-to-know basis. And you don't need to know," the gunman said and number two laughed like it was a funny joke.

He was a clump nugget.

"Then tell me what I do need to know," Romeo said.

"My boss is owed some money, money that her screw-up of an old man hasn't paid."

I knew it was going to be this. We knew. Still, it sucked to hear. I was being attacked just like my mother had been all those years ago.

"What the fuck does that have to do with her? Go get it from him," Romeo said, not a hint of regret in his tone for offering up my father.

"We could do that," he allowed. "But all that would end in is him being killed and my boss being out of the money he's due."

"Maybe your boss shouldn't loan people money who ain't gonna pay it back."

"Oh, he's gonna pay, just like they always do. There's always that one soft spot in someone's life to make anyone pay."

And that soft spot was me.

I laughed. "I don't really think my dad cares much about me right now. Or anything for that matter."

"No." The man agreed. "But he does." He grinned at Romeo.

"I don't have any money," Romeo lied.

Well, actually, I don't know if it was a lie. I had no idea how much money Romeo had. I knew he hadn't been paid yet for his NFL contract, but I never asked him how much he had personally. I didn't care.

Both men laughed. "You really think we would come in here like this if we didn't know you had money?"

"Big deal." Romeo shrugged. "So you snooped around in my business. You know I'm due a big payday for my NFL contract. Then you should also know I don't have that money yet."

"You can get it," the guy said.

Clearly, he had no clue how business and contracts worked. Or maybe he did. Maybe that's why he had to use threats to get what he wanted.

Romeo laughed. "I'm a rookie. I don't have access."

"We saw you sitting with Ron Gamble the other night. We know you're his new golden boy. Get it."

Romeo shook his head.

The logic and rational thought in this room was fleeting. These men clearly were idiots.

But that made them dangerous. Idiots didn't care how they got what they wanted so long as they got it.

"Five hundred grand. We want it tomorrow night. We'll be in contact with a meeting place. Be there with the cash or we're gonna kill her."

Rage burst through me, and without thinking, I lifted my foot and slammed it down the shin of the man nearby and stomped on his foot. He howled in pain and bent forward.

I elbowed him in the face.

Romeo leapt over to me, grabbing my arm and pushing me behind his body. His body was so tense that I was afraid he would snap at any second.

"Shit," the gunman swore. "She's a damn girl. You're an embarrassment."

The man I elbowed growled and came at me. Romeo blocked him. With his fist.

"Don't bother calling the police," fake reporter with the gun said once his friend fell back on his butt.

"We'll know, the deal will be off, and you'll be looking over your shoulder, wondering how we're going to kill you."

"You can't kill us!" I spat. "The cops will know it was you!"

"There's a lot of ways to kill someone. Car accident. Accidental overdose. Undetected carbon monoxide poisoning. A lot of those accidents are hard to prove as murder."

He finally lowered the gun and strolled closer on his way to the door. Thug number one was right behind him.

He stopped close to Romeo, who tensed.

"Imagine walking into a room and wondering if the air was filled with an odorless gas that could possibly kill you. Did you change the batteries on your smoke detector? Were they good batteries or bad? And what about the beer you just ordered at the bar? Did you look away for just a second? Is there something in there that could possibly kill you? Just living would be a torment. When death finally comes, it will be a relief."

I was shaking. The way he talked, so nonchalant about our deaths, made my skin crawl. It was like he just didn't care about human life.

Romeo stared him right in his eyes. "If I don't pay and you kill us, your boss will still be out the money he seems to desperately want."

The gunman smiled. "We don't like to kill people. We're peace-loving folk. It's why we're giving you this nice chance to make things right. But we only offer one chance. After that, the loss is just considered temporary. But your death?" he said. "And hers? Well, that will be forever."

The two men let themselves out of our room, quietly closing the door behind them.

Both of us stood there silently digesting the shit that just went down.

In all honesty, when all that stuff with Zach was going on, I never really thought he would kill anyone. I never thought Romeo or I could die.

But these men… they were in a whole other class.

They weren't unbalanced and unstable like Zach.

They were calm and in control.

And right now, they held our lives in the palms of their hands.

CHAPTER FORTY

ROMEO

I was a player.

Someone was trying to play me.

Good thing I was good at the game.

CHAPTER FORTY-ONE

Don't poke a bear with a stick and then be surprised when he attacks you.

... Alpha BuzzFeed

RIMMEL

Romeo recovered faster than I did.

It was like this air of certainty, of knowing, came over him and that was that.

He turned to me and held out his hand. I gave him mine, and he gently towed me into the bathroom and flicked on the light.

He didn't say anything when he lifted me and sat me on the countertop. He curved a finger beneath my chin and tilted my head back to give him a better view of my neck.

I wasn't sure if it was still bleeding. I couldn't tell. It was sticky, wet, and stung.

"Doesn't look too deep," he said and went about running water over a clean white cloth from the linen shelf nearby. Leaving the water running, he wiped away the blood, rinsed, and then repeated the action several times.

"I'm really tired of seeing marks on you, Smalls," he murmured as he worked. "This shit is enough to drive any sane man to murder."

I dropped my chin to glare. "*You* are nothing like those men. You are nothing like Zach or even my father. You're better than that, Roman Anderson. I don't ever want to hear those words out of your mouth again."

A half smile tipped the corner of his lip. "Is that an order?"

"Oh yes," I assured him. "And I'm serious." I wished I had a better one-liner to quip back, but I didn't. His words scared me. I would never forgive myself if he did something he could never take back because he thought it was what he needed to do to protect me.

He pushed up my chin and continued dabbing lightly. "Well then, I guess I better get a Band-Aid on this cut so I'm reminded of how much I hate it."

"Is it bad?" I asked.

"Nah. But it's deeper than I thought. That guy is a—"

I pushed my fingers against his lips so he couldn't finish the sentence. "He's gone."

Romeo nipped at my fingers playfully, and I jerked them back. He tossed the cloth into the sink and picked up my hand, pressing a kiss to the very fingers he'd just nipped at.

When he was done, a serious note crept into his tone. "They'll be back."

"We should call the police."

"I'm not calling the cops."

"What!" I shrieked. I swore when this was all over, I was going to need blood pressure medicine.

"You heard 'em. Don't call the cops."

"So you're going to do what a bunch of criminals tells you to do!"

"I'm not taking chances with you." He caressed my cheek.

"Romeo. You can't be serious. You just plan to hand over half a million dollars to a bunch of murdering extortionists?" Then I paused. "Do you *have* half a million dollars?"

He laughed. "Sure you want to know?"

I shook my head instantly. "I really don't care how much money you have."

"I know, baby." His eyes warmed on my face like the sun just burst through a dark cloud. He took a second to kiss me quickly. When he pulled back, he said, "I never said I was handing over any money."

"I think hitting my head has confused me." I groaned. He was talking in circles, and I really just didn't have the energy for that right now.

His eyes sharpened on my face. "You hit your head?" Romeo delved his fingers into my scalp and started moving around as he searched for a lump. "Do you feel dizzy? Disoriented?"

All trace of our conversation was gone. His sole focus was me.

I grabbed his wrist. "I didn't hit it that hard. Just bumped it when I fell off the bed."

He searched my eyes, making sure I was telling the truth.

"That was just a poor attempt at a joke."

"You're bleeding again," he said and started dabbing at my neck once more. When he was finished, he announced he'd searched through all the stuff hotels leave for guest use and found a small box with two bandages inside.

After one was applied, he lifted me off the counter.

"So you aren't going to pay them?"

"Hell no. If I pay them, it wouldn't be the end. If they didn't kill us to tie off loose ends, we would become their favorite plaything. They'd never stop trying to get money out of me, and if I keep playing in the NFL, my salary is only going to go up."

"But you don't want to call the police?"

"An underground gambling ring? A loan shark with enough money and power to have his guys find you all the way up in Maryland, then follow us back here? These aren't smalltime criminals, Rim. These guys probably have half the police force in their pocket. It's probably why they're still able to operate."

I gasped. "Do you think that's why they let my mother's death to go unresolved, because the cops on the force looked the other way?"

"I don't know. But frankly, after everything, I wouldn't rule it out."

"Romeo?" I asked and moved to sit on the side of the bed. All the covers were on the floor from when I tried to hang on to them as I was being pulled off.

"Hmm?" he said, clearly deep in thought.

"Do you think the men that were here tonight are the same men who killed my mother?"

"No," he answered definitively. "The men who killed your mother would be older. Those guys didn't look old enough. They would have been too young all those years ago."

"Do you think the guy my dad owes money is the same guy from all those years ago?"

A disgusted look crossed Romeo's face, and it made me feel ashamed. I knew he told me I shouldn't be embarrassed by the things my father did and it had nothing to do with who I was.

But I was.

Deeply ashamed.

Romeo dropped down in front of me and placed his hands on my bare knees. "I really don't think so. Gambling is an addiction, so I guess I can understand why he went back to it after all these years, even if it was the reason your mom died. But to then borrow money from the man that killed her? No one could be that sick."

"I think I need to see him," I announced. I needed more than a drunken encounter and more truth from his lips.

"We'll go as soon as the sun comes up." Romeo promised.

• • •

I nodded and touched his face. He didn't have a mark on him, but I knew he'd taken some punches. "Are you okay? Did they hurt you? How's your arm?"

"I'm fine," he assured me. "I take harder hits on the field."

"But your arm."

He shrugged. "I probably shouldn't have used it to throw some punches, but there was no helping or stopping that."

"Do you think you reinjured it?" I chewed my lower lip.

"I really don't, baby. It feels fine."

"Maybe you should wear the sling today. Minimize movement."

He rolled his eyes and I saw the denial on his lips when he glanced back at me.

But then he sighed. And gave in. "If it'll make you feel better."

I smiled.

He shook his head and stood. "Just so we're clear, this doesn't mean I'm whipped."

I smiled. "Maybe you should hand over your man card." I held out my hand. "I'm gonna need to tell Braeden about this."

He groaned. "Woman, don't make me come over there."

I laughed, and he pulled the sling on and positioned it in place.

"I might like it if you came over here." It surprised me that I was able to joke at all. It gave me hope that everything was going to be just fine.

"Baby, you know I would. But I can't. I got some calls to make. Shit to do."

Calls to make? What kind of calls?

When he didn't elaborate, I began to worry. "Romeo?"

He came across the room, grabbed his cell off the nightstand, and kissed me on the top of my head. "I'll pick up the mess out there."

"What are you going to do?" I asked.

"Take care of this."

That was *not* an answer.

That was just downright scary.

"What are you going to do?" I repeated.

He pretended like he didn't hear and walked out of the room.

He wasn't calling the cops; he said so. And he wasn't calling the bank; he said that too. So what was he doing?

CHAPTER FORTY-TWO

#EarlyMorningMusings
I could be a morning person. If morning started at noon.
#PassTheCoffee
... Alpha BuzzFeed

ROMEO

I made some calls.

Then a couple more.

I was aware of Rimmel watching and wondering. I didn't want her involved. Maybe it was macho. Maybe it was controlling. Maybe it was me being an asshole.

Or maybe it was all of the above.

But I loved her.

That was the bottom line. I was going to do whatever it took to keep her safe and out of harm's way. Someone had to.

Good Lord, this girl was like a walking disaster. And I thought her clumsiness was the worst hazard to her health. Until I met her family.

Even Dr. Phil couldn't fix that shit.

I wasn't even going to try to fix her family. Those relationships would fall where they may. I would leave that up to Rimmel. She could decide how much of them she saw and let them into our life. I would support her no matter what.

But I would also keep her safe.

I felt her trying to listen in on my calls. I felt her watchful eyes. Finally, I told her I was going down to the lobby to snag us some breakfast from the spread they set out every morning. She wanted to come. Of course she did. So I said yes. She was surprised, but really, it worked to my benefit.

I didn't want to leave her alone in the room. So we went downstairs together and into the dining area. I left her there and walked over to a vacant spot in the lobby and finished what I was putting together. I could still see her, but she couldn't eavesdrop.

When she saw where I'd gone, she frowned and then sat down and turned her attention to her phone.

I was calling in a Hail Mary.

A play that was a little desperate, a little crazy, but if I pulled it off, it would end all this once and for all.

Everyone I'd spoken to was on board so far, and my father was also helping set things up. I probably wouldn't have been able to do it without him. He knew a lot of people that were able to help.

I waited for a call back from him to let me know it was all a go.

While I waited, I dialed the last person I needed to call.

Ron Gamble.

Calling him was the biggest risk of all. The truth was what I was about to ask of him could get me tossed out of the NFL forever. It could end my career. I meant it when I told Rimmel I would give up my career for her. I hoped it wouldn't end that way, but if it did, I would accept my fate.

Ron was a big piece in this plan, but I'd waited to call him last because I wanted it to be a decent hour.

His secretary answered after a few rings, and I asked for him. The woman reminded me of a bulldog and almost refused to put him on the line. Frankly, I would have been impressed if it didn't piss me off.

"Look. I get it. Assholes call for him all time. This is Roman Anderson. His new quarterback. I need to speak with him. It's an emergency."

The bulldog in her went back to its cage. "Hold, please."

A few seconds later, Ron came on the line. "Anderson?"

"Yes, Mr. Gamble. I'm very sorry to disturb you so early."

"I'm always available for my players. Bonnie said it was an emergency."

Bonnie was a very nice name for a bulldog.

"Yes, I'm afraid it is. And unfortunately, this is going to sound very unprofessional and frankly, a little crazy, but I wouldn't ask if it wasn't absolutely necessary."

"Unprofessional and crazy you say?" he intoned.

"Yes. And yes, I'm aware if I piss you off, my career will be over before it starts."

"A career ender," he mused. "Then whatever this is must be important."

I glanced at Rimmel picking over her plate of food. "You have no idea."

"Let's hear it."

I didn't waste his time or beat around the bush. I laid it all out on the line. Everything I needed, crazy and all.

He was so silent sometimes I worried he'd hung up on me.

When I was finished, I fell quiet.

Ron whistled between his teeth. "I liked that girlfriend of yours. She was a breath of fresh air. Can't say I'm too thrilled to hear about someone threatening her like that."

I didn't say anything.

"And I know the season hasn't started, but you're a Knight. The ink on the contract is dry. I plan on getting a lot of years out of you on the field."

"I sure as hell hope so," I muttered.

"I don't take too kindly to two-bit criminals threatening my players and trying to extort money out of 'em."

Hope rose up inside me.

"I'll do it."

I pumped my fist in the air in triumph. "Just let me know if there's anything I can do in return."

"Oh, there is something I want," he said.

The feeling of victory vanished, and I was left with a pit in my stomach, wondering what he was going to say.

And then he told me.

I smiled.

CHAPTER FORTY-THREE

RIMMEL

YOU'VE BEEN GONE FOREVER!

The text from Ivy made me laugh.

IT'S BARELY BEEN TWO DAYS

YOU GONNA TELL ME WHY U LEFT IN SUCH A HURRY?

I wasn't sure how much I wanted to tell Ivy. Not because I didn't trust her, but because this was so crazy and I was still mortified. It seemed like I could barely wrap my head around it. How would she be able to?

Plus, I wanted to enjoy spring break. I didn't want the reason we were all here to begin with to ruin it.

WHEN U GET HERE.

It wasn't a lie.

Per se.

I could just tell her I needed to see my father, that he was sick. He was. Not necessarily physically, but he sure was mentally. I just didn't have to elaborate on that fact.

I ALREADY BOUGHT A NEW BIKINI

I giggled.

Romeo glanced at me from the driver's seat. "Ivy?"

I nodded, and he shook his head. "That girl is high maintenance."

"Hey, she's my friend," I said in her defense.

"I know." He reached across the seat and patted my leg. "She's grown on me. I like her too."

"Really?" I pressed.

"Yeah, really. Seems like she wants to make some changes in her life."

"I think what happened with Zach really shook her up. I mean, getting so drunk and not really knowing what she was doing? And with him? It was a wakeup call."

***I DON'T EVEN HAVE A BATHING SUIT,* I typed back to her.**

OMG!

It wasn't like Ivy was an alcoholic or anything. She did like to party, and drinking was definitely part of that. And it did seem for a while, she'd been searching for something. I wasn't sure what that could be until she told me she was going to get a man, but not *trying* to get a man.

It made me think maybe she was a little lonely. Maybe that was why she partied so much. To fill a void.

But then Zach happened. Getting so drunk and sleeping with him, letting him into our room where he violated my stuff… it was too much.

I was proud of her new resolve.

MISSY EXCITED? I asked.

I THINK SO. THINK IT WILL BE WEIRD WITH B AROUND?

ROMEO INVITED TRENT TOO

OOOH. INTERESTING.

Romeo pulled up to the curb at my dad's house. I really, really hoped he wasn't drunk again. I shot off a quick **TTYL** and then shoved my phone into my bag.

"This time next week, we're gonna be lying on a beach," Romeo murmured and wrapped his palm around the back of my neck to knead the knotted muscles.

"I've never had a vacation like that before. And definitely not with friends." I purred as the knots seemed to loosen.

"This is just the beginning," he said soft.

But I had to get through this first. I let go of the dreamy beach thoughts and focused on the house. I wasn't even sure what I wanted to say to my dad. But I had to say something.

"Rim?" Romeo said, pulling the keys out of the ignition. "Would you mind if I ran a couple errands while you're with your dad?"

"What kind of errands?" I asked suspiciously. Romeo was being so secretive about whatever he was planning. He told me he didn't want me to be involved, and he told me why.

But I just thought his reasons were stupid.

Well, okay, him wanting me safe wasn't stupid. But sidelining me was.

"I won't be gone long. I'll get you a latte while I'm out."

I tilted my head and studied him. "Make it a Frappuccino and we got a deal."

He held out his fist for me to pound it out.

I did it, but then I held out my pinky.

"Your finger got a cramp, Smalls?"

I laughed. "Boys pound it out. Girls pinky swear."

He looked at my finger like it was a baby alien from Mars. "I'm not a girl."

"I'm not a guy."

He ran a hand over his head and then chuckled. His pinky was like twice the size of mine. When he wrapped it around mine, I shook them. He seemed amused, but he didn't say anything else.

"Don't be gone too long, okay? I'm not sure how this will go."

"You think I'm going to dump you at the curb like a cab driver?" He shook his head.

"You aren't?"

He muttered something beneath his breath and got out of the car. I followed suit (without the mumbling), and he took my hand when we both stepped into the grass and walked forward.

"I'm coming in to make sure he's not in the same frame of mind as yesterday. If he is, I'm staying."

"I called to tell him I was coming. He didn't sound drunk when he answered the phone." I didn't add that I was surprised he answered at all. I chose to believe it was a good sign.

I knocked this time instead of walking right in. I felt this invisible line, this barrier between us that I never used to feel when I came home. But I guessed I should stop thinking of it as home because it wasn't anymore. Maybe that's why I felt the need to knock.

The first thing he said when he answered the door was, "You didn't have to knock."

He was dressed in clothes that weren't wrinkled or needed washing, a pair of jeans and a dark T-shirt. His eyes were still bloodshot and he still looked incredibly tired, but at least his expression wasn't glassy. At least he appeared sober.

"Hey, Dad. I just didn't want to intrude if you were busy."

He gave me a sad look and motioned for us to come in. Romeo followed me, so I figured he still wasn't satisfied he could leave.

Lord, I felt like I was suddenly being watched by an overprotective nanny.

My dad cleared his throat and looked at Romeo. A hint of embarrassment flushed his cheeks. "I regret we had to meet like that yesterday. As far as first impressions go, I would say mine was an epic failure."

Romeo smiled to soften the blow of his honesty. "We all have bad days."

Dad held out his left hand, and Romeo shook it. "What happened to your arm?" he asked.

"Broke it."

Dad lifted his eyebrows, and I knew he was going to start asking a million questions.

"You have the blinds open," I said in a lame attempt at interrupting.

"Yes, and I made coffee," Dad said, going ahead into the kitchen. "Would you both like some?"

"Actually, I'm going to go. Give you two a little bit of one-on-one," Romeo replied.

Dad stopped in his tracks and turned to meet Romeo's stare. "Checking me out before you leave her here, huh?"

"Yes," Romeo said without apology.

"I like that," he said, sizing Romeo up.

"I don't like the fact that I have to worry about leaving her with her own father."

Dad's face paled, and I gave Romeo a WTF look.

He ignored it and stepped forward to kiss my head. "I'll be back in an hour. Call if you need me." He let himself out.

I avoided looking at Dad until I couldn't. He was staring at me with an amused expression on his face.

"What?" I demanded.

"I like him."

"You like him," I echoed.

"Coffee?" he said and moved to lift the pot.

I followed behind him as he poured two mugs and got out a bottle of creamer that hadn't even been opened yet.

He probably went out and bought it this morning. He probably didn't even have any food in this house yesterday.

Sorrow swept over me. And so did guilt. I'd gone away to college only to return between semesters and on long breaks. The rest of the time, he'd been here, alone with nothing but his guilt and his pain.

I reminded myself that a lot of that was his own doing.

But it still didn't stop me from feeling bad about it. He was my father after all. I couldn't just turn off my love for him. I poured some of the cream into a cup and handed it to him. Then I poured some for myself.

"Rimmel, I want to apologize for yesterday. My behavior was totally unacceptable. I knew you were coming, and instead of making sure you felt welcome, I drowned my guilt and tried to hide in the bottle."

"Do you drink like that a lot?" I asked.

"More than I should," he admitted.

"I need to know why," I said, getting right into it. "Why did you let Mom's murder go unresolved when you knew what happened?"

He set his coffee down and walked away, over to the windows that once overlooked the pool in the backyard. He was quiet a while, and I waited.

"I could tell you a million different reasons. Half of them would be partially true. And the other half would just be lies," he said, clearing his throat. "But the truth is I was scared. Scared and so ashamed."

The pain in his words was so raw and so real that I knew this couldn't possibly be a lie. Plus, in all my life, I'd never heard my dad say that.

"I was scared of what would happen to me if I told people about the gambling debt. I thought I would go to jail or be charged with murder. I was scared those men would come back for me. Or for you. I was scared if I ratted them out, life would only get worse."

"Did you feel bad that Mom never got her justice?" I asked, my voice low and hoarse.

It was a hard thing to realize your parent was only human too. That they too experienced all the heartache and struggles that everyone else endured.

"Every single day of my life," he whispered.

"I don't understand why you would start gambling again. Wasn't what happened enough to keep you away from it forever?"

"One would think. And it did. For years and years. But then one night, I found myself standing in front of a bar with a poker tournament starting up. The next thing I knew, I was playing cards and falling deeper into that world."

"You ran up half a million dollars in debt, Dad. How could you do that?"

He turned and furrowed his brow. "I don't owe anyone that much money."

Frustration had my back teeth coming together. "Don't lie," I accused. "I know."

"I'm not lying. Who told you that?"

I told him about what happened this morning in our room. I told him about the guy following Romeo around and digging into all his personal information.

He seemed shocked and outraged all at once. Then the fear took over. "It's happening again," he whispered. "I can't pay, so they're going to come after you."

"It's not me this time, Dad. It's Romeo."

"And he'll pay the money, keep you safe?" His voice was hopeful.

"I'm not sure what Romeo is going to do." It wasn't really a lie, because I didn't have a clue.

"I'm losing the house," he said. "It's being foreclosed."

"Maybe it's better this way," I replied honestly.

He swung around. "You're not upset?"

"Why would I be?" I asked.

"Because this was where your mother was."

"She also died here," I said, frank.

He seemed taken aback and a little unnerved.

"I don't need a house to remember Mom. I remember her here." I laid a hand over my heart. "She wouldn't want us, you, living in this house day after day, tormented by what happened."

Tears filled my father's eyes.

I hadn't seen him cry since Mom died.

"You're a good girl."

"You raised me," I said gently. "You're a good guy, but, Dad, you need help. Like serious help."

He pressed his lips together and nodded. "I'll get it. Right after I take care of the guys who are harassing you."

"No," I said firm. "We don't need your help. What you need to do is focus on yourself."

"So that's it?" he said, heat coming into his voice. "*We* doesn't include me anymore. It's just you and him?"

"Romeo has been there for me. Really there. And it's not fair for you to be angry when you're the one who put me in this position."

"Let me make it up to you."

"You can make it up to me by getting help. Rehab."

"I don't know if I'm ready."

"Well, I guess that's a choice you're going to have to make. But if you want me in your life at all, you will do it."

"Are you saying you'll cut me out?"

"Yes," I replied. It was the hardest thing I ever had to say and mean. But I did. "And, Dad? I can't promise when all this is said and done the police won't be paying you a visit. I won't protect you like Gran and Grandpa did for all those years."

He hung his head. "You shouldn't have to."

The weight of the conversation was almost too much to bear. So I went to the sink and started washing all the mountains of dirty dishes.

As I washed, we talked some more. There was so much to say yet nothing at all.

The truth was out, and the truth didn't need disguised by excuses or pretty words. The truth was what it was. Talking about it wouldn't change a thing.

Eventually, he asked me about school and classes. I never told him about the scholarship thing and the plagiarism I was accused of. It seemed pointless to bring up something that was already resolved. I told him a little about Zach and the attack, but I didn't go into a lot of detail.

By the time I was finished with the dishes, cleaning the floors, and generally tidying up, I was exhausted. I didn't want to talk anymore.

The doorbell rang a short time after that, and I think both Dad and I sighed in relief, grateful for a distraction from the tension between us.

I ran to open it and smiled wide because I knew I'd see Romeo.

But he wasn't alone.

Someone was standing on the tiny porch beside him.

My eyes bounced back and forth between them.

Finally, I put my hands on my hips and gave them both a stare. "What's he doing here?"

"Tutor girl!" Braeden said and burst forward to sweep me up in a hug.

"Braeden, I'm thinking you got on the wrong flight. Spring break isn't for days," I said against his shoulder even as I hugged him back.

Behind us, my father watched me interact with my two guys, but he didn't say a word. I felt bad again because he probably felt like I'd moved on, made my own life that didn't include him. I had found a life and people I loved, but cutting him out wasn't part of that. Yet.

"I knew you missed me. I had to come," B said. When I stepped back, he grinned down at me.

I rolled my eyes and looked behind Braeden at Romeo. He was holding a giant Frappuccino with chocolate drizzled over the huge pile of whipped cream and smiling his most charming smile.

That only meant one thing.

I wasn't going to like this.

"Braeden?" I said. "Why are you here so early?"

He threw his arm across my shoulders and grinned. "I'm your new babysitter!"

CHAPTER FORTY-FOUR

#ISmellTrouble
A last minute press conference?
Something is up.
#KnightFootball
... Alpha BuzzFeed

ROMEO

He just had to announce it like that.

"I'm your new babysitter," I mimicked and then grimaced.

He just liked causing little ripples between Rim and me. It was the big brother way. But I didn't like it. I thought it was time Braeden found himself his own lady so he had someone else to focus on other than mine.

Rimmel glared at me. "You flew him out here to babysit me?"

"I flew myself out here." Braeden objected.

"Be quiet," we both told him at the same time.

"A guy flies all this way," he muttered, "and no one's glad to see him."

We ignored him.

"I just thought it would be a good idea for him to be here right now," I said, not wanting to go into a lot of detail, but also fully aware of the watchful eye of her father.

"You didn't think it would be a good idea to talk to me about this?" she pressed, hands on her hips.

She looked cute trying to be all rawr with me.

"You two can have your little spat later," B said. "Introduce me."

Rimmel seemed to deflate like an old balloon. I noticed the exhaustion that wrapped around her like a thick blanket. Quickly, I glanced around, looking for signs of any kind of argument. I didn't see any broken glass. In fact, the place was a lot cleaner than it was yesterday.

When I saw the huge pile of freshly washed dishes drying on a towel, my mouth flattened. She cleaned while she was here. She felt responsible for him. I didn't want that for her. It shouldn't be that way.

"Dad, this is Braeden. He's Romeo's best friend," Rimmel said, gesturing between the two men.

Braeden cleared his throat. Loudly.

Rimmel rolled her eyes. "He's also my self-appointed big brother." Then she smiled and added, "And one of my best friends too."

Braeden ruffled her hair and then held his hand out.

"Brock," her dad said as they shook. "Nice to meet you."

When the introduction was over, silence fell over the room.

Brock cleared his throat. "Anyone want coffee?"

"Sure," B replied before anyone else. He followed Brock into the kitchen, and I shut the front door.

Rimmel stepped up close. "Why would you involve him?"

I sighed. "Because having someone I can trust here to keep an extra set of eyes on you is important."

"Romeo," she sighed.

I pulled her against me and whispered into her hair, "This will all be over tomorrow night. Just hang in until then."

"Fine."

"How'd it go here?" I handed her the coffee.

She took it, wrapped her lips around the straw, and shrugged. "It was fine. Good, actually. We talked."

"He willing to go to rehab?"

"I think so." She frowned. "That is if he doesn't go to jail first."

"It's gonna be okay," I said again.

The sound of phones going off echoed through the room. Rimmel made no move to dig hers out of her bag.

"Rome!" Braeden called. "What's this all about?"

Rimmel and I walked into the kitchen where B and Brock were standing. Braeden was starting down at his phone.

"What is it?" I asked.

"The newest Buzz." Rimmel held out her hand for his phone, and he gave it to her while I pulled mine out of my pocket.

Ron Gamble announced a special press conference later this afternoon. The plan was being set into motion.

"Do you know what this is about?" Rimmel asked, looking at me.

"I have an idea," I allowed.

By the look on her face, I knew she knew I wasn't going to say anything else. To my surprise, she didn't say anything, just took another pull of her drink and sat down at the table.

It made me feel bad because clearly she was too tired to even argue with me.

But then I reminded myself why I was doing this and my resolve strengthened.

When the press conference went live on a local station in Maryland, I knew it would hit the sports channel and other news outlets right after, but instead of waiting, we pulled it up online. Back in the hotel room, the three of us gathered around the screen while Ron Gamble took his position at the microphone.

"I called this conference today because I have an announcement. It's rather disappointing and will likely come as a surprise, which is why I decided not to just release a statement to the media."

Flash bulbs were going off in front of him, but Gamble didn't even flinch. He acted like he didn't even see them.

"The recent signing of Roman "Romeo" Anderson as the Knights newest quarterback is no longer valid."

A ripple went through the crowd. Rimmel gasped and glanced at me.

"This is highly unusual because once a contract is signed, its iron clad. However, due to recent information that has come to light, I have made the decision to dissolve the offer. Our highly skilled team of lawyers have voided the contract, and all parties have been notified. Mr. Anderson is no longer part of the Maryland Knights. There is no additional interest in him as a player by the NFL at this time. Mr. Anderson is no longer a free agent with the National Football League."

The people gathered at the conference all started talking at once, yelling out questions and demanding a larger explanation.

My stomach turned a little because even though I knew what was really going on, I didn't like any of this.

Ron held up his hand and the crowd quieted. "I am not at liberty to discuss any further details at this time. This is a private legal matter, and the institution of the Knights would appreciate you respect those boundaries."

With that, he walked off the stage.

The station cut to the news anchor, who talked a little more about the announcement, and then it went to commercial.

Rimmel pushed out of her seat. "What the hell is going on!"

"I'll explain later," I said.

She looked at Braeden, who didn't seem the least bit worried about the conference.

"Why aren't you two going crazy with this news?"

"Do you trust me?" I asked.

"You know the answer to that."

"I'll explain everything tomorrow night."

I don't think any of us really slept that night. Rimmel was too worried about what was going on, and I didn't want to go to sleep and miss someone trying to break in here again.

Instead, I surfed the internet and watched Ron Gamble's news spread like wildfire, farther and faster than I even hoped. The pure fact that he said he legally couldn't discuss his reasons for kicking me off the team fueled the fire.

Everyone loved a good secret.

It was what I was counting on.

When the three of us went out to breakfast, reporters were waiting. They swarmed around us and tried to get quotes and pictures.

After breakfast, we holed up in the room again, but even still, the reporters waited downstairs.

In the early afternoon, my cell phone rang. It was the men I was supposed to meet.

"Do you have the money?" a low voice demanded.

"I tried to get it. It cost me my job."

"You get that money or we'll kill the girl."

"Where do you want to meet?"

He named off some random address, probably in the worst part of town.

"Are you kidding?" I said. "I can't make it there alone. There are reporters camping out in the hotel, following my every move."

There was some silence and some swearing on the end of the line. "Make it happen."

"You want me to lead a bunch of reporters to you, I will. Maybe they can run a story on the fact you're extorting money from me, threatening murder, and got me fired from the NFL."

"We have nothing to do with your job."

"You think Ron Gamble is stupid?" I said. "You know he's powerful. The minute I tried to get an early advance on my salary, he knew something shady was going on. He's accusing me of illegal gambling. Of betting."

"Just bring us the money."

"Come get it," I countered. "You can get in here unnoticed. Me leaving will draw too much attention."

There was some silence on the line. It stretched so long I started to worry they wouldn't go for it. That all these lies would be for nothing.

"Fine. We'll be there tonight. After dark. Be alone."

"Okay." I didn't have to fake the nerves or anxiety in my voice.

"You better have the money. If you don't, those reporters are going to be reporting your murder."

The line went dead.

Braeden and Rimmel were watching me.

I tried not to show them how freaked out I was getting. If this went wrong, we could all end up dead.

"We got work to do before nightfall," I said.

And then I got to work.

• • •

CHAPTER FORTY-FIVE

RIMMEL

The sun was dropping lower in the sky when Romeo ushered Braeden and me out into the hall.

I felt the way he watched everything and stared into every corner of every space we were in. His hawk-like attention made me extremely nervous.

I couldn't understand what he was doing.

Or where we were going.

Then he knocked on the hotel room door beside ours.

After several seconds, the door opened soundlessly and Romeo motioned for us to go inside. The three of us walked in, and the door shut and locked behind us. I spun to see a man in a black suit and red tie standing there.

"Mr. Anderson," he said. "I'm Agent Marks. We spoke on the phone."

"Of course," Romeo said and stepped forward to shake the man's hand.

"Agent?" I asked.

"Ma'am," he replied and then produced a very shiny official-looking badge. "I'm with the FBI."

My eyes widened. "The FBI," I echoed. I turned to Romeo. "I thought you said no cops."

"He's not a cop." Romeo shrugged.

I narrowed my eyes.

He sighed. "Well, he's not local. None of them are." He gestured farther into the room where there were several other men dressed just like Agent Marks.

"I couldn't take any chances that the local cops weren't involved."

Agent Marks nodded and moved into the other room. "We've actually had this area on our division watch list for a while. Several of the police officers are suspected in illegal activities. We just haven't come up with enough evidence to make any arrests."

Romeo called the FBI. He set up an entire sting in just one day.

This was the kind of stuff that only happened in movies. It was so hard to wrap my head around it being real life.

"Just breathe," he murmured against my ear.

"So you're sure they will come here?" Agent Marks asked. "You sold it to them?"

Romeo stepped forward. "If you've watched the news or the sports channel at all, then you know I sold it to them. Gamble and I went to extremes to make sure I was being followed by reporters so I couldn't leave this hotel."

"You're not really fired?" I asked.

Romeo smiled. "Hells no."

Braeden laughed.

Agent Marks signaled three guys in the room who nodded and grabbed up bags full of God only knew what.

Romeo produced our room key, and they took it and disappeared.

"The room will be wired heavily so you won't need to be," Agent Marks told Romeo.

What did that mean?

"You have the money?" he asked.

The agent gestured to a black briefcase on the nearby table. "May I?" Romeo asked.

The man inclined his head. Romeo popped the top, and when he opened the lid, rows and stacks of money stared back at us.

"You're going to pay them!" I gasped.

"They won't get out of that room with that case, ma'am," Marks said.

"It's a trap, tutor girl," Braeden whispered.

"A trap," I echoed.

Romeo moved across the room and offered his hand to Agent Marks. "Thanks for coming through. I really appreciate this. These guys are scum."

"Of course. We were quite excited when your father called. As I said, we've been trying to take down this ring for a while now."

"So they know everything?" I asked nervously.

Romeo glanced at me, a little regret in his eyes. "Everything."

Agent Marks turned to me. "We're going to need a full statement from you. I've reviewed your mother's file, and I'm certain I can have the case reopened immediately."

"What about my father?" I chewed my lower lip. I know I said if he had to do jail time, that was his price, but that didn't mean it wouldn't be hard.

"He's not innocent in all this," the agent said. "But he's also not the big fish we're after. We're hoping he will cooperate with this case and give us names and additional evidence we can use to bury these guys in jail for the rest of their lives."

"Will my father go to jail?"

"I can't make promises. But I can tell you if he is cooperative, we'll be willing to cut him a deal. He'll get more leniency."

At this point, it was the best I could hope for. "And what about us?" I asked.

"We'll be free," Romeo said.

The agent moved away and pulled up a laptop and a few tablets. He did some things and then the sound of the men over in our room came through.

"What if they suspect something when we give them the money?" I asked.

Romeo shook his head. "You won't be in the room. You're going to stay here. With Braeden."

I shook my head adamantly. "You're not going alone!"

A hard look came into Romeo's blue eyes. "You're staying here. And I won't be alone. That's why the feds are here."

"This is all very elaborate," I said, weary.

Braeden put his arm around me. "Go big or go home."

Going home sounded pretty good at the moment.

"Ma'am," the agent said. "If you could come over here. I'll take your statement and get a report started."

I answered so many questions I lost track of them all.

But the one thing I didn't lose track of was the clock. Darkness was approaching quickly and with it was danger.

CHAPTER FORTY-SIX

ROMEO

All we could do was wait.

Because they never gave a specific time, I had no idea how long this could take.

I was sitting in the hotel room with only a briefcase full of cash to keep me company. Rimmel was in the next room with Braeden, and I knew she wasn't happy about it.

Once this was over, I would have all the time in the world to make it up to her. Assuming something didn't go wrong and they killed me.

It was well after midnight when I heard a sound at the door. My body tensed, but I stayed where I was. I wasn't about to go open the door and make it any easier for them.

Seconds later, two men slipped into my room and shut the door behind them.

I clicked on the lamp nearby, and they jerked around to face me.

"Evening fellas," I said.

Their eyes bounced around the room with paranoia, and that made me nervous.

"Where's the girl?" the man who pretended to be a reporter asked.

I snorted. "You threatened to kill her. You think I wouldn't keep her away?"

"You better have every last cent of that money or it won't matter where you stashed her. We'll find her. We'll kill her. Just like that mother of hers."

My blood ran cold, and I jumped up. "You killed her mother?"

The men enjoyed the reaction they got. "Regretfully, no. But her killing set a precedent among the underground world of gambling. It's what inspired our boss to go into business for himself, and that old man was such an easy target."

"What the hell are you talking about?" I growled.

"A couple drinks, a few free games of poker, and some organized wins was all it took to get dear old daddy back in the game. He racked up a whole pile of debt before he even knew what hit him."

"You son of a bitch," I growled and launched across the room. My fist connected with his jaw and his head snapped back on his neck. "You fucking conned him."

The man rubbed his jaw and smiled. "Well, with his daughter cozying up to a rising football star, how could we not? The possibilities are endless."

How long have they been watching Rimmel? Months? Years? The thought made me sick. Even though this had been a big gamble, I knew then it was the right thing. They wouldn't have stopped here. They would have kept trying to extort money from me, or worse.

I pulled my fist back to pound him again. The sound of a gun cocking stopped me.

"I wouldn't if I were you." his friend said, taking aim at me.

"You shoot that gun," I said, slyly alerting the agents next door, "and kill me, this room will be swarming with people before you can get out."

"That's what silencers are for," he rebutted and casually screwed it onto the end.

"Where's the money?" reporter guy demanded.

"Over there." I pointed.

I stayed where I was while he went to get the case. After he opened it and was satisfied it was all there, he snapped it shut and smiled.

"Pleasure doing business with you." He moved toward the door.

"Wait," I said and then gave the signal the feds needed to get here. Now. "That's it, right? You'll leave us alone? You'll leave Rimmel alone?"

Not even two seconds later, the door burst in and several agents dressed in head-to-toe gear swarmed the room.

"Freeze!"

The man with the briefcase shrieked and tried to run. He was knocked down and his hands were cuffed behind his back. "We're going to kill you for this!" he roared. "You son of a bitch."

The other man, the one with the gun, stood there in shock, like it never occurred to him that he would get caught.

"Put down your weapon!" one of the agents said and aimed at the man. "Hands in the air!"

It seemed to jerk him back to reality. He glanced at the man holding a gun on him, and this dark look crossed his features.

Oh shit.

He didn't drop the gun, he turned toward me with revenge dripping from every pore and took aim.

"Drop the gun!" the agents yelled.

He pulled the trigger.

It all happened in slow motion.

The bullet cut through the air, a clear path right for me.

Another shot went off and then another.

The bullet hit its mark. The force of it threw me backward.

Pain, white-hot and sharp, was all I knew as I fell to the ground.

Chaos broke loose around me.

CHAPTER FORTY-SEVEN

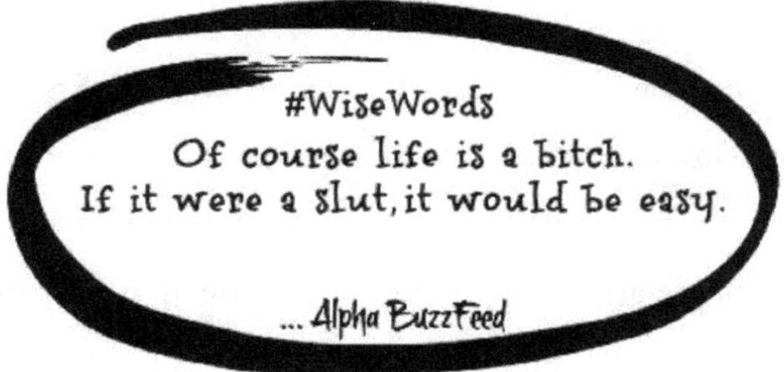

RIMMEL

The second I heard the shot go off, I ran for the door.

Braeden tried to pull me back, but then more shots were fired.

Both of us went rushing out into the hall, ignoring the orders from Agent Marks, and into the room next door.

There was a man in handcuffs screaming.

A forgotten briefcase full of half a million dollars on the floor.

The other man, his name I would never know, lay slumped half on the floor and half against the wall. He was dead from multiple gunshot wounds.

"Romeo!" I yelled, desperately trying to locate him in all the chaos of the room. Braeden saw him first.

"Rim, why don't we just move back for a minute." His voice was hoarse and his face had gone white. I avoided the attempt he made to pull me in; it only made me more frantic.

I rushed around one of the agents standing in my way.

And then I saw him.

He was sprawled out on the floor with an agent leaning over him.

A cry ripped from my throat, and despite the orders for me to get back and the demands that someone "get her out of here," I ran forward and dropped to my knees beside him.

I couldn't even see clearly. I was too busy sobbing. The tears taking over my vision were unstoppable. I ran my fingers through his crazy blond hair and whispered his name through my tears.

"Ma'am," I heard someone say but ignored them.

Someone tried to pull me away, but I fought them until Braeden appeared and pulled them off.

"Just give her a minute," he said. I heard the pain in his voice, and it only made me cry harder.

I heard the agent talking, saying something to Braeden, but I was beyond listening.

I laid my head against his stomach and sobbed. I would never forgive myself for what happened here today.

Never.

I might still be breathing, but my life was over.

Seconds later, a hand brushed at my hair.

"No," I pleaded. "Let me stay with him."

"Wouldn't have it any other way." The familiar voice jarred me.

My sobbing stopped instantly.

"Romeo!" I sat up and looked down at his eyes, his incredible blue eyes, which were staring back at me.

"Hey, baby." His lopsided smile made me start crying all over again.

"I thought you got shot!"

"I did."

I gasped and began searching his body for the wound, looking for a place to apply pressure. "Why aren't you bleeding?" I demanded, my brain still not catching up to everything that happened.

"I'm bulletproof."

"Roman Anderson, you are a lot of things, but bulletproof is not one of them!" I yelled. "Now is not the time for your big head!"

Above us, Braeden laughed. "He's good. Just give them a minute."

The agent and B moved away. Romeo sat up, a grimace pulling at his mouth.

"You shouldn't move!" I said, dashing away some of the tears staining my face.

"I'm wearing a vest, sweetheart. I'm fine."

I grabbed his T-shirt and tugged it up. Sure enough, there was a bulletproof vest strapped to his chest.

"You're an asshole!" I yelled and then collapsed into his arms to cry some more.

"I know." He agreed and held me close. "But I'm an asshole who loves you."

I snorted and then wiped my snotty mess of a face on his shirt. It already had a bullet hole in it; it's not like I could make it worse. "I don't ever want to go through this again."

"Me either." He agreed. I looked up at him, and he wiped a tear off my cheek. "It's over. We won the game."

"Everything's going to go back to normal?" I asked.

He smiled. "I don't think we'll ever be normal. But I can guarantee we're going to be happy."

It was more than this #nerd could ever ask for.

HAPPILY EVER AFTER

RIMMEL

The stadium was packed full and the crowd was going wild. The Knights were having their best season yet, and the entire state was absolutely thrilled.

From my seat near the field, I cheered and clapped louder than the rest of them.

Instead of wearing Romeo's Alpha U hoodie, I was wearing Knights purple, a team hoodie with Romeo's number twenty-four on the back.

After everything that happened last year with Zach and my family, it took a while to get over. But we did; we did it together.

After the feds helped us at the hotel, they arrested the "reporter" and the case moved fairly fast. The man in custody rolled over on everyone he was involved with. Romeo's testimony and the recordings from the room that night were more than enough to put them all away.

My dad cooperated with them, and my mom's case was solved. Dad didn't get away without punishment. He went to jail for a while but then was released early for good behavior.

He was currently in a private rehabilitation center and would remain there for at least a month. I didn't fool myself into thinking his treatment and finally serving his time for the things he'd done made everything that happened to me, Romeo, and my mom okay.

But it was a start.

Romeo worked hard for months when we got home. He dedicated almost all his time to physical therapy and getting back the strength in his arm.

His hard work paid off, and he left Alpha U in early summer and went to training camp. It took a while for him to get back into the swing of things, for all the strength in his arm to come back. But even so, he made a name for himself. Being ambidextrous on the field was quite the achievement.

Of course, I already knew he was the best.

Now here we were halfway through his first season as a Maryland Knight. He'd already been offered and accepted a new extended contract.

I missed him at Alpha U, but Braeden was more than enough to keep me busy.

In just another year, I would graduate and then I would have to make some decisions about my career. Go off to vet school or use my bachelor's degree to work with animals here at home. Since the shelter raised so much money, we were able to remodel and were in the process of expanding and hopefully opening another shelter across town.

Michelle already offered me a position to run it.

I was thinking it over.

Out on the field, Romeo threw a completed pass and moved his team into the end zone, where they were perfectly positioned for a touchdown.

I stood up and cheered and shouted like everyone else in the stands.

Instead of going back into the play, Romeo lifted his hands and signaled a time out.

Players called timeout in games a lot. But really, there was no reason to call this one. Not right now. We had a game to win!

Everyone sat down and waited. I picked up my phone to text Ivy.

Before I could type anything, the crowd started going wild. The cheering was insane.

I looked up.

I started to laugh.

Romeo was running across the field, helmet in hands, toward where I was sitting.

I got up and ran to the railing. I glanced up at the giant Jumbotron, and of course, the little scene was being broadcast all over live TV.

Romeo leapt up onto the railing and grinned.

"We've got to stop meeting like this," I told him.

"There you go again, Smalls," Romeo quipped. "Making me interrupt another game for you."

"Me!" I yelled. "I wasn't doing a thing."

"Maybe not, but there's something I really need to ask you."

I laughed. "It can't wait 'til after the game?"

"No." He stared at me like he'd forgotten we were in a stadium with thousands of people and every move he made was live on TV.

"I can't imagine Ron Gamble is very happy about this."

He grinned. "Oh, he knows. He's been waiting for this moment."

"I don't understand."

From out of nowhere, Romeo produced a black velvet box.

The crowd went nuts, like beyond anything I'd ever heard.

"Romeo," I breathed.

He smiled and lifted the lid.

Everyone around us ceased to exist.

I stared down at the most sparkly, beautiful ring I'd ever seen.

It had a huge round diamond in the center and then was surrounded by even more, smaller round diamonds. The light reflected off it in a million different directions and caught my breath. It was all held together by a thin gold band.

I tore my eyes away from the ring and back up to Romeo. He wrapped his arm around the railing and gripped the ring with one hand. His free hand reached up and wrapped around the base of my neck.

Even with the crowd roaring, I heard everything he said.

"Marry me, Smalls. Nothing in this entire world means more to me than you. Marry me because I really fucking love you."

A tear ran down my cheek, and I could feel my body trembling. "You really need to stop cussing so much."

He threw back his head and laughed.

I lost myself in his eyes, in his face. In the way I felt about him. My chest was so full I thought it might burst at any moment.

I don't know how I got so lucky, I don't know how I found a love so pure.

But I was going to spend the rest of my life thanking God every day.

"Uh, Rim?" Romeo said, a small smile playing on his lips.

The moment came crashing back in and the crowd was chanting yes over and over again.

Yes. Yes. Yes.

"I am gonna need to get back to the game," he said, sheepish. "You gonna give me an answer?"

I grinned. "What they said." I gestured to the crowd.

"Yes?" The happiness on his face was all I would ever need.

"Yes."

He gave a great shout and pumped his arm in the air. He pulled the ring free and tossed the box behind him onto the field.

And then he slid it home.

It took up my entire finger.

"It's huge." I laughed.

"It still doesn't match how much you mean to me."

I threw my arms around his neck and he pulled me close with one arm as he balanced us with the other.

His kiss was familiar and hot. And so full of promise.

I stood at the railing and watched him run back out onto the field.

My future husband.

My everything.

My #player.

#SELFIE

The Hashtag Series #4

It's all about the #Selfie.

She was the one girl I never wanted.

Until I had her.

One night.

One mistake.

Something we both wanted to forget.

I got rid of the proof. The one piece of evidence that could remind us both.

At least, I thought I did.

When it shows up on the school Buzzfeed, rumors fly. Friendships are tested and the feels get real.

I don't do relationships. I don't open my heart.

Especially for a girl everyone knows I hate.

What happens during spring break, stays in spring break.

Until it follows you home.

AUTHOR'S NOTE

I don't even know how I got to this point.

Like for real. I can't remember half the stuff I wrote in this book. The re-read sure will be interesting… haha.

It's like I sat down at the computer and a lot of it literally bled out of me. I'm sitting here just moments after putting THE END, and I'm kind of still in shock. This book was a weird experience for me, because I love these characters and this world so much they've become part of me. And a lot of times I felt like I was trying to exist in two different realities: theirs and mine.

It can be very challenging to switch back and forth between the two and sometimes it's quite overwhelming. There is also the pressure of this being the third book in the series. #Nerd and #Hater have been very well loved. Trying to take the story even further and still keep that freshness and love that everyone wants so much is stressful.

But this time around, I trusted the characters. I let them lead the way. I wrote what they told me to write, and hopefully you will all enjoy it.

And I'd also like to issue a small disclaimer: this is FICTION. That means it's made up. While I try to make it as believable as I can, sometimes I mess up (gasp!). I realize I might not have all my football facts correct, but again, it's fiction and I know next to nothing about football. I do research what I can, but again, my interpretation of the things I find might not always be correct.

I hope most people will enjoy the story for what it is—a good read.

In many ways, I'm sad to type the end on this one because Romeo and Rimmel mean so much to me. I'm not ready to say good-bye to them.

But really, we aren't. They will be in #Selfie with Braeden. Who's looking forward to that book?!

I'd like to thank all the readers who have supported this series and me. The notes, the shares, and the emails have totally kept me going.

Now, if you will excuse me, I need to go attempt to rejoin the real world before I start in with Braeden.

Happy Reading!

XOXO—CAMBRIA

Cambria Hebert is a bestselling novelist of more than twenty books. She went to college for a bachelor's degree, couldn't pick a major, and ended up with a degree in cosmetology. So rest assured her characters will always have good hair.

Besides writing, Cambria loves a caramel latte, staying up late, sleeping in, and watching movies. She considers math human torture and has an irrational fear of chickens (yes, chickens). You can often find her running on the treadmill (she'd rather be eating a donut), painting her toenails (because she bites her fingernails), or walking her chorkie (the real boss of the house).

Cambria has written within the young adult and new adult genres, penning many paranormal and contemporary titles. Her favorite genre to read and write is romantic suspense. A few of her most recognized titles are: *Nerd, Text, Torch, Tryst, Masquerade,* and *Recalled.*

Cambria Hebert owns and operates Cambria Hebert Books, LLC.

You can find out more about Cambria and her titles by visiting her website: http://www.cambriahebert.com.

CPSIA information can be obtained
at www.ICGtesting.com
Printed in the USA
BVHW071528220620
581986BV00003BA/396

9 781938 857683